PRAISE FOR VANISHING LEGACY

Vanishing Legacy is a fast-paced, action-packed, suspense story with twists and turns. It will leave you on the edge of your seat as you race through the pages until the end.

ALLYSON, GOODREADS

This is such an exciting read! I could not put this one down, the story pulled me in from the opening pages and it was a thrilling read all the way to the end. My favorite thing about the book though was Penny. As a mom to a special needs child, this touched my heart in so many ways. A truly excellent read!

MELISSA, GOODREADS

This was a truly awesome read, and I am not using that word loosely. Terrific plot, awesome characters, non-stop suspense, and a really great ending. This was a book that was difficult to put down, and I couldn't wait to get back to it when I did have to set it down.

MARK, GOODREADS

Tighten your seatbelt for this wild ride! On the edge of your seat suspense and action will keep you turning the pages. Definitely worth the read!

JONI, GOODREADS

VANISHING LEGACY

ELITE GUARDIANS: SAVANNAH | BOOK ONE

LYNETTE EASON

KATE ANGELO

sunrise
PUBLISHING

Vanishing Legacy
Elite Guardians: Savannah, Book 1
Copyright © 2024 Sunrise Media Group LLC
Print ISBN: 978-1-953783-92-9
EBOOK: 978-1-953783-95-0

This book is a work of fiction. Names, characters, places, and incidents are either products of the author's imagination or used fictitiously. Any similarity to actual people, organizations, and/or events is purely coincidental.

All Scripture quotations, unless otherwise indicated, are taken from the Holy Bible, New International Version®, NIV®. Copyright ©1973, 1978, 1984, 2011 by Biblica, Inc.™ Used by permission of Zondervan. All rights reserved worldwide. The "NIV" and "New International Version" are trademarks registered in the United States Patent and Trademark Office by Biblica, Inc.™

For more information about the authors, please access their websites at lynetteeason.com and kateangelo.com.

Published in the United States of America.
Cover Design: Hannah Linder

For God, Who fills me daily with unimaginable peace and joy.

For Jerry, my prayer warrior, trusted advisor, biggest supporter,
and best friend.

And for Cash Thomas, whose name inspired the character in this story.
May you grow to become a man of faith and integrity.

"But store up for yourselves treasures in heaven, where moths and vermin do not destroy, and where thieves do not break in and steal. For where your treasure is, there your heart will be also."
Matthew 6:20-21 NIV

PROLOGUE

SAVANNAH, GEORGIA

THURSDAY, 1:42 P.M.

Why was everything in the world so easy for grownups? Penny Thomas struggled to tear the crinkly granola bar wrapping with her teeth. Libby had said she'd open it, but she was driving.

That was the routine. On Thursdays, her nanny picked her up from school early and drove her to see the speech lady while Penny ate a granola bar on the way.

Grownups always wanted to do things for her, but she wanted to do stuff for herself. Like opening her own snack. Penny tugged the top edge with her teeth. The wrapper ripped down the middle. Yes! She did it! The noisy paper peeled off and she—

Penny's body slammed forward. The seatbelt jerked tight against her chest. Tires screeched and glass shattered as another lurch flung her back against the safety of her booster seat.

Penny blinked. Tried to comprehend.

1

It was so hard to breathe. Thoughts whirled in her head, but she couldn't grasp a single one. Something bad had happened.

Libby twisted around. "Penny, are you okay? Are you hurt?" Her nanny had never used such a shrieky voice before.

Penny opened her mouth to speak. Instead, she burst into tears.

"Oh, baby girl. I'm so sorry. Hang on a sec." Libby unbuckled her seatbelt and leaned across the console. The contents of her purse lay scattered on the floorboard, and her golden-brown hair bun wobbled while she searched. "Ugh, where's my phone?"

Could it be back here? Penny craned her neck and studied the dark floor. Nope. The only thing she saw was...was...oh no! Her granola bar! She...she'd dropped it. Every *Thursday, she* ate a granola bar before therapy, and now...now it was all dirty. She screamed.

"Oh, Penny! Penny, it's okay. Hang on, I'll get you." Libby gave up the search for her phone and slipped out of the car, leaving the door open. She froze.

Libby's eyebrows rose. "Wh-what are you—"

A bang stung Penny's ears. Libby crumpled to the ground. Was she sleeping? A shadow passed Penny's window. A man in black clothes leaned inside and pressed a button on Libby's door. The locks released with a click.

Penny's door creaked open, and the man ducked his head inside. His dirty black hair flopped over his forehead. He unlatched her seatbelt. "C'mon, kid, let's go."

Her heart froze at the drawings on his neck and arms. The black scorpion on his neck moved when he spoke. Her body screamed, trying to call Libby's name, but no words formed. She shook her head and waved both hands. No, no, no. Daddy said never ever go anywhere with a stranger, and she would not go with this scary man.

Tears flooded her eyes. She wanted to speak but her tongue seemed glued to her mouth. She tried again and again. Still no words came. They were stuck. Why did it always happen when too many things were going on all at once? When she really needed her words, they would get all tangled up and only yelling came out. That's why Libby had to take her to see the speech lady. To help her get her words unstuck.

Her thoughts slipped out of control. The hot tears rolled down her cheeks, which only made her cry harder. Deep, heaving sobs, making it hard to breathe. Her body vibrated.

"Geez, what's wrong with you, kid? Calm down. I'm not gonna hurt you."

The bad man tried to grab her, but she pitched herself sideways and scurried across the back seat. A sweaty hand clamped down on her ankle. "Oh no you don't." He dragged her toward him.

She shrieked louder and kicked her free leg. The toe of her shoe landed somewhere between his eyes.

The man screamed a curse and covered his face with both hands. "Now look what you did!"

A red line of blood dribbled from his nose and pooled around his mouth. He ran his forearm over his face, smearing the blood across his arm. Mean black eyes squinted down at her. "Yer gonna pay for that one, kid. Now stop yer bawlin', cuz one way or 'nother, you're comin' with me."

Now she was in big trouble. She stopped screaming, but her hands started to shake. The man seized her wrist and dragged her out of the car. He hoisted her over his shoulder and carried her toward his smashed-up car.

Daddy had taught her to fight. If someone tried to take her, she should throw a fit and fight. She pulled the man's hair. Kicked his ribs and stomach. Screeched in his ear. Arched her back and tried to wiggle out of his arms.

It was no use. The man was too strong and she was too little.

Why didn't someone help? Libby was there, on her stomach

beside the car. "Luh! Luh! Luh!" Penny tried to call her name. Begged her to get up and help.

Libby lifted her head and looked at Penny. "Run," she rasped. "Penny...ruuuun!"

A buzzing noise filled Penny's ears and vibrated through her body. She thrashed her head side to side. Kicked and pounded her fists on his face and neck and shrieked her best high-pitched scream ever.

The bad man tugged the handle on the back door of his car. Locked.

"No! Penny, no! Do *not*...get...in...car!" Libby coughed the words. "No matter what...do *not*...get...in...his car!"

"Quit yer squirming, kid." He shifted her to one arm while he unlocked the doors and opened the back door.

Penny bit the arm wrapped around her waist. Her new front teeth weren't big, but they were sharp. They sank deep into the flesh of his arm, and she clamped her jaw so hard her face shook.

He let out a howl and released his grip. Penny fell. Her bottom bounced off the backseat, and she tumbled to the pavement. She tucked her arms in and rolled under the car, then belly-crawled to the other side. She scrambled to her feet and bolted to the woods.

"Get back here, you little brat!" The car door slammed shut, cutting off a string of naughty words.

A low ditch ran alongside the street, and Penny ran into the marshy weeds. Cold water oozed into her shoes and socks. She slogged through tall grass and burst into the underbrush. Mud squished under her feet with each step.

"Hey, kid, why you runnin'? Come on back and I'll take ya on over to see yer daddy," the deep voice boomed.

She didn't believe him. He was big and angry. He would hurt her if he could. All she could do was run. She ran deeper into the woods and darted left, then right. Leaped over a fallen tree limb and sprinted left again. Spanish moss dripped from the tree branches, and she dodged around it. If she touched it, the tiny bugs hiding inside would make her itch for a week. The forest closed in on her. A tangle of green and shadows threatening to swallow her whole. But she couldn't slow down. Couldn't let the bad man catch her.

Penny zigzagged and ran in different directions until she was all turned around. The forest was an endless maze of trees that gobbled her up. No matter which direction she turned, everything looked the same. She couldn't find her way back to Libby even if she wanted to. Oh, why hadn't she stayed with her? Libby was more than a nanny. She was Penny's friend.

But she hadn't stayed. She'd run. Now she was lost and all alone.

Footsteps crunched the leaves from somewhere behind.

"You think you got away from me, Penny, but you didn't! I will find you! That money's mine, and I ain't givin' it up just 'cause o' one dumb kid!"

Her whole body froze at the sound of his voice.

The bad man was right there. He was coming for her.

And all she could do was run.

ONE

FORSYTH PARK, SAVANNAH, GEORGIA

THURSDAY, 2:07 P.M.

How anyone could be obsessed with a fiction author, Alana Flores would never understand. As a bookworm herself, she loved reading. Even completed an annual book challenge. But stalking a famous writer? No way.

Yet here she was. Close personal protection to none other than celebrity author, S. M. Warren.

Alana couldn't complain. The job protecting Warren paid well, and she could use the extra cash. It had been a risk joining the new Savannah branch of the Elite Guardians Agency, but so far it was paying off. Every extra dollar she earned was squirreled away in savings to fund her dream of opening a community outreach for kids in foster care—and those who probably should be in care.

After Warren's team hired the agency to provide executive security for a local publicity event, Alana had spent the weekend reading the author's latest. She'd only planned to skim a few pages. Enough to make polite conversation. But she'd gotten sucked in from page one with the fast-paced action and complex characters. What had really captivated Alana was the vivid scenes that brought her new hometown of Savannah, Georgia, to life.

Even though she liked the book, she couldn't understand why someone would want to hurt the author. She scanned the hundreds of adoring S. M. Warren fans. All who chose to gather on the paved walkway in front of Savannah's iconic Forsyth Park Fountain to hear the author. At least one who wanted to kill her.

Alana had to admit, it was a glorious day to be outside. Massive live oak trees bordered the walkway. Their gnarled limbs stretched out in all directions to offer shade beneath their branches. Park benches scattered throughout the park offered a place to sit and take in the beauty. There was a reason Forsyth Park drew tourists from all over the world. It was downright picturesque. All of it, the perfect backdrop for the day's event. .

Warren stood on a two-foot-tall dais with the fountain behind her. The fifty-something author had a tumble of short blonde hair and wore a sleeveless cream silk top with peach-colored pants. A wooden podium served as a barrier of protection while she read an electrifying scene from her latest novel.

Alana was one of three Elite Guardians in a loose diamond formation around Warren. Noelle Burton, the branch manager, remained within arm's reach on Warren's right. Juliette Montgomery watched for threats from the sides and back, while Alana took point. Today, their agency was concerned with one threat in particular: Bethany Gould.

It'd all started with Gould calling and sending letters to Warren claiming Warren had promised to launch Gould's writing career. At first Warren had responded to the letters, but when Gould's manuscript was rejected, the woman had snapped. In Florida, she'd rushed at Warren, demanding she get the book published. A plainclothes detective in line to have her book signed had intervened and arrested Gould on the spot. An order of protection issued by the judge hadn't deterred Gould, who began stalking Warren.

Last month, things had escalated when Gould followed Warren to a writer's conference in St. Louis, Missouri, and attempted to kidnap the author from a parking garage. Warren had fought back and thrown herself out of the moving car, suffering a knee injury during her harrowing escape. Though the injury had required surgery, Warren refused to let it stop her from showing up for her fans here in Savannah.

Alana admired Warren for her bravery in the face of such danger. Protecting her was an honor, as it was with all their clients.

Of course, it had taken some reprogramming for Alana to get used to the bodyguard job. Her training and instincts led her to charge headfirst into danger, but as an Elite Guardian, her mission was to shield and retreat with their client. Except in her current position as point bodyguard. If anyone attacked, Alana would run interference while Noelle and Juliette removed Warren to safety.

A delicate breeze carried the spicy, sweet fragrance of blooming azaleas from the nearby gardens surrounding the concrete fountain. Alana listened to Warren read.

"A second explosion rocked the yacht and knocked Brady off-kilter. Shoot. Where was Kendra? He clutched the rail and searched the churning water for any sign of her," Warren read.

That would be one crime scene Alana would love to investigate. As a former member of the Los Angeles Underwater Dive Unit, she was no stranger to water crime scenes. She'd conducted countless dive operations in the aftermath of explosions like Warren described in her book. Alana had spent her workdays salvaging evidence and retrieving decomposing bodies from the murky depths.

Diving alone in swift water with almost zero visibility electrified her. Thrilled her to the core. Each recovery was like searching for buried treasure. Far more interesting and exhilarating than standing around waiting for an unbalanced Warren devotee to step out of line.

She sighed and shifted her weight. Maybe she shouldn't have turned down the job with Georgia's underwater dive team. After all, what could be more exciting than working beneath the surface of the water?

Alana's earpiece chirped. The small, high-tech device allowed her to covertly communicate with Noelle and Juliette.

"Any sign of Gould?" Noelle tugged the sleeve of her dark suit to cover her wrist. A habit Alana had noticed.

"Negative, but possible threat, three o'clock," Juliette said. "Caucasian male, hoodie pulled up."

Alana spotted the suspect near a park bench. Posture hunched, face obscured by a dark hood, and hands concealed within the pouch of his sweatshirt.

"Good eye. On it." Alana strolled the path, keeping her eye on the suspect. If this dude planned to harm Warren, the ninety-some-odd people in front of him created a pretty big obstacle. She circled around him and got a good look at his face, but he wasn't what she expected.

A gaunt face with dark circles around sunken eyes peered at Alana. Knowing sliced through her. Smooth, pale skin. Shoulders hunched from the sheer exhaustion of holding himself upright. All the telltale signs of a body ravished by chemotherapy.

The man turned and gestured for Alana to pass.

"Thanks," she said, managing a weak smile.

"Status?" Noelle asked.

"False alarm," Alana whispered into her comms.

"Copy. Ten minutes till Warren's signing. Stay alert."

"Copy," Juliette said.

"I'm doing a little recon along the way back."

The crowd grew restless. They shifted their weight and inched closer to the stanchions. Once Warren finished reading, a horde of fans would make a mad dash for the book signing line. They'd have to ensure Warren didn't get trampled in the excitement.

"Hey, you can't cut!"

Alana stood on her tiptoes and zeroed in on two women. A doughy woman with ragged bangs blocked the path of a tall woman with frizzy red hair. Great. The last thing she needed was a cat fight. She made a beeline for the two women. "Checking a disturbance at your nine."

"What's your problem?" The redhead glared at the shorter woman. "I ain't got no beef with you."

Alana plastered a smile on her face and adopted her best law enforcement voice. "Ladies, ladies, let's take this over to the shade so we don't disrupt the event for others."

"I ain't goin' nowhere." The shorter woman shoved a finger in the redhead's face. "Carrot Top here tried to cut in line, and I've been waiting for hours!"

"Get your finger outta my face!" The redhead slapped the finger away.

Seriously. These two were fighting over one spot in line? "Hey, if you two don't knock it off, you're both outta here."

"Not me. Carrot Top can leave." The woman planted two hands and shoved.

The redhead stumbled and lost her balance.

Alana caught her by the waist, trying to keep her steady.

"Take your hands off me!" The redhead jerked her arm away and glared at Alana.

The color of her green eyes seemed off. Too...vibrant.

Bethany Gould.

She'd changed her hair. Appeared taller somehow. Lifts in her shoes? The facial features were different too. Possibly a prosthetic nose. If Alana hadn't been standing within inches of the woman, she wouldn't have recognized her.

"It's Gould. Get the principal off the X. Execute Beta Plan." Alana issued the command to shield Warren and immediately withdraw to their safety vehicle.

"Copy," came the voices in her earbud.

Now she had to distract the woman and keep her from making a scene. "Take it easy, Ms. Gould. I know you'd love to visit with Ms. Warren, so how 'bout we step into the shade and have a chat?"

Red raced up Gould's neck. "I'm not going nowhere with you!"

Alana stepped closer. "Look, there's no need for—"

"Guuuunnnn!" Gould pointed at the weapon at Alana's waist. "She's got a gun!"

Screams erupted from the crowd.

"Everyone calm down. I'm security." Alana shouted over the chaos, but her words died in the air.

People pushed and shoved. Exactly what Alana didn't want. A panicked mess. Worse were those who pressed in, jockeying to get closer. Phones held up to record the whole thing.

Alana flicked her gaze toward the dais. Noelle and Juliette were rushing Warren around the concrete fountain, using it as protection. From there, it was just shy of fifty yards to the armored personnel vehicle where Rose Lawson, a contract bodyguard, waited behind the wheel, ready to whisk Warren away. Savannah PD could handle the rest.

Gould's eyes darted past Alana. "No! She can't leave!"

Alana stepped in front of Gould and blocked her view. "I need to inform you that you're currently under a restraining order, which legally prohibits you from being in close proximity to Ms. Warren. I strongly advise you respect the terms—"

"I don't give a spit about your terms!" Gould launched her fist at Alana.

She blocked the punch with one hand and grabbed Gould's wrist with the other. She twisted Gould's arm behind her back.

The woman howled in pain, but it didn't seem to slow her down. She spun out of Alana's grip and took off running.

Alana groaned and sprinted after her. Why did they always have to run? There were few things she despised more than running. "Gould evaded. She's on the move."

"Copy," Juliette said.

The woman was fast, but Alana was in better shape. She lengthened her strides and closed the distance. She reached to grab Gould, but the woman dodged left and slipped through her grasp. Alana growled and pushed herself harder, sidestepping innocent bystanders.

Gould ran to the wrought-iron fence surrounding the fountain and rolled over the rail. She landed hard on her shoulder but scrambled to her feet. Alana hurdled the fence and landed in stride, eyes fixed on the woman's back. Arms outstretched, Alana launched herself forward and tackled Gould from behind. The momentum propelled them forward, and they crashed into the fountain pool.

The icy water stole Alana's breath, but she quickly slipped a forearm under Gould's chin and rolled to her back. The woman came up coughing and spurting.

Alana dragged Gould to her feet as two uniformed police officers jogged up.

A stocky female cop put her hands on her duty belt. "Hey, you two! There's no swimming in the fountain!"

"Yeah, yeah. I know." Alana used one hand to pin Gould in an arm lock and drew her other arm over her mouth. She wiped the disgusting water off her lips. She was soaked head to toe. "I'm with the Elite Guardians. This woman is violating a protection order."

Even as Gould was being handcuffed, she swore at Alana for getting in between her and Warren. "You stupid woman! You ruined everything!" She writhed and tried to escape the officer's grip. "You haven't seen the last of me!"

Alana followed the officers out through the gate. The crowd had dispersed. Warren's assistants righted the overturned book table. What a mess.

Car doors thudded shut. Alana's eyes followed the SUV carrying Warren. Any thoughts of a bonus sped away with the author.

Regardless of the payment, at least she'd apprehended the stalker and Warren was safe. She'd just work extra hard to secure the funds for her dream project.

SAVANNAH GENERAL HOSPITAL

THURSDAY, 2:44 P.M.

Dr. Cash Thomas respected the Second Amendment more than most Americans, but he'd be a happy man if he never operated on a gunshot wound again. This was the third GSW this week. It wasn't the responsible gun owners shooting each other in the streets. Illegal firearms accounted for the majority of wounds Cash saw in his operating room. The trigger man was almost always too young to legally own the weapon.

The patients seemed to get younger and younger too. This one? Well, Cash doubted he was old enough to shave. And the kid never would if Cash didn't get the bleeding under control.

A bullet to thirteen-year-old Dante Johnson's chest had ripped through his scrawny body. Cash hadn't seen a gunshot wound this bad since Morocco. And that'd been a two-hundred-fifty-pound Navy SEAL. This kid? A hundred ten soaking wet.

Cash determined the bullet had entered just below the heart and punctured the left lung, tearing through tissue and organs before exiting. Now he and his surgical team worked to control the life-threatening bleeding in the spleen.

Alarms blared.

"Pressure's eighty over fifty." His surgical nurse, Brooke Newton, shifted beside him and silenced the alarms so they could concentrate without the ear-splitting sound.

"Calling for two units of type-specific and running five hundred saline," the anesthesiologist said.

Cash held out his hand. "Clamp."

The steel hit his palm, and he clamped the section of tissue he'd been repairing and moved to the heart. The bullet had grazed the pericardial sac. Blood pooled inside the sac, causing pericardial effusion.

Brooke called out vitals. "He's not responding to the fluids."

"Page Dr. Shiro," Cash said.

Generally, he could handle these types of heart injuries, but with so many other complications, Cash needed the heart surgeon to repair the sac and drain the blood while he continued to locate all the bleeders in the spleen.

The machines went haywire. The boy's heart rate and blood pressure crashed again.

"He's in bradycardia," Brooke said.

"Not good. Not...good," Cash muttered. The blood filling the pericardium had too much pressure on the heart. "The left ventricle's collapsed. He's in tamponade. We need two more units! Where's Dr. Shiro?"

"On his way. Five minutes," someone said.

"We don't have five minutes! Call him again!" Cash flicked his eyes to Brooke, then back to his work. "Start needle decompression."

"Urine's dropping," the anesthesiologist said.

"Can't worry about the kidneys until I've got Dr. Shiro here."

"Pushing more fluids to stabilize the pressure."

He focused on relieving the pressure around the heart while the anesthesiologist focused on pushing fluids to stabilize the pressure.

The OR door opened and closed.

"Hey, Dr. Thomas. Read me in?" Dr. Shiro asked.

Brooke didn't look up. "Pulse zero."

The sac was filling again. Fast.

The team began resuscitation procedures. Compressions. Epinephrine. Defibrillator. Every possible procedure. Cash and his team fought hard for ten minutes, but Dante remained pulseless.

"Enough," he said. "Enough."

Giving up wasn't in his nature, but he wanted to spare Dante's body more abuse.

He stepped back and called the time of death.

Cash tore off his mask and surgical gown, stuffed them into the biohazard bin, and headed for the locker room for a breather. After all these years, some patients got under his skin more than others. And facing Dante's family was the last thing he wanted to do right now.

At the sink, Cash splashed cold water on his face and watched the water swirl down the drain. Just like that kid's life.

A knot formed in his stomach. He ran a wet hand over his eyes and let out a soft groan. Informing the family a loved one had died was the worst part of his job. But the family had a right to answers. He wouldn't shirk the responsibility, no matter how difficult.

He turned off the water and dried his hands. Ready or not, it was time to face them. On the way out of the locker room, he almost bumped into Brooke rushing across the lounge that connected the men's and women's locker rooms.

"Oh! Sorry, Dr. Thomas. I was checking to see if you were in here before I paged." She ran her thumbs under the brim of her surgical cap and tucked the dark hairs back in place. "The family is asking for an update."

"Thanks, I'm on my way. I needed a minute." His words came out a tad more defeated than he'd intended.

Brooke sat on the arm of the couch and stared at her shoes. "Yeah, that was a rough one. It's hard to lose them so young."

"Senseless." Cash put his hands behind his back and leaned against the wall. He studied his own shoes and pictured the operating table. "That kid didn't deserve to die. They come in, clinging to life, and we have no idea who we're working on or why he was near a gun in the first place. Then they die and it's like I failed them. I couldn't buy him a few more years. I couldn't even buy him a few more hours to say goodbye. And the biggest gut punch of all...did he even have a chance to hear the gospel before he died? I never know, and it's all so frustrating sometimes."

"Don't be too hard on yourself. No one else could have kept that boy alive as long as you did. One thing's for sure—I know I'll be hugging my husband and son tighter tonight." Brooke stood. "Shift's almost over. Maybe you can cut out early?"

Cash sighed. "I'd love to but can't. If I want to make chief, I need to prove I can handle the hard things."

Chief of surgery would mean more responsibility but regular hours. No more on-call rotations. He could be home with his daughter instead of entrusting her to a nanny. Something he'd been working toward since his ex-wife had died and he'd become a single dad.

"The unspoken rule is you can go home after two traumatic events in a shift and no one can say anything. This makes three today."

Three? Had it really been that many in one day? He must've blocked it.

His first case this morning had been an abused infant. When the father'd realized the police were on the way, he'd tried to take his baby and leave. Cash intervened. "That dad needs to work on his right hook. Easy block."

"Well, yeah." She laughed. "You managed to handle things just fine, but I was referring to the condition of the infant."

"No one should see a baby in that condition." Knowing it'd happened at the hands of the father made his blood boil. All he'd wanted to do after he'd handed off the patient was leave, drive straight home, and hold his daughter so she knew how much he loved her.

"You know, maybe I will head out a bit early. Give the nanny the evening off," he said. "I'll take Penny out to dinner on the Riverwalk. Then a nighttime ferry ride."

"Penny likes the ferry?" Brooke had been one of the few who'd helped him come to grips with the diagnosis of autism spectrum disorder and suggested he take Penny to a speech-language pathologist specializing in ASD.

"Well, she's not wild about the boat part, but she sure loves to watch the lights of River Street from across the water."

Brooke smiled. "Sounds like a wonderful daddy-daughter date."

Penny's curiosity around all things shiny and sparkling never grew old. The awed look on her little face as she pointed out the purple, orange, pink, and blue hues reflecting off the water always made him smile. "Yeah, that's exactly what I need tonight. A daddy-daughter date." He straightened and retucked the back of his undershirt into his waistband. "But first, I'll update the family."

Brooke stood and headed for the coffee. "Dr. Shiro offered to handle the family if you want to—"

"No, it's my responsibility. I'll go now while I have time. Thanks for the offer though." Cash smiled and headed for the door but paused when his name was announced on the intercom. The pager on his waist vibrated.

"Spoke too soon." He read the message aloud: "Twenty-year-old female. GSW to the abdomen. Right lower quadrant." He glanced at Brooke.

"Should I ask Dr. Shiro to inform the family?"

"Yeah, I'll take him up on the offer if he's still available. If not, inform the family I had another emergency and I'll be out as soon as possible."

"Yes, doctor."

Cash stood at the surgical sink just outside the operating room and began the five-minute-long scrub-in, carefully washing every nook and cranny of his fingers and hands.

Two gunshot wounds in one day. Unbelievable. And this victim only a few years older than Dante. With a GSW to the abdomen, there was no telling what type of trauma he'd be dealing with. Surgery could last thirty minutes or hours. Good thing he hadn't texted Libby. Penny didn't do well when plans changed. No sense in upsetting her if he ended up being late.

If he didn't make dinner, they'd go to Bitty & Beau's Coffee for a smoothie. Just the two of them. Still getting that daddy-daughter date. Penny loved the cafe, and Cash loved to support the company whose passion was to employ individuals with intellectual and developmental disabilities.

With his sterile hands raised, he hit the door with his back and entered the operating room ready for battle. The scrub nurse had his gown held up. He slipped into it while listening to the stats and vitals of his patient.

"The bullet entered the right lower quadrant of the abdomen. Fractured the pelvic bone. Possible bowel perforation and urogenital injuries," the ER doc said. "She's stable, but at her age we were worried about permanent damage to her reproductive system."

"Of course," Cash said. Twenty years old? The young woman

had her whole life ahead of her. He'd do his best to ensure she had the option to have children in the future.

Cash approached the surgical table and stared down into the face of the patient. His mouth fell open. The room began to spin.

"Dr. Thomas?" He barely registered the voice. "Everything okay?"

He blinked, hoping he was seeing things. But no. It was...it was her.

"This...this patient," he said. "I think it's Libby. She's...she's my nanny."

The surgical nurse checked the woman's wristband. "The patient's name is Libby Hendrix. Are you saying this girl is your nanny?"

"Yes. And if Libby is here...where's my daughter?"

TWO

Well, she may not be a dive detective anymore, but at least Alana still got wet on the job. Oh, how a steaming shower beckoned. Or a hot bath. Soak some warmth into her chilled skin. She'd have a nice evening with Rocco, then slip into the fluffy pink robe her sister, Christina Parker, had bought her for Christmas, and snuggle up with a book. Maybe even another S. M. Warren novel.

Now that Gould was in police custody, the author would need less security on her book tour. Rose had taken the assignment on contract since it required traveling with Warren for the next few weeks. While Alana was a tad disappointed at missing out on the bonus money, she was looking forward to a low-key spring break with her son.

Alana parked her Jeep in her garage and hopped out, bare feet smacking against the cold concrete floor. She'd long since shed her sopping wet shoes and socks and was seriously kicking herself for not having her go-bag in her vehicle. At least an extra pair of dry socks. A small oversight, but who knew protecting an author would land her in a historical landmark filled with dirty water?

She shook her head. Time to step out of bodyguard mode and into mom mode. She smacked the garage door button with her palm.

"Hey, Rocco, I'm home!"

Her son didn't need the announcement. The door rattled and rumbled down like a steam locomotive, announcing her arrival to the whole neighborhood. Yet another thing on her ever-expanding to-do list.

"You better have your chores and homework done," she bellowed through the laundry door.

The moment Alana crossed the threshold, a gentle sigh escaped her lips. Her shoulders sagged, shedding the heavy weight of the day. She paused in the oversized laundry room which served as the mudroom and peeled off her wet jacket. Tossed the sodden socks into the washer and hung her blazer on the drying rack.

"Hey, Rocco?" She headed toward her room in the back of the house. "I'm gonna hop in the shower and—"

Alana stopped dead in her tracks.

One look at the disaster in the kitchen sent her blood pressure through the roof. The sandwich bread lay open. Crumbs scattered. Lid off the peanut butter jar. Globs of jelly on the counter. At least he'd put the sticky knife on a paper towel.

Rocco's homework was spread out all over the breakfast table. His jacket and backpack tossed on the floor. Oh, that kid...

A pile of chocolate chip cookies caught her attention, but she didn't recognize the plate. She plucked one off the plate and took a bite. The rich, buttery flavor flooded her tastebuds.

"Rocco, you better get in here and clean up this mess," she said around the last bite of cookie. "What were you thinking?"

She marched down the hallway, bare feet padding against the cool hardwood floors.

Hands planted firmly on her hips, Alana surveyed her son's room. The bed looked neat and tidy, but her eagle eyes spotted his pajamas in a pile on the floor instead of in the hamper. Wires, resistors, circuit boards, and bits of colored plastic littered his desk. Parts for the robotics project Rocco was building for his upcoming competition. She was proud of his passion, but she'd remind him to be more organized.

Stupidly, she checked his walk-in closet. Unlikely he'd play in there at his age, but a mother's worry knew no bounds. She ran a hand over her damp hair. Where was her son?

The cookies.

Oh no, how many had he eaten? More than one and his blood sugar could skyrocket. Couple that with the PB&J and he could be in serious trouble. The joint glucose monitor and insulin pump Rocco wore managed his diabetes, but it didn't always respond quickly to a sugar spike.

"Rocco, where are you!"

The lack of response only fueled her to search every room of the house faster, calling his name as she went. Her mom brain went into overdrive. Visions of Rocco tied to a chair, lethargic and unresponsive, popped into her brain. Last Christmas was the closest she'd been to losing her son. Until now.

Please, please, let him be safe.

She jogged back to the kitchen and grabbed Rocco's cell phone off the table. Her fingers fumbled the screen. "Stupid hands. Stop shaking."

She found the one she was looking for and tapped it. The glucose monitoring app said his sugar was in range. In fact, it had been all day.

Okay. Good. He was fine, but still...missing, which didn't make sense. Rocco was responsible and always checked in. She scrolled through the calls and texts on his phone. Besides her number, he'd only been in contact with Miss Martha, the elderly neighbor who kept an eye on him from time to time. She hit the speed dial for Miss Martha and paced the kitchen as it rang.

"Hello?" Miss Martha answered in her slow Savannah drawl.

"Miss Martha? It's Alana. Have you seen Rocco today?" Her heart pounded as she spoke. Ridiculous for someone with her skills in crisis management. But honestly, she'd been a bit more of a helicopter mom ever since the terrorist Tomás Muñoz had held them hostage at church last Christmas.

"Oh, hello, Alana." Each time she said Alana's name, she pronounced it *Uh-lawn-uh* which made Alana smile despite herself. "Yes, Rocco came by after school like he always does. I sent him home with a plate of fresh-baked cookies."

"I saw that, thank you." She'd remind Miss Martha about Rocco's diabetes another time. "It's just...I came home a few minutes ago, but I can't find him. Are you sure he didn't come back to your house?"

"Oh, I'm sure, dear." Miss Martha's cat mewed in the background. "But if you cain't fine 'im, maybe we should call the po-lice?"

Alana stopped pacing and stared outside. The floor-to-ceiling windows overlooking her backyard had been a key selling point when she bought the place a few months ago. The door to her shed was cracked. "I don't think we need to call the police."

"Why not?"

"Because I think I just found him," she said on a sigh. "He's in the shed." Alana kept an eye on the door, waiting for Rocco to emerge.

"Oh, I thought I heard a ruckus outside earlier. Musta been him. He taking the lawnmower apart again?"

"He better not be. And if he is, he's in big trouble. He knows that shed is off-limits without permission." More than once, Alana had tried to start the mower only to have Rocco confess he'd *borrowed parts* for his robotics project. She'd finally put her foot down. No more scavenging household electronics without permission *first*.

"Pshh...now, don't you be too hard on him. He's a bright boy, and we grownups should encourage a child's natural curiosity, not squash it."

"Oh, in that case, don't *you* have a lawnmower?"

They laughed and Alana said, "Thanks for looking out for Rocco. I don't know what I'd do without you."

"No trouble, dear. Just let me know when you've laid eyes on the boy," she said. "Oh, and you make sure to eat dem cookies too. You're awful skinny, child."

"Yes, ma'am. I will." Alana smiled to herself as she disconnected the call and dropped Rocco's phone onto the table. She didn't care what Miss Martha said. If Alana found her mower in parts again, Rocco would be doing pushups until his bony little arms fell off.

She opened the sliding back door and called for Rocco. Somewhere in the distance a dog barked. She heard muffled noises coming from the shed and hopped off the low deck.

"Rocco? Hey, are you out here?"

She rounded the corner as the shed door flung open, then bounced back, slamming shut with a bang. A man burst out of the wooden building, his face a blur as he slammed straight into her. His shoulder caught her in the chest and knocked her off her feet. A child's legs were tucked under his arm.

Alana had her gun in her hand and was on her feet before she knew what was happening. Her brain put it together on the fly. The man was taking her son.

"Rocco! Rocco!"

The child was crushed against the man's chest, screaming like a banshee. Arms and legs flailed, but the man held tight.

"Stop!" Alana yelled, chasing after the man.

He was wearing a dirty white T-shirt, motorcycle boots, and jeans so loose he was in danger of losing them. The veins in his neck corded, making the scorpion tattoo under his ear appear to be moving. Long blonde hair snaked around his arm and flapped in the wind.

Rocco didn't have blond hair.

Her bare feet dug into the grass faster and faster until she was only a few feet behind. She closed the distance. Waited for the right moment. When he was midstep, she reached out and caught his foot as it came up behind him. It was enough to throw him off-balance. Momentum did the rest. He stumbled and fell forward, landing on his face.

Alana was over him, wrenching the little girl out of his hands. The crying girl wrapped herself around Alana and squeezed her neck. Her tiny body wracked with sobs.

The man with the scorpion tattoo staggered to his feet. His chest heaved with each breath. He shuffled backward and pointed at Alana. "You ain't seen the last of me. That money's mine, and I ain't givin' it up just 'cause a dumb broad stuck her nose where it don't belong!" He stabbed a thick finger in the air. "I'll get you. I know where you live, and one way or another, I'll get you!"

Police sirens pierced the air somewhere in the distance. The man took off running. He rounded the corner of the house and disappeared.

Alana was breathing too hard to speak. She held tight to the girl with one arm and kept her gun aimed in the man's direction. He knew where she lived. He knew...where she lived.

He would be back.

Rocco! She had to find her son. She lowered her gun but didn't holster it. The warm, wet spot on her shoulder registered. The tears had soaked through her shirt. "It's okay, baby girl. We're okay. I've got you."

She reached for her phone, but it wasn't in her pocket. Either she'd left it inside, or it was somewhere in the yard. She

couldn't waste time looking. Rocco could be hurt. He could be…
no. She wouldn't go there.

The girl clung to her neck as Alana ran to the shed. She
pulled the door open with her heel and used her hip and
shoulders to wiggle it open.

"Rocco! Where are you?"

"Mom!" Rocco was at her side. Arms around her waist. Head
buried in her stomach. "Mom, I was so scared. I tried to stop
him, but I…I couldn't." His words rushed out.

She holstered her gun and set the little girl down, but the
girl's arms snaked around Alana's leg and squeezed. "It's okay,
baby. Are you hurt? Did he hurt you?" He looked okay, but she
ran a hand over his head in a cursory inspection.

Rocco shook his head. "I was doing my homework at the
table when I saw her crawl through the hole under our fence
and run in here. She looked so scared, so I came outside to see
what was wrong. Then that scary dude came in and said he was
taking her. I wanted to stop him, but—"

"I know." She kissed his forehead and hugged him tight.
"You did your best, but he was much bigger than you. Bigger
than me too. He's gone and everyone is safe. We'll go inside and
call the police. See if we can find her family."

A muffled whimper came from the child at her side. For the
first time, Alana really looked at the little girl. Cerulean blue
eyes peered out from a rat's nest of long blonde hair that fell
around her shoulders. Mud caked her pants, the shoe missing
from her left foot. Didn't she have both shoes earlier?

"What about you, baby girl? Did the man hurt you?" She
brushed the tangles out of her face. A delicate puffiness
encircled her red-rimmed eyes. The child looked exhausted.

"That man bad. He good." She pointed at Rocco. "Him's
friend. Him's help."

"Yes, Rocco is a very brave boy. You're safe and we're both

going to help you. My name is Alana. Can you tell us your name?"

She ducked her chin and pinched her lips with two fingers. Shy all of a sudden. "I Penny," she whispered.

"Wow, what a pretty name." Alana had pegged Penny at six or seven years old, but her verbal skills appeared delayed. It could be the trauma, though. The brain did weird things when it came out of an adrenaline dump.

Her own body had the jitters. She managed to keep her voice calm, but her insides crackled with energy. She had to get the kids inside in case that guy decided to come back.

She hoisted Penny and settled her on her hip. "C'mon. I want us to hurry inside."

Alana scanned the backyard. All clear. She carried the little girl in one arm and wrapped her other around Rocco's shoulder.

Rocco stiffened and stepped in front of her. "Don't worry, Mom. I'll protect you."

That was her son. Courageous to the core. Fearless enough to stand up to anyone if it meant protecting another. Even a grown man.

A grown man who knew where they lived.

And promised he'd be back.

THURSDAY, 4:44 P.M.

If Cash didn't get out of here soon, he just might punch something. He stalked the hospital conference room. Long legs eating up the space like a caged tiger. His daughter was missing. He should be out there searching for his little girl. Not stuck in here. He wanted to run. Or scream. Or...or...

Cash stopped.

His brain wasn't working right. Why hadn't he thought to

call his contact at the FBI? They could get things moving. He unlocked his phone and scrolled through his contacts.

The door creaked open and Detective Matt Williams strode in. After handing Libby's surgery off to another doctor, Williams had escorted Cash into the conference room and peppered him with questions until his blood boiled. Weariness etched the man's features. Dark circles ringed eyes heavy with exhaustion, and a day's beard growth sprouted from his tired face. "Sorry for the delay, Dr. Thomas."

"Please tell me you found my daughter."

Williams took a deep breath. "I'm sorry, but no. Believe me, we're doing everything we can. Detective Slaton is at the crime scene. She'll update us when there's new information. I know you'd rather be out there looking for your daughter, and honestly, I don't blame you. But right now, the very best thing you can do is stay put in case she calls."

Cash was tired of pleasantries. He didn't need coddling. He needed details. Facts. Something besides the barrage of horrific scenarios his imagination conjured up.

"Look, Detective, I'll do whatever it takes to find my daughter, but you should know I deployed with the SEAL teams as a combat surgeon. I'm not the sit-back kinda guy. I thrive in crisis. It's my job. You know as well as I do, intel is an incredible resource, so whatever information you have, I can take it."

"Fair enough." Williams ran a hand through his disheveled hair and released a long breath. "We found blood in Penny's car seat and a few drops leading into the wooded area east of the crime scene. Officers started a door-to-door canvass in the surrounding neighborhood, and we've called in a trailing dog. We're mobilizing additional personnel to conduct a grid search of the woods, and we'll expand our search to the waterways if necessary. If she's in the area, we'll find her."

Words appeared in bold behind his eyes. *Blood. Waterways. If she's in the area.*

His stomach churned. How could this be happening? His little girl. The mere thought of a stranger laying hands on Penny tied him in knots. He'd taught her a few self-defense moves, but she was so small. No way she could take down an adult on her own. There had to be more they could do to find her.

Cash had an ace up his sleeve, but if he played it now, he could expose an undercover agent. Not something he wanted on his shoulders. Better to try a different route. "Has anyone contacted the FBI? Aren't they supposed to get involved in cases like this?"

There was a slight jut of Williams's chin. "The field office has ERT on standby."

"The Evidence Response Team? What do they have to do with this?"

"They specialize in cases of missing and abducted children."

Cash tightened his jaw and tried to force the emotions back down. "Abducted? You...you think she was abducted?"

Williams held up a palm. "We're not sure that's what happened. It's completely possible your daughter ran for help and got lost in the woods."

"Or?" Cash all but shouted the word.

The trill of a cell phone startled him. He snatched his phone off the conference table.

"It's me." Williams waved his phone at Cash and answered it. "Yeah. Okay." He nodded and gave Cash a half-smile. "Great, we're leaving now. Be there in fifteen." He disconnected the call and clapped a hand on Cash's shoulder.

"You found her?" Cash's throat tightened.

"Yes. A woman and her son found her. She's safe in their living room. My partner is with them and says Penny couldn't be in better hands. Ready to go get your girl?"

He nodded. "I've never been more ready in my life."

Fifteen minutes later, Cash slid to a stop in front of a charming lowcountry home with dark green trim. He flung his door open, hopped out of his truck, and jogged up the steps to the porch. A uniformed officer lifted his chin in a nod of acknowledgment, but Cash didn't speak. Right now, he was focused on seeing Penny.

Chest heaving, he pounded three hard knocks on the door. It boomed louder than he'd intended, and he hoped the noise didn't scare Penny. He shifted his weight. The wooden planks groaned under the weight of his steps. He rubbed his hands together. What was taking so long?

After a million minutes, the door creaked open. The woman standing in the doorway wasn't at all what he'd expected.

Dressed in all black except bare feet, the woman studied him with dark eyes lined with thick lashes. Her inky black hair was pulled into a ponytail that didn't quite contain the soft tendrils framing her brow. Every feature was razor-sharp yet carried an alluring softness. And she was tiny. Petite in a way that made him feel like a giant looming in her doorway.

His brain halted. Mind blurred. In his haste to see Penny, he hadn't even considered who might live here and how to ask for his daughter.

The woman's soft smile widened. "Hi, you must be Dr. Thomas. I'm Alana Flores." Her voice held a faint Hispanic accent.

The sound of his pulse thrumming in his ears drowned out every thought other than Penny. He willed his brain to function. Say something. Anything.

"Are you?" she waited. "Dr. Thomas?"

He nodded, finally. "Cash, yes."

"I believe you're here to see your daughter." Alana opened the door wider. "She's right in here."

Cash crossed the living room. Penny. His beautiful, special little girl was on the couch with a book in her lap. He almost laughed. Reading! As if she didn't have a care in the world.

The young boy beside Penny smiled when he saw Cash and closed the book.

Penny looked up. "Daddy!" She raised her arms and squirmed her little body.

He scooped her up and enveloped her in a hug. "Oh. My lucky Penny. It's so good to see you."

Penny held him tight and nestled her face into the crook of his neck. Her tiny fingers traced the collar of his scrubs. He alternated kisses on her head with whispers of comfort and prayers of gratitude.

His focus was drawn to the oversized window behind the couch, where a buzz of police activity consumed the backyard. Detective Williams stood with his hands on his hips, nodding to the officer talking and pointing. A woman holding a boxy camera squatted near the fence. A white flash strobed with each photograph. Behind the photographer, an officer walked a wide perimeter around the shed, a fat roll of yellow crime scene tape unfurling from his hands.

"That's where Rocco found her." Alana had moved beside him and nodded at the shed.

The boy scooted off the couch and thrust out his hand. "Hello, Dr. Thomas. I'm Rocco Flores. It's a pleasure to meet you, sir."

Wow. Polite kid. Didn't see too many of those these days. He shook the boy's hand. "Please, call me Cash. And the pleasure is all mine."

"Can I get you anything? Water, soda, coffee?" Alana gestured to the kitchen.

He lowered Penny to the couch. "Coffee would be great, thanks." Exhaustion tugged at his muscles. A combination of the long hours and the adrenaline crash. Caffeine might not be the right answer, but in his experience, it usually was.

Penny patted the cushion beside her leg. "Here, friend. Sit."

Rocco plopped down beside her. "Have you ever seen a fidget

spinner?" He showed her a small toy, then held it between his thumb and index finger and gave it a quick flick. It set the small toy in motion. Tiny LED lights lit up in a blur of color and light as it spun between his fingers. Penny was mesmerized.

"They'll be fine there. Let's talk in the kitchen." Alana's eyes widened and she tipped her head.

He slid his eyes over to Penny. An invisible string tugged his heart to her, and he wasn't sure it would stretch more than a few steps away.

"It's okay, Dad. She'll be right where you can see her." Alana gestured to the chairs at her kitchen counter, where he'd have a clear view of the living room.

He sat at the kitchen island and ran a hand over his hair. "I'm sorry. I'm still in shock, I guess." The aroma of rich coffee wafted through the air. At first, he wasn't sure his stomach could handle coffee, but yeah. He'd take a cup or ten.

He watched Alana as she moved around her kitchen. She found two coffee mugs in the cabinet and set them next to the pot. "Coffee will be a few minutes. Can I make Penny a snack? I didn't before because I didn't know if she had food allergies."

"No, don't go to any trouble. I'll get out of your hair in a few minutes. I'm just so grateful you found her."

"Penny is a brave girl, Dr. Thomas. She's in good spirits despite all she's been through today."

"Please, call me Cash."

"Cash and Penny." Alana smiled. "Cute."

Cash lifted a shoulder in a shrug. "My wife's idea."

"Oh, please tell your wife she's welcome to come—"

"I misspoke. *Ex*-wife. And she passed away when Penny was a baby. It's just the two of us." His eyes drifted to Penny, who was trying to balance the fidget spinner between her tiny fingers without much luck.

"I'm sorry to hear that. It's just the two of us too." She filled a mug and placed it in front of him. "Cream or sugar?"

"Black is fine." He rested his elbows on the counter and laced his fingers around the cup. "Back to your earlier statement. Penny doesn't have any food allergies, but I'm sure you noticed her communication skills aren't that of a normal seven-year-old. She's on the spectrum. Autism. She seems to have bonded with Rocco awfully quick. She's not normally like that."

"That's what I wanted to talk to you about." Alana rested her elbows on the counter across from him and leaned close. "Rocco was the one who found her in our garden shed. He saw her crawl through the hole in our fence. The previous owner had a dog that kept digging. I've been here a few months but never got around—" She waved a hand. "Sorry, that's not relevant. What I'm getting at is, there's nothing but woods behind my house. What was she doing back there?"

"I don't know. I still don't have the full story. My nanny, Libby, was driving her to speech therapy when they were rear-ended. Detective Williams said it's what they call a bump and run. Libby stopped at a four-way intersection, and a car intentionally crashed into the back of her car. When she got out to check the damage, the guy shot her."

Alana's eyes went wide. "Wait, Libby was shot? Right in front of Penny? Is she okay?"

"Like I said, I still don't have all the details. Libby's...alive, but not talking." He stayed away from breaking medical privilege. "Penny's the only witness for now. I won't allow the police to interview her without me present. Because of the ASD, her verbal skills are limited. It can be a challenge to get her to communicate. We're working on it with speech therapy, but when she's stressed, it interferes with her ability to speak. If you can imagine how frustrating that could be for an adult, you can begin to understand what it's like for a child still learning to express her emotions appropriately. When she's in an unfamiliar place, has an abrupt schedule change, or when everyday life becomes too much, she'll shut down and scream until someone can help her calm down."

"Well, she hasn't said a lot, but considering what you described, I'm amazed she was able to speak at all."

"Is it wrong to say it's a blessing of ASD? She doesn't quite understand the severity of what happened. She's likely to be more upset about the change in her routine than what happened. But so far, she seems happy to play with Rocco." His eyes drifted to the living room. Penny giggled with Rocco. The fidget spinner whirred between her fingers. "I came so close to losing her today. Thank God you were there."

He took a sip of his coffee. It was so good a sigh slipped out.

"That good, huh?" Alana's soft smile brightened her dark eyes.

"Yeah. It's been a long day." He chuckled. "Anyway, what were you saying? Rocco saw Penny crawl through the hole in your fence?"

"That's right. I came home from work and couldn't find Rocco anywhere. I started to worry, but then I saw the shed door open. I figured he was in there taking parts from my lawn equipment for his robots again."

"Hang on, I think we might have to come back to that later. Robots?"

"Yes, he's a budding engineer. Too smart for his own good, really." Pride filled her eyes. "Rocco said she looked terribly frightened when she ran into the shed, so he went to check on her. A few minutes later a man came looking for her. He tried to stop the guy, but I guess that's about the time I saw the shed door open and went outside."

"Whoa, Rocco tried to stop a grown man from taking Penny?"

"Yep. I walked up right as the man ran out. I chased him across the yard. Eventually tripped him and pulled Penny out of his arms."

He chuckled. "I guess we know where Rocco gets it."

"Maybe." One corner of her mouth turned up in a smile, but it disappeared. Her eyes fixed on his. "Here's the kicker. This guy gets up, turns to me and says, 'That money's mine and I ain't giving it up.'"

"What? That doesn't make any sense. What money?"

Her shoulders lifted. "The thing that really bothered me was when he said, 'I know where you live, and one way or another, I'll get you.' And the way he said it, I tell you...I believe him."

"He threatened you?" Cash forced himself to stay seated. "Did you get a good look at him?"

"Yeah, I don't think I can forget that face. Or the tattoo. An ugly black scorpion right here." She drew her index finger from her ear, down her neck, and along her jawline. "The officer who took our statement asked us to go down to the station and look at some photos.

"But here's the thing, Dr. Thomas." Alana leaned in. They were inches apart. Her eyes fixed on his. "I don't think he was talking to me. He was talking to Penny."

Good thing he hadn't jumped to his feet, because every muscle in his body turned to water. "Are you—" His mouth went bone dry. He swallowed and tried again. "Are you saying Penny's still in danger?"

Alana's eyes scanned his face. "That is exactly what I'm saying."

THREE

Alana forked a bite of taco salad and watched a three-inch strip of crime scene tape flutter in the wind. The yellow plastic stuck in the shed door was the last remnant of all that had transpired in her yard.

"I hate that the guy who tried to kidnap Penny is still out there. I should have offered security services to Cash before they left."

"Good excuse for you to spend more time with Cash." Noelle sat across from Alana and grinned.

Alana ignored her and pushed the food around on her plate.

"Seriously, though." Noelle talked around a mouthful. "Are you sure you don't want me to stay over tonight? It sounds like there's a chance that dude planned to come back."

"So the bodyguard needs a bodyguard now?"

"Hey, we all need someone to watch our back now and again."

"True. And you know we love it when you stay, but I think I need space to get things back in order around here."

37

Noelle made a show of looking around Alana's house. "Yeah, right. This place is a disaster. I can see why you need time to clean up." She smiled and stuffed a bite of Spanish rice in her mouth. "Although, I was surprised to see SPD packing up when I got here."

"Being best friends with former Detective Burton has its benefits after all."

Noelle huffed a laugh. "You mean besides bringing takeout and free babysitting?"

Half an hour ago, Noelle had shown up with dinner from Rocco's favorite restaurant and an overnight bag. The former detective might be Alana's boss, but she was also her closest friend here in Savannah.

"Those are good benefits." Alana grinned at her friend. "But I guess they heard you were coming and processed the scene in record time. Never seen locals move that fast. Did you get any updates when you talked to them?"

Noelle held her finger up while she finished chewing. "Stop asking me questions right when I take a bite. I swear you do that on purpose."

They both laughed and Noelle drained her water glass. "Rumor has it the nanny is awake and flipping through the mug book like it's a fashion magazine and she's picking out a prom dress. If the gunman's in there, they'll have more than enough evidence to put him away. All they'll need from you and the kid is confirmation."

"You got that from Williams?"

Noelle grinned, tapping the side of her nose. "We have a little insider exchange program. A tidbit here, a tidbit there."

"I do love your special connections."

"Oh, but wait. There's more." Noelle wiped her mouth and tossed her napkin on her plate. "Dr. Cash Thomas has an interesting connection to our very own Jonah."

Alana stopped chewing. "Jonah? As in your friend Jonah Harris the M.E.?"

"Yeah. Jonah worked in the ER before he left to work at the medical examiner's office. Cash was his replacement. Jonah showed him the ropes for a month or so during the hand off."

If there was a clue from Cash's past to explain why someone would try to abduct his daughter, Alana wanted to hear it. "What else do you know about him?"

"Not much, really. Let's see..." Noelle folded her arms and looked up, searching for answers. "They work out sometimes. I think Cash has a friend who owns a gym or something. He was a surgeon in the Navy, and according to Jonah, excellent under pressure. Knows how to take orders without getting his feathers ruffled. I remember Jonah saying it was nice to talk to someone else who'd lost a spouse."

"Single dad. Former Navy. ER doctor. Quite the package."

"Speaking of packages." Noelle pulled an envelope out of her back pocket and slid it across the table. "Your heroic escapade today has attracted some attention."

Her gaze shifted to the handwritten cursive script on the outside of the envelope. "What's that?"

"Only one way to find out."

Alana slid her finger under the flap and tore the seal. Inside was a personal check and a handwritten note. The amount took her breath away.

Noelle leaned in. "What's it say?"

Alana had to swallow before she could speak. She read the note aloud. "Ms. Flores, please accept my gratitude for your heroic effort today. I couldn't have written a better action scene myself. I consider you a true Elite Guardian angel." Alana glanced at Noelle. "It's signed S. M. Warren."

Noelle raised her glass. "Cheers to literary-inspired heroics."

"And check out the amount." Alana held it up.

Noelle sputtered and coughed. She wiped the water from her lips. "Whoa, that's generous."

"I'll say." Alana chuckled and examined the check again.

"What's the plan? New Jeep? Trip to Australia? College fund for Rocco?"

"It's all going straight into the ministry fund."

Noelle nodded. "A smart move. That'll give your dream a significant boost. How long till you get things up and running?"

"I'm holding off until Rocco's in high school. Gives me time to secure a building. With this and more overtime, I'll have enough for a down payment. Then the real work begins."

"Alana, what you're building is incredible. You'll be changing lives, one step at a time. And just so you know, I'm right behind you. Even if it means losing my favorite bodyguard."

"Don't worry, you're stuck with me," Alana said. "The Elite Guardians is where I belong."

"Good. I was half worried you'd miss the thrill of SWAT or the deep-sea dives and sail off into the sunset."

Alana waved her check. "Believe me, this job is plenty exciting."

When their laughter subsided, Alana rose to clear their plates. A quick glance at the microwave told her Rocco's shower time was nearly up. He'd grumbled when she'd insisted they stick to the routine, but routines were the backbone of success. The only way she could ensure he'd grow up to be successful and manage life with diabetes was to teach him self-discipline now.

"Speaking of today," Alana said, moving into the kitchen with their plates. "What's the lowdown on Bethany Gould?"

Noelle followed Alana with the empty containers. "She was arrested for violating the protection order. She's due for arraignment tomorrow."

"Why not stalking charges?" She turned on the water and rinsed her plate.

Noelle took the plate and placed it on the bottom rack of the dishwasher. "Public place loophole. Savannah's playing it safe. The order of protection was issued in a different state, so prosecution falls to them."

"I can't believe she went through all that trouble with the disguise and everything." Alana shook her head. "It's like she's upping the ante. Someone needs to give her a reality check before things get ugly. So where are we with Warren? Is she still planning to stay in Savannah while they film the movie?"

Noelle organized the silverware by type and dropped them into the dishwasher caddy. "Warren's a tough bird. She refuses to let anyone intimidate her. She'll be under Rose's wing. There's standard set security, but Rose is glued to her side."

Alana smiled. "Rose is growing on me. Any chance she'll join us full time?"

Noelle sighed. "I keep trying, but she's a free spirit. Likes the flexibility of being a contractor."

"One of those wild roses," Alana said.

"A bit less thorny, though." Noelle loaded the soap packet and closed the dishwasher. "I should get out of your hair and let you guys do your bedtime thing."

Noelle'd always respected Alana's structured life. She didn't mind following Alana's routine when she watched Rocco overnight so Alana could take a night shift.

"Hold up a sec." Alana dried her hands on the tea towel. "I've been thinking about Cash and Penny. That guy was willing to shoot an innocent woman just to get his hands on that little girl. What if he comes back? Catches Cash off guard. I hope you don't think I'm out of line, but I'd like to offer our services."

Noelle bit her lower lip and nodded. "The police probably have some kind of protection in place already. They might even have a lead by now. But I'll check."

"Thanks," Alana said. "And thanks for dinner. It was amazing."

Rocco emerged from the hallway. He wore black pajamas with a science lab print on the bottoms. He hugged Noelle in the foyer. "Yeah, thanks for bringing tacos. That's my favorite."

"I thought so. You deserve them after today. You were incredibly brave." She shot a smile at Alana. "He takes after his mom."

"I hope Penny is okay and they catch the bad guy," Rocco said.

Noelle ruffled his wet hair and gave his shoulder a gentle squeeze. "I have a feeling they'll catch him soon. But hey, speaking of exciting things, are we still on for the robotics expo?"

Rocco turned to Alana, who arched an eyebrow. "As long as he keeps up with his chores and his daily workout routine."

Rocco flexed his arm and grinned. "Did a hundred pushups before my shower."

Noelle tapped his arm. "Impressive, muscle man."

"All right, enough muscles for now," Alana interjected, stepping in and pulling Rocco closer. "Time to get to bed."

After another round of goodbyes, Alana got Rocco settled. She knelt beside his bed and brushed his hair away from his eyes. It was getting a little unruly, even though he'd had a haircut a few weeks ago. Another sign he was growing up too fast. Alana listened to Rocco's prayers for Penny, his heartfelt concern for the little girl palpable.

"And please keep Mom and me safe forever and ever. Amen," he said.

"Amen," Alana said.

Rocco shifted to his side and rested his cheek on his hands. Dark eyes that mirrored her own studied her. "Mom, do you know how Penny is doing?"

"I believe she'll be fine. Her dad is taking good care of her and making sure she gets checked out at the hospital."

Alana didn't want to delve into the emotional toll such an

experience could have on a child, but they both understood it all too well. Three months ago, Rocco'd nearly died right before her eyes. The bullet fired by a terrorist may have missed her son by mere inches, but it had left an indelible scar on their lives. Penny and Dr. Thomas would have their own wounds from today. In time they'd heal, but the scar never went away.

"You know, I really like Dr. Cash. He was so nice and he's cool like Uncle Grey." Rocco's eyes lit up as he shifted the conversation. "Did you know he's lived in Afghanistan and Japan? That's so awesome."

Alana smiled at her son's enthusiasm. "Yeah, he does sound like an interesting person. Kind of like you, always curious about the world."

Rocco's eyes twinkled. "You should date him."

Alana couldn't help but laugh. "Oh, really? And why is that?"

One shoulder went up in a shrug. "You never go on any dates, and I just think he'd fit in with us pretty well."

Rocco had never known his father. That hadn't been Alana's plan, of course, but he still paid the consequences for her poor choices. She'd always thought she could love her son enough for two parents, but maybe he longed for a loving father in ways she couldn't fulfill. But no sense in raising false hopes.

She planted a kiss on his forehead. "Dr. Cash is a good man, and I do like Penny. But dating is not on our agenda."

A deep furrow creased Rocco's brow. "Why not?"

She had to tread carefully, revealing enough but not everything. He was her son, not her confidant. "Well, I'm not looking to date right now. Our lives are complex as it is, and adding dating to the mix only complicates things."

"Life isn't always about perfection, Mom. Sometimes it's okay for things to get messy, you know?"

The weight of Rocco's words landed with unexpected force. Perhaps she'd been too focused on maintaining the appearance of perfection and hadn't given him enough room to enjoy the spontaneity of being a child. It was a hard pill to swallow, especially considering Rocco's unique qualities. His intellect and talents surpassed her own in many ways, offering him a world of possibilities she'd never had. Yet she couldn't shake the belief that control and order were crucial for Rocco to harness his potential and navigate life's challenges.

But that was a discussion for another time. "Messy is fine, but that doesn't include your bedroom. Tomorrow you need to clean this place up before you do anything else." She tucked the covers around him and patted his back. "And remember, go easy on Miss Martha's cookies, okay?"

Rocco sighed and snuggled his head deeper into the pillow. "Yes, ma'am."

In the dim light of her son's room, Alana eased the door shut and padded down the hall to her own bedroom. The weight of the day bore down on her. Exhaustion settled into her bones.

The conversation with Rocco stirred thoughts she wasn't quite ready to face. His childhood was slipping away, and perhaps he finally saw a chance at having a father figure in his life. Cash did seem like a wonderful man. A gentle, loving father whose tender embrace of his daughter stirred Alana's soul. She couldn't imagine the kind of comfort and security that would come from being held by a parent like that.

Rocco had experienced that type of love his whole life because she'd given it to him. But her past held a more skeptical truth. One Rocco remained unaware of.

When life turned messy, most people walked away.

Not Alana, though.

Which was why she was determined to make sure Penny Thomas stayed safe until her kidnapper was off the streets. She'd just have to figure out a way to protect Penny and keep her distance from Dr. Cash Thomas.

SAVANNAH GENERAL HOSPITAL

THURSDAY, 9:30 P.M.

Cash lingered in the doorway of Penny's exam room, watching his daughter sleep in the golden hue of the pediatric lights. Special lights allowed the children to choose their favorite color and Penny had chosen yellow. "Because it's Thursday, and I always wear yellow on Thursday," she'd chirped.

The image of Penny escaping such a dangerous man gnawed at him. He should have been there. He should have protected her. A renewed sense of purpose ignited within him. He would do anything to keep her safe from now on. Anything.

A reassuring hand landed on his shoulder. "Hey, man, how's our girl?" Dr. Jonah Harris thrust his chin in the direction of Penny. Cash's friend and fellow doctor wore tactical khakis and a collared shirt with the medical examiner's seal on the breast.

Cash motioned for Jonah to follow him into the hall and closed Penny's door behind him. Better she rest while they waited on the myriad of tests he'd ordered to come back.

"She's in good spirits. Complained of a headache and nausea, so I ordered X-rays and blood work to start."

"Good call. No need to subject her to the big machines and risk traumatizing her without cause."

"Oh, the blood work was bad enough."

"Didn't go well?"

Cash shook his head. "Screamed bloody murder."

Jonah acknowledged a passing doctor with a nod. "I stopped by to check on Libby, but Matt—Detective Williams, I mean—kicked me out after a short visit. Seems to be doing great, all things considered. What about her parents? How are they holding up?"

Cash folded his arms over his chest. "They've been surprisingly understanding."

Jonah's eyebrow shot up. "You lost me there. Why do you say surprisingly?"

He dropped his gaze to the linoleum floor. "It's my fault. Libby was shot because she was taking Penny to speech therapy for me. If Libby's recovery wasn't going so smoothly, I'm pretty sure they'd unleash all their anger on me, right where it belongs."

"Dude, you can't seriously be carrying that weight on your shoulders. This isn't your fault. You can't predict every crazy thing that might happen. And blaming yourself for things out of your control won't do anyone any good."

He paused, letting Jonah's words sink in. While the logic was there, Jonah didn't quite grasp the truth. "I get what you're saying, but it's like I've got this track record of leaving a trail of pain behind me. Today, for instance. I wasn't even scheduled to work. I took on an extra shift, thinking it'd improve my shot at becoming chief of surgery, and look what happened."

Jonah's eyes softened. "Cash, I hear you, but don't discount the fact that being here is important too. You save lives. And Penny, she's safe now. Everything worked out."

Cash looked through the glass doors at Penny's small form in the hospital bed. "I appreciate that, Jonah. I really do. But you don't understand. The woman who found Penny told me the man threatened to come back." Cash lowered his voice and stared at Jonah. "He knows where we live. My gut tells me she's still in danger. And Libby too, if she keeps working for me."

"Have you thought about bringing in some extra protection until the police apprehend this guy?"

"I'm Penny's father. I'm more than capable of keeping her safe." Even as he said the words, he knew he'd have to work at some point—he just wasn't able to be with Penny one hundred percent of the time.

"Alana Flores—the one who found Penny—is part of Noelle's agency. She's an expert in martial arts. Used to be on the LAPD SWAT team. Trust me, if anyone can keep Penny safe, it's her."

"Listen, I'm sure Alana is amazing. She saved Penny and opened her home and her life to the investigation. I'm grateful for what she did, but I don't need anyone else."

"I hear ya." Jonah's thumb traced a deliberate path over his beard as he spoke. "Look into the Elite Guardians and get to know Alana. Consider it your backup plan."

"Yeah, okay." Alana Flores. She was unlike any woman he'd ever met. Tough, smart, and fierce, yet soft and kind. Everything he found attractive in a woman. And her past as a detective made her even more intriguing. It couldn't hurt to google her. That wouldn't be stalking or anything.

The overhead speaker crackled to life, summoning the medical team for a triage category one. The area came alive with nurses and doctors as they rallied to respond to an incoming patient in need of resuscitation.

Cash glanced at the nurse jogging by. "Hard not to jump in, isn't it?"

"Took me a while to suppress that instinct. I'd take half a step before I realized I don't work here anymore." Jonah chuckled. "So how did Penny do with the police interview? I worried about that for her."

He blew out a breath. "Rocky start, but Penny found her voice. Somehow, she managed to describe the perpetrator in her own way. Her description matched up with Alana's and Libby's. Savannah's finest are on the hunt now."

"Good. Let me know when they find him. In the meantime, hungry? Need a fresh set of clothes?"

Being in the hospital and wearing scrubs was so natural, Cash hadn't thought to change. He couldn't remember the last time he'd eaten, but the thought of food made his stomach roil. "Nah, I'm all right. Thanks for swinging by, though. Means a lot."

They did a bro handshake, interlocking thumbs in a firm grasp that morphed into a steadfast hug.

Jonah thumped Cash on the back. "Just remember, I'm here whenever you or Penny need. Don't hesitate to reach out, brother."

Cash didn't want to think about how much he needed this moment with his friend. The last time they'd been locked in a hug, they'd been pummeling each other in the ring. It was good to have a friend like Jonah to lean on when times were tough.

Cash let the embrace linger a beat longer. "You know, if we keep hugging like this, people might start to talk."

Jonah chuckled and released him. "Guess I better go before the single nurses get jealous." He gave a resigned sigh and walked down the hallway.

Cash slid the door open and stepped into Penny's room. He paused at the familiar sensation of his phone vibrating in his pocket and fished it out. The caller ID was Detective Williams.

He stepped back into the hall and closed Penny's door. "Hey, Detective, what's up?"

"Hey, Cash. You still at the hospital?"

"Yeah, why? What's going on?"

"I've got something to share with you. Mind if I swing by?"

"Sure thing. Trauma room three in the pediatric ER. It's just down the hall."

"Got it. I'll be right down."

Cash slipped inside Penny's room and took a moment to check the computer for updates in her chart. The results from her blood work looked great. A note from radiology said they were backed up and it would be another half hour before her film was processed. He could call in a favor to speed things up, but with Penny resting comfortably, he didn't see the point.

A soft tap echoed against the glass doors. Williams waited as Cash slid the door open and stepped into the hall. "Good to see you again, Detective Williams."

"Call me Matt. Everyone else does."

"Thanks, and I'm just Cash. How's the investigation? Any updates?"

Matt ignored the question. His chin jutted toward Penny's room. "How's the little one doing?"

Cash's gaze flitted to Penny, then back to Matt. "Doing great. Waiting on one more test to clear, then we should be able to go home."

"Glad to hear it. I came down to let you know we've made a breakthrough in the case. We have a lead. Ms. Hendrix picked the suspect out of a photo lineup. Name Jeremy Black mean anything to you?"

He shook his head. "No, not that I can remember. That's the guy?"

"He's a low-level dealer. Arrested for possession a few times. Aggravated assault, assault during the course of arrest, evading arrest, trespassing. The rest is pretty much more of the same. He's been on parole for about six months."

Oh, he couldn't wait to lay eyes on the scumbag who'd shot Libby and attempted to abduct his daughter. What he really wanted was to call up a few of his old SEAL team buddies and teach Black a lesson about hurting innocent people.

Of course, he'd never do that. He'd settle for the perp walk and parking himself at every court hearing to have a front row seat at justice being served.

"So you caught the guy. Sounds like great news," Cash said.

"Depends on how you look at it." Matt paused. "He's dead."

The air seemed to thin around Cash as he absorbed Matt's words. "He's...dead?"

Matt ran a hand over his hair. "It's been a wild day. There was a shooting over near Baker Street Park. We just got word the victim matched the BOLO description. His prints matched the evidence we found in the car and the shed. It's him, no doubt."

"Okay..." Cash processed the information. "So, what now? It's all over?"

Matt was silent. His eyes traced back and forth across Cash's face, weighing his words before he spoke. Finally, he said, "Cash, I need you to brace yourself for what I'm about to say. We believe Jeremy Black was hired to kidnap Penny. This isn't over. She could still be in danger."

FOUR

Whoever was ringing her doorbell this early in the morning must have a death wish. Alana glanced at the clock. She groaned and pulled the covers over her head to block out the brightness of the sun filtering through the windows.

"Go away," she muttered into her pillow.

Who on earth could be at her door this early? Miss Martha was well aware of Alana's long working hours and that she slept late to make up for working the graveyard shifts.

"Take a hint, would ya?"

The ringing persisted.

She hauled herself out of bed. "Fine, I'm coming!" She grabbed a sweatshirt and quickly tugged it on over her sports bra.

She padded toward the front door and caught a glimpse of herself in the hallway mirror. Whoa, she looked like she'd been dragged through a hedge backward. She finger-combed her hair, trying to tame her frizzy bangs. The obvious sleep creases wouldn't budge no matter how hard she rubbed.

As Alana flung open the door, her frustration dissipated at the sight of Cash and Penny standing on her doorstep. The little girl held a stunning bouquet of spring flowers. The aroma of the fresh blooms filled the air. A surge of warmth spread through her chest at the sight of the father-daughter duo.

"Well, look who it is. What brings you by this morning?"

"Penny wanted to thank you for yesterday. I would've called, but I didn't have your number." Cash jerked his thumb over his shoulder. "We can...uh...come back later if it's not a good time."

"No, no, not at all! I'm just a little surprised, that's all. Please come in." She stepped aside to let them pass. "Forgive my appearance. I was just about to get ready for the day." Or sleep until noon.

Cash followed Penny inside. "Not a morning person?"

Alana quirked an eyebrow. "Are you?"

"Can't help it. I'm a surgeon."

Penny giggled. "Here! Flowers for Alana! Thank you for Alana!"

Alana smiled. Not only at the sweet gesture, but she loved hearing Penny's sweet voice. "Wow, thank you, Penny, they're beautiful."

She accepted the flowers, not sure if she could give Penny a hug or not. Since she hadn't brushed her teeth yet, she opted against it. "You guys must get up with the sun."

Rocco stumbled out of his bedroom, eyes heavy with sleep. When he saw Penny, his face lit up. Penny raced to Rocco and hit him with a hug. "Whoa, what are you doing here? Missed me already?"

"Missed you, friend," Penny said.

Alana kept smiling. Amazing how well Rocco and Penny had bonded in such a short time.

"Morning, Rocco. Sorry to wake you," Cash said.

Rocco yawned. "Morning, Dr. Cash."

"Hey, bud." Alana hugged her son. "Did you make your bed?"

Rocco moaned and shook his head. "I forgot. I'll do it later."

"You always say that. Go do it now. Maybe Penny can help?" She glanced at Cash and he nodded.

Penny tugged Rocco's hand. "I help!"

"Fine." Rocco drew out the word and led Penny to his room.

Cash handed Alana a gift bag. "I brought a little something for Rocco. Hope that's okay."

Alana took the bag and heard the rattling sound of Lego pieces. "If it's what I think it is, he'll be thrilled." She strode into the kitchen. "But really, you didn't have to bring us anything."

"I'm just so grateful for all you and Rocco did. For Penny and for me. It meant the world to us." He settled onto one of the barstools and rested his hands on the counter. "I also wanted to talk to you about something."

"Oh yeah?" Alana stole a glance at Cash. The way his broad shoulders filled out his shirt meant he worked out. Probably before sunrise.

She pushed Rocco's words from last night out of her head. It'd been a long time since she'd let a man into her personal life, and she wasn't quite sure what to think of the one sitting at her counter. One thing was for sure, she'd have to set some boundaries so Rocco wouldn't continue playing matchmaker.

"You know, Penny sure loves Rocco. You should've heard her chatting nonstop about him last night. She woke up talking about you both this morning."

"She's really sweet. Rocco hasn't been around a lot of children, so it's great to see him step into a sort of protective big brother role."

Well, that came out wrong. She wasn't trying to insinuate anything, but maybe Cash would let it slide. She reached for the bag of coffee beans and filled the grinder. "How's the other girl? Libby, I think you said."

"Good. We stopped by to see her before we came here. She'll make a full recovery physically. Emotionally, well, we'll have to keep praying for her there."

Thank goodness they'd gone to the hospital first. Alana would've died if he'd shown up any earlier. The grinder whirred as she pulverized the beans into fine grounds. Alana readied everything and flicked the coffee maker on. The gurgling sound of the brew began to fill the kitchen.

"Speaking of getting up early," she said. "You mind if I run freshen up while the coffee brews?"

Cash stood. "Oh, yeah, of course. I should probably check on the kids. See if their bed-making skills would pass my commander's inspection."

She thanked him and hurried to her bedroom. She changed into a black T-shirt and running pants and pulled her hair into a ponytail. While brushing her teeth, she swiped deodorant under her arms. One last check in the mirror. Good enough for now.

On her way to the kitchen, she noticed a dark stain on her shirt and lifted the hem for a closer inspection. Was that a grease stain? Her head collided with something hard that knocked her off balance.

Cash's strong hands caught her shoulders. "Whoa, there."

Oh. That solid surface she'd hit was his toned chest.

They danced around each other, exchanging a fluster of apologies.

When they finally stopped, she tilted up her head and scanned his face. Think. Think of something to say. Wow. His eyes were blue.

A small smile played at the corners of his lips. "Are you okay?"

"Um, I'm fine. I wasn't looking where I was going. Obviously." Alana became aware of how close they were standing and shuffled back, smoothing her shirt. Now if only she could get her pulse to stop racing. "Anyway..." She drew out the word. "I'm sure the coffee's ready."

"I could definitely use a cup of coffee right about now." He made a sweeping gesture toward the kitchen. "After you, madam."

In the kitchen, the coffee aroma revived her brain. She poured them each a cup as Cash settled himself back on the stool at the counter. The soft hum of the whirring refrigerator and muffled giggles carried across the house.

Alana stood across from Cash and savored the first sip in silence. This morning thing might not be so bad if it meant sharing a peaceful cup of coffee.

Cash set his mug on the counter. "So, I hope it's okay, but I really wanted to stop by and ask you about the Elite Guardians."

"Oh. Of course." How dumb of her to think he was here for any other reason than to hire protection for his daughter. She'd planned to bring it up, but now she wouldn't have to. "What do you want to know?"

"Let me back up. You might have heard already, but the cops found the scorpion guy."

"Whoa, that was fast."

"Fast, yes, but not the way anyone hoped." Cash glanced over his shoulder. A total dad move. Little ears and all. "His name was Jeremy Black, and he was discovered dead in his car."

"Murdered?" Alana asked in a low tone.

Cash nodded. "You remember what Black said to you, right? About money? Penny mentioned it too. Detective Williams thinks Black was contracted to abduct Penny and murdered because he failed. She could still be in danger."

"That's where the Elite Guardians come in?"

He shook his head. "No, I wasn't saying I needed to hire a bodyguard. I believe I can handle protecting my daughter on my own. But I need insight. Knowledge on how to shield her properly. What to look out for. Your expertise."

Her eyebrows shot up. "You're seeking guidance, not a bodyguard?"

"Exactly. I know Penny is still at risk, and I can't afford to underestimate the danger. I'll do whatever it takes to keep her safe. Even if it means admitting I need some help and advice. So, can you teach me what I need to know?"

He expected her to teach him a lifetime of skills in what? One conversation? "Oh, Cash, I don't know about this. I've been in law enforcement for years. Even with my background I had to go through a rigorous training program to provide effective private security. How could I possibly teach you everything I know?"

"I'm not asking for everything you know. Just a few basics. My military training can handle the rest."

She chewed her lower lip. Last night she'd been determined to make sure Penny stayed safe, and helping Cash was one way to do it. "You'd really be better off hiring a bodyguard. If it's a money thing, we could—"

"The money is not an issue. Believe me. It's just...I know you've seen Penny generally in good spirits, but it's not always that way. Like tonight, we'd planned to go to the hot air balloon festival, and if we don't go, it could throw her off for days."

"The hot air balloon festival? Cool! Can we come too?" Rocco appeared behind Cash with Penny by his side.

"Please, please, Daddy!" Penny begged, tugging on Cash's sleeve.

Alana put a fist on her hip and narrowed her eyes at her son. "What have I told you about eavesdropping?"

Rocco lowered his head. "I'm sorry, Mom. I didn't mean to. We were coming to ask if I could show Penny my robot in the living room. But can we go, Mom? Please? I love hot air balloons. It's going to be so cool!" Rocco bounced on his toes.

"It would be a great opportunity for me to pick your brain." Cash grinned. "I mean, unless you have plans or something."

Plans? She almost always had plans. The day was reserved for Rocco's robot. They had to work out the kinks before the upcoming competition. Even though Cash had given her an out, the eager faces of Rocco and Penny, both pleading with clasped hands, stirred her heart.

She faltered. "I mean, I guess we could go. We don't want to intrude."

"It's no intrusion," Cash said. "We'd love to hang out, wouldn't we, Penny?"

Penny and Rocco erupted into cheers. It was good to see Rocco so happy. Acting like a kid. Especially after their heavy conversation last night. How could she deny him a bit of fun after all they'd been through?

"All right, all right," she said. "You've twisted my arm. We'd love to come along."

"Great! It's a date," Rocco said.

A warm smile spread over Cash's face, and he locked eyes with her. "Yes, it's a date, then."

Cash's words hit her.

A date? No, no, no. She'd been so focused on protecting Penny and helping Cash, she hadn't considered the implication of two single parents hanging out on a Friday night.

Cash scooped Penny up and tossed her in the air. Amid the joy and laughter in her living room, Alana was unsettled. In a matter of minutes, a new layer of complexity had woven itself into her life.

Now she'd have to figure out how to untangle it.

———

HUTCHISON ISLAND

FRIDAY, 7:45 P.M.

What on earth had possessed Cash to go and use the word *date* with Alana? The word sort of fell out of his mouth. Probably because he'd had the daddy-daughter date on his mind.

Now everything was all sorts of awkward. Or maybe it was just him, because Alana acted as cool as a cucumber, strolling through the bustling crowd at the hot air balloon festival, enjoying a box of popcorn.

They walked shoulder to shoulder along a line of deflated balloons waiting to be filled. Pilots and crew members busied themselves with checks and rechecks of their equipment to prepare for the night flight.

"Nice evening." He cringed at his lame attempt at small talk. Could he be more awkward right now?

"It is." Alana offered him the box of popcorn. "Want some?"

The savory aroma of butter and salt wafted up to his nose. His mouth watered. "Thanks." He took a handful and popped a few kernels into his mouth.

Rocco and Penny held hands and skipped a few steps ahead, leaving him and Alana alone in a way that made him feel like the fifth wheel. She didn't want to be here with him. Inviting her had seemed like a great idea in the moment, but now it was plain weird. He needed to give Alana an escape. "You and Rocco can feel free to explore on your own. You don't have to stay with us."

Alana nodded to the kids. "They seem to be having a great time together."

The kids were cute together. Rocco really looked out for Penny. But no one could mistake them for siblings, with his thick, dark hair and sepia skin that mirrored Alana's. Penny's pale skin and straight, strawberry-blonde hair came right from his side of the gene pool.

"Okay but let me know if you want to leave early. I don't want to keep you out too late."

"No worries. I can handle a late night if it means getting everything sorted out for Penny's safety. Besides, Rocco and I are night owls, and I let him stay up a little extra on the weekends anyway."

"Oh, right, it's mornings you're not so great at."

"Well, they aren't my favorite, especially after a long shift."

This seemed like a good segue into the real reason he'd invited Alana to come along. "Speaking of long shifts, how does the Elite Guardian Agency manage to protect a client when the threat is so vague?"

Alana didn't answer right away. Her eyes scanned the crowd on high alert. "Much of what we do is provide security for a VIP during a specific period of time. Say, a movie premier or a speaking engagement. When the potential threat is imminent, we can provide round-the-clock protection."

"Round-the-clock? How does that work?"

"We do it all the time. The agency will assign a regular rotation of as many bodyguards needed. Usually, two on a rotating schedule of twelve-hour shifts."

"Ah, I see what you mean by long shifts."

"About the same for doctors and nurses, right?"

Cash nodded. "Those hours tend to fly by most days. What about Rocco? Can you ever take him to work?"

Alana waffled her hand. "It's not ideal. Rocco could be a pretty big distraction. If there was a threat, I'd have to choose between protecting my son or protecting my client."

"Makes sense," he said. "Doesn't it make clients nervous to have someone following them around twenty-four seven?"

"We try and stay invisible and blend in where we can."

"Like how you blended in with the crowd at Forsyth Park

yesterday?" He suppressed a smile, testing the waters to see how much teasing Alana could handle. The short article about Alana's stalker takedown didn't share many details, but the multiple videos on social media painted a pretty good picture of her capabilities.

"Oh, yeah. That. Well, all in a day's work, I guess." She laughed. "But really, we try to be invisible until we're needed. And then we're not."

"I know what you mean. It was like that with the SEALs. Those guys were invisible until they wound up on my operating table." They were wading into serious topics he'd rather not delve into. At least, not now. Not in public. He shifted the conversation. "It must have been quite a culture shock moving from Los Angeles to Savannah."

She made a puffing noise with her mouth. "It's definitely different. But it's worth it to have more time with Rocco. Give him a better life than I could in L.A."

"I don't mean to pry, but divorced?"

Alana sputtered a laugh. "No. I've never been married."

"Okay, so not married. Not divorced." He twisted his lips and pretended to think. "Dating anyone?"

She laughed again. This time the sound caught in her throat. "Nope, no way. What about you?"

"Me? No, I'm clueless about women. I'm no ladies' man. In fact, I married my first girlfriend." And look where *that* had landed him.

Alana glanced at him, skeptical. "You haven't dated all this time?"

"Oh, sure, I've been dragged to a few social events where some well-meaning friends tried to set me up, but honestly, I wasn't the slightest bit interested." He shrugged. "I always thought I'd bump into the right woman when I least expected it. But with my grueling hours at the hospital, chaotic on-call schedule, and Penny, a social life is pretty much out of the question."

"I get that. All of it. Add in being the new girl in town with a brand-new career, and our situations are identical."

The sky darkened and the hot air balloons began to inflate. The low roar of the burners intensified, and the fabric of the balloons rustled and crinkled as they expanded. A rock band had started playing. Blue and white lights flashed over the audience packed in front of the stage. The music ratcheted up. Cash watched Penny for any sign of overstimulation. It didn't seem to bother her. She stood beside Rocco, transfixed, watching the massive hot air balloons grow to towering heights. The warm, multicolored glow of the balloons illuminated the night sky.

Cash leaned close to Alana to speak over the music. "It's moments like these I want to remember forever." Was it his imagination, or did she shrink back?

"I meant the kids," he hurried to say, nodding toward Penny and Rocco. "Seeing them so entranced by all this."

She gave him a crooked smile. "Absolutely. It's one of the best things about being a parent, right? Making memories with our kids."

"I couldn't agree more." Cash grinned and listened to Rocco as he explained to Penny how the balloons worked.

The inflation noise subsided, replaced by the gentle rustle of the fabric and the occasional hiss of gas as the pilots made adjustments to the burners.

"I love these colors. I've seen pictures, but there's something about standing here seeing them in person that takes my breath away." Alana's dark eyes shone.

"Mom, look at that one!" Rocco pointed to the next row, where a hot air balloon in the shape of an elephant slowly took form.

Penny hugged Cash's waist. "Can we see it? Can we?"

He chuckled. "Of course."

Rocco and Penny hopped and turned to run.

"Whoa, you two," Alana called. "Stay where we can see you at all times."

"Yes, ma'am." Rocco took Penny's hand, and together they skipped a few steps ahead.

They skirted the concert crowd and walked along the row of balloons "You know, it's great to see Penny so happy," he said over the music. "Especially after yesterday. Sometimes...well, it can all become too much. Her emotions can swing from calm to meltdown in the blink of an eye."

"That sounds challenging for a child," Alana said.

"For everyone. But moments like this? So excited and making friends—it's all worth it. These small victories remind me it's possible to help Penny navigate the world around her."

Alana looked at him with something of a smile on her lips. She squeezed his shoulder. "You're a great dad, Cash."

A man with acne-scarred skin and sunken eyes appeared in front of Cash, blocking his path. His greasy black hair was slicked back from his forehead, and a scruffy goatee clung to his chin. "Hey, I know you! You're that doctor who killed my brother!" Spittle flew from the man's lips, and he slurred his words.

Cash stepped back. "I'm sorry?"

"My little brother. Emilio Trejo. He was shot and *you* let him die." The man closed the distance and thrust his face in Cash's. His hot breath reeked of alcohol and mingled with the bitter tang of rage that hung heavy in the air.

Trejo. Trejo. The name didn't ring a bell. "I—I'm truly sorry, but I have no idea what you're talking about."

Trejo's face twisted into a mask of fury. His dark eyes blazed with anger. "He was my only blood, and you let him die!" He slammed both palms into Cash's chest and shoved him back a couple of steps.

Cash's hands flexed into fists.

Alana was in the space between them. "Hey now. I think it's time for you to back off." The threat came out menacing considering she had to crane her neck up to give it.

Cash touched her shoulder. "Hey, it's okay. I got this. Just call the police before this guy hurts himself." People grieved in different ways, and he'd dealt with the whole spectrum from anger to depression. He didn't need Alana to shield him from the worst part of his job.

Her eyes needled him with intense concern. "Subduing suspects is the work of a bodyguard, not a surgeon."

Cool fingers brushed the back of his hand. The gesture was equal parts comforting and infuriating. It was part of her job to step in, but he wasn't the one in need of protection. Over her shoulder he saw Penny and Rocco watching a clown twist long balloons into the shape of a hot air balloon, oblivious to Trejo and his tirade. "Please, I can handle this. Keep Penny and Rocco safe, and call this in."

Cash turned to face Trejo. His loss of a patient was nothing compared to this man's grief. "I promise you, I did everything I could to save your brother. Emilio. There was too much damage to repair. I did my best, but sometimes it's just not enough." Trejo didn't need to know Cash was speaking about Dante Johnson, not his brother, the kid he couldn't remember.

Trejo's face twisted into a mask of hatred. "You liar! You see another thug on the table and think he's better on ice." He spat and reared his fist back.

The shot was wild. Cash easily ducked. He really did not want to fight with this guy. Trejo lunged, his body low like a linebacker going for a tackle. Cash sidestepped and drove his heel into the back of Trejo's knee. The man let out a grunt. His leg buckled, and Trejo crashed to the ground.

A scream sliced through the air. Cash's heart seized as he recognized his daughter's voice.

Penny!

His head snapped around to look at her. Trejo punched him in the face so hard he saw flashes of light. Cash saw it coming but didn't move quick enough. He deflected the second strike, and jabbed Trejo in the kidney. They both went to the ground and scrambled away from each other. He was on his feet seconds before Trejo.

That was when Cash saw the gun pointed at his head.

FIVE

Penny's scream had sent Alana into bodyguard mode, and she was on the move, dodging through the crowd that had formed around Cash and Trejo. Where was that goofy balloon-making clown?

"Mooooom!" Rocco's voice pierced the air. "Mom, he's got Penny!"

Alana's eyes followed Rocco's trembling finger. A thin man with a hoodie over his head pushed his way through the swarm of people listening to the concert. He carried Penny against his chest. A hand clamped over her mouth. An image of the hoodie-wearing guy from Forsyth Park flashed in her mind. It couldn't be the same guy.

"Stop that man! He's kidnapping a child!" Her shouts hit the wall of music. No one could hear over the music and singing.

Alana skidded to a stop and dropped beside Rocco. "Are you okay?"

He was nodding before she finished. "Help Penny."

Alana thrust her phone into Rocco's trembling hand. "The police are on the line. I want you to talk to them. You know the drill, right?"

More nodding.

"Cash might be in danger, so don't go to him without the police. Are you sure—"

"Go, Mom! Go!"

The last thing she wanted to do was leave her son, but Penny needed her. She kissed the top of his head and bolted into the crowd. Eyes glued to the back of the abductor.

Running was her least favorite activity, but she was good at it. While never a great sprinter, she could outlast most marathon runners. The man holding Penny kept looking over his shoulder. He wasn't the same guy from yesterday. She could tell by the color of his skin. The other guy was pale. This guy had a dark complexion, like her. Probably Hispanic.

He maneuvered between the hot air balloons, putting obstacles between himself and Alana. His body blocked her view of Penny. She kept calling for someone to help, but either they didn't hear over the music, or they didn't want to get involved. Either way, Alana refused to give up. She couldn't let him get away. Not with Penny.

She cut down the middle of the row, hurdling and ducking ropes stretched out to anchor the balloons. The man saw Alana and skirted around the next row. He dropped Penny into a wicker basket attached to a glowing red and gold hot air balloon. Oh no. He wasn't about to...no. No way.

He tossed his leg over the basket and climbed in. The gondola was narrow and held four people max. It was anchored with a single tie-off line that the kidnapper worked to unlatch.

"Stop that man!" Her voice rang out with authority. "Stop him! He's trying to abduct a child!"

The ground crew appeared confused. Their eyes widened and they stared at Alana, completely ignoring the man working to untether the line.

They couldn't fly without a pilot. No telling what would

happen. Alana had to get to Penny before the balloon took flight.

A burly man with a bushy white beard, wearing a baseball cap and overalls, waved his hands at the kidnapper. "Hey, get out of there! You can't be in the baskets."

The kidnapper dropped the rope and pulled a small silver weapon out of his pocket. A gun or a knife, maybe. "Get in."

The burly man's hands shot up. He shuffled backward. "Hey, I don't want any trouble."

The balloon jolted and lifted a few inches off the ground. Arms pumping, legs moving in a blur, Alana locked eyes onto her target. She was close. So close. Five yards.

With everything in her, she launched herself off the ground. Her fingers found the side hole used as a stepping aid. One hand clung to the opening as the balloon ascended into the sky. She looked between her dangling feet. Oh, what was she doing?

The rough texture of the woven wicker cut into her skin. Her fingers and triceps screamed for relief. Above her head were two other holes she could use to climb up.

If she could reach them.

The muscles in her arms stretched as she reached for the second hold. Her fingertips brushed the edge. Not. Quite. There.

She swung her legs back and forth like a pendulum, building momentum until she had the force to extend her reach to the hole. Her free hand found the edge and clamped down. She held tight.

A sigh slipped out. She closed her eyes and rested her forehead on the rough wicker. Now what? She opened her eyes and watched the ground below shrink. Her sweaty grip was the only thing keeping her from falling. Probably to her death. She gritted her teeth, determined not to let go.

Alana's hand slipped. She couldn't hang on much longer.

———

Cash worked hard to keep his tone calm and sympathetic. "C'mon, Trejo. This won't bring Emilio back. Put the gun down and we'll talk about what happened." His eyes darted between the gun and Trejo, searching for options. There weren't any. A firearm in the hands of a drunk was always a bad thing, but in this crowd, it would be catastrophic.

Trejo shook his head. "What's left to talk about? You let my brother die, and now it's your turn. A life for a life!" His finger curled around the trigger.

Cash took a quick look behind Trejo. Three men fanned out, each with a weapon trained on Trejo's back. The question was, could they shoot Trejo before he shot Cash? Cash didn't think so. He was standing less than six feet away, staring into the black eye of the muzzle.

The music had stopped. Emergency lights flashed somewhere beyond his peripheral vision. He'd been stalling Trejo so far, but the only way out of this was to convince him to lower the gun. "Emilio was a great kid, wasn't he?"

Trejo nodded. "The best."

"How old was he?"

"Too young." His voice cracked. "Nineteen."

"That's right. Way too young. I want to hear more, but your finger on that trigger is making me nervous. Can you..." Cash patted the air, indicating lowering the gun.

Trejo glared at Cash a beat. The gun went down.

He forced himself not to exhale. This wasn't over yet. The officers had their guns pointing straight at Trejo. Cash caught a flash of the bright yellow grip in one officer's hand. Taser gun.

The words clicked into place as two hooked probes shot out at a speed of over 160 feet per second. The tiny barbs latched onto Trejo's back and neck. Fifty thousand volts screamed through his body. Trejo went limp. The officers swarmed. Wrenched his hands around and clamped handcuffs on his wrists.

"Dr. Cash! Dr. Cash!" Rocco stood beside a female officer, waving his hands.

He ran to Rocco and scooped him up. He pressed his palms into the boy's back. "Rocco," he breathed. The last few minutes came crashing down around him. He hadn't had his head blown off. Trejo hadn't been killed. Rocco was safe.

Cash's cool started to slip. He put Rocco down and squatted to eye level. "Where's Penny? Where's your mom?"

Rocco turned and pointed.

Cash craned his neck upward. It took his eyes a second to focus on the object. A glowing hot air balloon suspended in the night sky with Alana hanging from the basket.

SIX

If she survived this, someone should tell Alana she was stupid. She had no idea what she was doing. Never even been rock climbing. But somehow, she'd managed to get the toe of her shoes into the steps and shift her weight to her legs.

The air was so cold her teeth began to chatter. She could hear Penny crying and the kidnapper mumbling words she couldn't make out. She was out of options. If she stayed here... well, she couldn't even think about that. Penny needed her.

Heart pounding, she pulled herself up and peered over the lip of the basket. The kidnapper was young, with wild eyes that darted around. He had tattoos on every part of skin showing. Splotches of red sores around his mouth told a story of long-time drug abuse. His grip on Penny was tight, holding her in front of him like a human shield.

Then she saw what he held in his hand. The silver weapon wasn't a gun. It wasn't a knife. It was an uncapped syringe.

Now or never. She swung her leg up and over the edge and threw herself into the gondola. She fell on her hands and knees, pausing to let the swinging motion of the basket settle before scrambling to her feet.

Startled, he fumbled with the syringe and put his thumb over the plunger. "Stay back," he hissed.

"Wait, wait, wait. I won't hurt you. I just want to talk. Can you tell me your name?"

He glanced over his shoulder. They were still rising, but slower.

"Let's start with something easy. Just your first name."

"C-C-C-Carl."

"Okay, that's good, Carl. You're doing good." Carl's pupils were blown out. He was as high as the hot air balloon, which made him dangerous. "I'd like you to let go of the girl. Can't you see you're scaring her?" Alana reached for Penny.

Carl tensed and raised the syringe. Penny screamed.

"Are you deaf, lady? I said stay back."

"Okay, easy. But look around. There's nowhere to go. If I move any farther back I'll be flying." The instant the words were out of her mouth she wanted to snatch them back. She didn't need to give him any ideas about throwing her overboard.

Carl turned Penny to face him. "I'm sorry, okay?"

He lowered the syringe. Oh, thank goodness. He'd come to his senses and—

Carl stabbed the needle into Penny's stomach and pushed the plunger.

Penny shrieked.

"No!" Alana lunged and snatched Penny out of his grasp. She pushed Penny behind her back, shielding her from Carl. Penny clung to Alana's waist and buried her screams into Alana's shirt. "What did you give her?"

Penny continued to scream.

"Tell me, Carl! Tell me what you gave her!"

A blank expression had come over his face. Something was wrong. He stared over the side, scratching his neck with dirty fingernails. In one languid motion, Carl tossed the syringe out into the inky blackness. It sailed to the ground.

"No!" Alana grabbed him by the shoulder and spun him around. "Hey, look at me!" She snapped her fingers in his face. "What was in the needle, Carl? Tell me!"

"I don't...I don't know." His hands clutched the edge of the basket. He leaned backward, staring at the ground over his shoulder.

She needed to know what he'd given Penny, but they weren't in a good place. His furtive glances and jittery movements were telltale signs he was coming down from his high. She had to keep him calm.

"Okay, look. There's nowhere to go, so we may as well work together to get this thing on the ground."

Penny's screams settled into sobs.

"No way." His expression darkened. "We're taking this thing as far as it will go."

Alana's stomach dropped. This man had some sort of death wish. "Do you know how to fly this thing, cuz I sure don't."

He lifted himself and sat on the edge of the basket, hands clutching the suspension cables. His hair fluttered in the wind. "We'll fly to Mexico. Think this thing can go to Mexico? Or Fiji! I always wanted to go to Fiji."

"We're not going to Fiji. We're gonna end up crashing into something, and then where will we be?"

Carl shrugged. "What do I care? I'm dead already."

It happened in slow motion. Carl leaned backward and released his grip. His thin body dropped out of the basket and plummeted to the ground below.

Alana whirled away. Eyes squeezed shut, she knelt and held Penny tight. "It's okay."

Tears pricked her eyes, but she wouldn't let herself cry. Lord, please say Penny hadn't seen what had happened. Let the injection, whatever it was, not harm her.

"Hurt," Penny whimpered.

"Oh, baby girl." She thumbed Penny's soft cheeks and studied her face for symptoms from the injection.

Penny's eyes were red, and her pulse raced, but then, so did Alana's. "It's okay, honey. We're okay."

At least, they would be as soon as she figured out what to do. She rubbed Penny's back and blew out a shaky breath. "All we have to do is figure out how to land this thing."

Penny sniffed and ran a hand under her nose. "I know. Rocco teached me."

"Are you kidding? You...you really know how to drive this thing?"

Penny gave a small nod.

"You are so amazing." Alana smiled and tucked Penny's hair behind her ears. "Well, Captain, what do we do?"

Penny's small voice instructed Alana to pull a nylon cord to open the vent and allow hot air to escape. Alana alternated working the red and orange cords, trying to steer the balloon back toward the field of brightly lit hot air balloons dotting the ground. It took a few attempts to find the sweet spot, but eventually, they began a slow descent.

The balloon basket finally touched down, swaying gently as it settled onto the grassy field. She must've done something wrong, because the balloon deflated and fell to the ground behind them.

They climbed out of the basket. Her knees gave out. She sank to the ground and hugged Penny. The girl's small frame shuddered each breath, but she wasn't screaming or even crying. Simply breathing. Alana closed her eyes and took another deep breath. If the injection had a physical effect on Penny, she couldn't see it.

The blare of sirens cut through the night. Alana's eyes flew open, and she turned her head toward the horizon. A line of emergency vehicles flashing red and blue lights raced across the field. The sound was almost deafening, drowning out everything else. As Alana struggled to her feet, several emergency vehicles raced past them. Probably headed for wherever Carl had landed.

A pickup slid to a stop in the ankle-high grass. Rocco and Cash jumped out and sprinted toward them.

Alana lifted Penny and thrust her into Cash's waiting arms. "The man...he gave her something. An injection. In her stomach."

Cash's eyes widened. "What was it?"

She shook her head. "I-I-I don't know. He wouldn't say. Is she going to be okay?"

Cash didn't respond. Holding Penny against his chest, he ran to the ambulance, shouting instructions to the paramedics. The doors slammed shut. The ambulance took off, sirens wailing.

Alana hugged Rocco and kissed his head. Images of Carl's face flashed unwanted in her mind. The realization hit her hard. Tonight, she'd risked everything to save Penny but had come so close to losing her own son. She'd left him standing alone in a crowd and charged into danger. Nearly fallen to her death like... like Carl had.

There were sacrifices she'd have to make to be an Elite Guardian, but her son wouldn't be one of them.

"Mom? Will Penny be okay?"

Alana squeezed his shoulders. "I don't know, baby. I don't know."

Whatever was in the injection, Alana prayed Cash would find out before it was too late.

SEVEN

ELITE GUARDIANS AGENCY

SATURDAY, 7:49 A.M.

Cash was dead tired after a long night at the hospital. He hefted a sleeping Penny up the bricked steps of the Elite Guardians office. The historic three-story home near Lafayette Square ate up half a block of prime Savannah real estate. The cream and black exterior maintained the details of the traditional mid-nineteenth-century homes of the area.

Inside, a young woman with a midnight-painted smile stood behind the reception desk. She embodied the essence of goth culture in a lacy black corset-top dress, chunky combat boots, a thin choker necklace, and thick eyeliner rimming smoky eyes. Her hair gleamed with an iridescent sheen of ebony that shimmered with hints of deep blue and purple. "Good morning—oh…" She covered her mouth and whispered, "Sorry, I didn't realize she was asleep."

Cash hoisted Penny higher on his shoulder. He didn't bother

to lower his voice. "No worries. She slept through the extraction from the car and the trek up here. I think she's good."

"Cool. I'm Raven, administrative assistant to the Elite Guardians. Alana asked me to make you comfortable in our client room while they finish up. Shouldn't be long. Follow me."

Raven led him to a parlor behind the reception area. The room had gorgeous wide-plank hardwood floors, a marble mantel over the gas fireplace, and ornate finial and garland decorative plaster moldings. The windows flanking the fireplace offered a view of a massive live oak tree in the center of the garden. "Wow, is that the original crown molding?"

"Most of it. This home has been in Juliette's family for generations. Her grandmother handed it down when she passed away. Juliette moved into the ground-floor apartment while the upper floors underwent restorative renovations but decided the big old house was too much for one person."

He surveyed the refined details of the room. His ex-wife had been an interior decorator, and he'd learned to appreciate the intricacies. "It's exquisite."

"I'll be sure to let her know." Raven dipped in a half curtsey. "Take a seat wherever you like. Can I bring you a hot or cold beverage?"

"Coffee?"

"You got it."

The door closed with a soft click, and Cash sank into a silk striped armchair. He shifted Penny off his shoulder and cradled her in his arms. He probably should let her rest on the couch, but he couldn't bear not holding her. At least, not right now.

He brushed Penny's tangled hair away from her forehead. It needed washing and brushing, but Penny's sensitivity made it near impossible to get through without tears. It was a daily battle, and today he didn't have the heart to put her through the fight.

The door opened and Alana crossed the room with a soft

stride. She wore black pants and a white silk shirt under a leather tactical jacket. "Hey, how's she doing this morning?"

Cash shifted the sleeping Penny in his arms. A bit of drool had trickled out of her open mouth and dried her cheek to his arm. "She's sacked out. Has been for a few hours."

Alana sat in the matching chair beside him and angled herself to face him. "Good. And emotionally?"

He bobbed his head side to side. "Too early to tell. But by the way she screamed bloody murder about the needle last night, I wonder if the blood draw was more traumatic than the abduction."

She flashed a tight smile. "I get it. I hate needles too."

Interesting. So there was something that scared the woman. Seeing her dangling from a rising hot air balloon last night had him thinking she was fearless.

"So, what changed your mind about professional security?"

He huffed a laugh. "Are you kidding? I've done some death-defying things in my life, but you did it without gear or backup. All to save my daughter from a kidnapper. Seeing you in action sealed it. I don't think I'll ever forget watching you pull yourself up and into the basket. The image is burned into my brain."

"It's my job." She averted her gaze and focused on smoothing an invisible crease on her pants.

He caught the flicker of doubt in her features and put his hand over hers. She stilled and stared at his fingers. "You charged headfirst into danger to save Penny, and I know it meant leaving Rocco alone in a dangerous situation. It takes one decisive, brave person to make a choice like that. My daughter over your son." He shook his head. "I don't know how I can ever thank you for what you did."

Her dark eyes fluttered up to look at him. The muscles of her neck jerked with a hard swallow. "It wasn't the smartest thing I've ever done, but—"

"I have beverages," Raven said, carrying a silver tray with

bottled waters and a cup of coffee. The coffee cup clinked against the tray as she lowered it to the wooden console.

Noelle and Juliette came in and each took a seat on the Crillon sofa opposite him. They made polite small talk while Raven placed their drinks on coasters and arranged them on the glass coffee table.

"That should do it," she said. "Buzz if you need anything."

Cash was still getting to know each of the women in the office, but he had to admit the team stood up to the Elite name.

Noelle Burton headed up the Savannah branch of the Elite Guardians and came across as a tough-as-nails rule follower. Could've been a hard lesson learned during her time as a Savannah PD detective.

Juliette Montgomery's soft brown eyes and delicate features framed by a honeyed pixie cut made her appear gentle. Harmless, even. But he wasn't fooled. Underneath that unassuming exterior, the former Army Ranger harbored a concealed fatal power.

"So, Dr. Thomas. Any clue about what was in the injection?" Juliette asked.

"Please, call me Cash. The doctor thing makes me feel like I'm at work." He grinned, letting her know he wanted to keep things casual. "The tox screen came back clean. It wasn't a narcotic. She has a slightly elevated white blood cell count. Other than that, her blood work is normal."

"Elevated whites? Is that bad?" Noelle didn't take her eyes off him while she smoothed the folded sleeves of her blouse.

"Not necessarily. Stress could cause it, and Lord knows she's been through the wringer the past few days. There's one more test we're waiting on, but the way everything is reading, I think it's possible she was injected with nothing more than saline as a scare tactic."

"Or maybe God protected Penny from something more sinister," Alana said.

He nodded. "That would be an answer to my very fervent prayers over the last twelve hours."

"Mine too," Alana said.

"I'll keep monitoring her for symptoms and keep you posted. How about Rocco? How's he doing after all the excitement last night?"

"He can't stop talking about it. He's out there right now telling Raven how cool his mom is." Juliette's eyes glinted and she gave Alana a single nod.

"All I know is she's a force to be reckoned with. You guys should have seen her hanging from that hot air balloon basket. If Alana hadn't been there...well, I don't want to think about what could have happened."

"How'd you manage to land without crashing?" Juliette directed her question to Alana.

"It was all Penny. She was paying attention when Rocco told her how they worked."

"Still," Noelle said, shaking her head. "I'm impressed."

"Yeah, well, let's discuss options," Alana said, changing the subject. "First, Jeremy Black tries to kidnap Penny. Then Trejo throws a punch and pulls a gun while Carl Bizik steals Penny and injects her with something." She shook her head. "You're being targeted. If it were me and Rocco, I'd want around-the-clock protection and investigative services until I had some answers."

Cash looked at Noelle. "Okay, so can I request Alana? She already has a relationship with Penny, and it helps to keep her on routine, in familiar surroundings, and with familiar people."

"That can be arranged," Noelle said with a smile.

"And Rocco? I know it's a lot to ask, but can he hang out with Penny at times? His friendship has done wonders for her already. He has a way of making her feel safe when her world doesn't make sense."

Alana flicked her eyes to Noelle, then back to him. "They do have a special bond we want to see flourish, but not if it means putting either child in danger."

Noelle said, "I suggest we consult the threat assessment. We often work with Detective Matt Williams, and he's on board with our agency handling some of the investigative work. We've run down the risks you might face and planned the security measures required. I'd like to wait and go over it when Matt arrives. But in low-risk situations, I don't see why Penny can't have a friend around if the parent agrees."

"Sounds reasonable. I can't ask Alana to put her son's life at risk to indulge Penny." He shifted the subject. "Did you ever figure out why that Carl guy jumped?"

"Yeah," Juliette said. "The whole thing was strange. It's not normal to pick a hot air balloon as an escape plan."

Alana shook her head. "I think he was high. Not thinking clearly. I don't know what his plan was, but I tried to talk to him, and right before he jumped, he said something about being dead anyway. I don't know what he gave her, what his plan was, or who put him up to it. He seemed despondent and just...let himself fall."

Cash's stomach twisted into a knot. "And now we may never know."

Alana touched his arm. "Maybe Trejo was a distraction, giving Carl a chance to grab Penny, or maybe it was a legit coincidence. Either way, this involves both you and Penny, and we'll figure it out."

"You're right. It's better to be safe than sorry. I need to know that Penny is protected no matter what."

"Good," Noelle said. "Now let me ask you, could any of this be connected to your time in the Navy? Maybe something happened during your service that's coming back to haunt you?"

"If someone has a vendetta against you, they might see your daughter as a way to hurt you," Juliette said.

"I can't think of anything like that." Cash rubbed his

forehead. A dull ache lingered behind his eyes. He shifted Penny to alleviate the numbness settling into his fingers.

Penny's eyes popped open, and her body tensed.

Cash braced himself for what was coming before the first scream tore from her lips.

———

Alana sprang to her feet along with Noelle and Juliette. Penny's continued screams shredded the mother's heart within her chest. There had to be something she could do. Some way to comfort the crying child.

Her fingers brushed the little girl's hand. "Penny, honey—"

Penny released an earsplitting shriek. She thrashed Cash's arms. Her hands flew to her head and clawed her hair.

Cash dodged Penny's flying elbows. "Hey, um...no offense, but it would be best to give her some space." He deposited Penny on the floor and hovered on the edge of the chair. "Penny, Daddy knows you're overwhelmed, so we're going to give you some space, okay?"

Tears streamed down Penny's face. She balled up. Clutched her knees to her chest and rocked like a tiny wrecking ball.

Alana had made a huge mistake. She knew how to calm kids and adults in a crisis but hadn't considered Penny's ASD. Her colleagues had beelined it to the door the moment the screaming began. She should've done the same. Instead, she'd made things worse.

She turned to leave.

"Alana, wait." Cash's voice froze her to the spot. "Can you get Rocco and come stay with us? A familiar face sometimes helps her make sense of unfamiliar places." His eyebrows arched high, waiting for a response. "Please?"

Her head was nodding. Feet moving toward the door.

Two minutes later, Rocco sat cross-legged on the floor

beside the wailing Penny. He cupped his hands over his ears. "Hey, you don't have to be so loud, ya know. You're hurting my ears."

"Rocco, be nice." She glanced at Cash from her spot near the fireplace. If he had a problem with Rocco's method, it was hidden behind his broad smile.

"It's cool if you're scared," Rocco said. "I get it. This old house is kinda creepy. Know what I do when I'm scared? I focus on my breathing. Ever tried that? My uncle Grey taught me. He said take one deep breath, then suck in another breath before you push it all out. Do it like this." Rocco sat ramrod straight and closed his eyes. He sucked in a deep breath, then a second, smaller one before pushing the breath out in a slow, even stream.

Penny emitted a soft sniffle and used her knee to wipe away the clear mucus dribbling from her nose. A delicate puffiness encircled her red-rimmed eyes. She watched Rocco repeat the breathing exercise. Penny seemed to understand and followed his example. A double inhale followed by a long exhale. A few minutes later, both children were laughing as if nothing had happened.

Cash patted Rocco's shoulder. "Good job, bud. I gotta remember that one."

Rocco looked at Alana with that same twinkle in his eye from the other night. A conversation about how much he liked Dr. Cash and Penny was sure to come up. Again. She'd have to be firm and help Rocco understand that her personal life was separate from work.

Rocco handed Penny a fidget spinner. "You wanna go hang out with Raven? She's so cool."

"Yay!" Penny bobbed her head.

Once the kids were settled with Raven, Cash and Alana joined Noelle, Juliette, and Detective Matt Williams in the smaller conference room near the reception desk. With the double doors open, Alana had a clear view of Rocco and Penny taking turns spinning in Raven's cool chair.

Noelle slid a folder to each of them. "Alana compiled our initial threat assessment and made copies for each of you. Matt was kind enough to drop by to update us on the investigation."

"Thanks, Noelle. I can't stay long, but certainly happy to give an update. The man who assaulted you last night is named Luis Trejo." There was a slight jut of Matt's chin. Something the detective did often before he delivered hard news. "Trejo is a distributor for the Madrina cartel. Word on the street is he wants vengeance for the death of his brother. We'll do what we can to hold his arraignment until the weekend, but it wouldn't matter if we held him for years. Trejo is a dangerous man who doesn't get his hands dirty. He doesn't have to. He has a small army willing to follow his orders."

Alana didn't like the sound of that. As a distributor, Trejo would be at the top of the Colombian-based organization, second only to the leaders. The Madrina cartel had a reputation for ruthless killings. Last week, the bodies of two teenagers had turned up in trash bags somewhere outside Hatchet, New Mexico, after they'd tried to escape working in a cocaine processing plant. Kidnapping and murder were all in a day's work for the cartel.

"I can't believe this is happening. How is this my fault? I wasn't the one who pulled the trigger." Cash stared at Matt. "If this guy is a known drug lord, why can't you arrest him and everyone who works for him?"

"We're working on it, but we need more evidence for a big arrest." Matt's chin jutted again. "Like I said, if Trejo wants to kidnap Penny for revenge, jail won't stop him from getting it done."

Alana touched Cash's arm. As a doctor, his whole life was probably spent anticipating what came next. Thinking three or four steps ahead. Running scenarios and preparing for possibilities. She got it. It was her job too. "Jail might not stop Trejo, but the Elite Guardians will."

"I can't argue with that," Matt said. "This is complicated. Attempted kidnappings, shooting, murder, and now a suicide. We're putting a lot of man-hours behind this. If Trejo is involved, we'll get him." The detective pushed back from the conference table and stood. "I need to run down a few leads from my informant. I'll be in touch."

"Thanks, Detective." Alana stood and shook his hand before he slipped out the door.

Noelle opened her folder and shuffled papers. "Alana has compiled a thorough threat assessment, but we have a few questions. Alana?" She lifted an eyebrow to offer the floor.

The chair creaked under Alana's weight, and she angled herself to face Cash. "I'm sorry if our questions seem invasive, but my gut says there's more to the attempted kidnappings than Trejo's revenge."

Cash leaned back in his chair and tossed his hand up. "I'm all ears."

"In a crime like this, the police always look at the parents first. If they haven't ruled you out already, they will soon."

"Wait, you think I could be a suspect? I was in surgery when Libby was shot."

"True, but you could've hired someone—" She held up a hand. "I'm not saying that's something you'd do, but part of the investigation is ruling both parents out completely."

"Fair enough. And that rules out Penny's mom."

Alana glanced around the room. Juliette nodded, urging her on. "We understand your wife is deceased, but we'd like to ask a few more questions. Do you mind?"

"What did you want to know?"

"Start at the beginning?"

"Sure, the beginning. The beginning is easier than the end, that's for sure." Cash paused, rubbing his jaw and fixing his stare at a spot on the table. "We met in high school. I was on the swim team with her older brother Darian, and I'd seen Sonia a few times at meets. I didn't realize she was a swimmer until my sister, Bailey, joined the girls' team. The four of us ended up as friends."

"And you eventually ended up dating?" Alana prompted.

"It was natural, I guess." He shrugged. "After high school, I joined the Navy to help pay for medical school. The long-distance thing was difficult, so we got married thinking it might fix things. We were young. Too young."

Juliette tapped a paper in front of her. "She stayed to finish college while you deployed overseas?"

"Yep. For some reason, I thought she wouldn't miss me being around. You know? She'd be busy with school and friends. But it was tough."

Alana could imagine. Those days of holding her son for the first time, embarking on a whole new journey as a mother but going at it alone. It was more than tough.

"After college, Sonia's older sister, Ziva, helped her start her own interior design business. Introduced Sonia to a few big clients and it took off. She decorated several historical homes on Jones Street, and later, big name celebrities hired her to decorate their beach houses on the island. She was great at it. Bought the house where Penny and I live now and decorated it herself. Said it was a surprise for me, but my guess is it was some kinda live portfolio for her clients. I didn't realize how much money she was making until...until her death."

Noelle had helped Alana pull Cash's financials. The numbers in his bank balance had left her speechless.

"How long were you married before Penny was born?" Noelle asked.

"Let's see..." Cash tipped his head back and squinted. "About four or five years. Somewhere in there. Penny was only two when Sonia died. But Sonia had filed for divorce around

Penny's first birthday. I knew she was unhappy, but man, I had no idea things were so bad. I was deployed with the SEAL team as a combat surgeon. Living in constant high-stress, dangerous situations. I refused to take leave and come home. The weight of my responsibility to the team was so heavy I simply forgot about the court date and was divorced by default. Goes to show what kind of husband I really was."

Alana's heart twisted at the pain in his voice. She carried her share of guilt over all the times she wasn't home for Rocco because she was out saving the world. Or so she thought. "Can you tell us more about how Sonia died?"

"I was deployed when Hurricane Irma came through here. People in Savannah don't worry too much about hurricanes. There hasn't been a direct hit in decades, so maybe Sonia didn't think twice about driving to a client's house on Tybee Island during the bad weather. But her car got caught up in a flash flood and swept away. Pulled her car right off the road and into the ocean. Somehow it disappeared, but I don't understand how that could happen."

Tybee Island was a barrier island east of Savannah, popular with tourists. The charming coastal beach town also drew celebrities looking for a tranquil vacation home. "The storm surge could've pushed her car toward a low-lying area where it could be submerged in floodwaters and carried away by the current," Alana said.

"That's what the Coast Guard said. After searching over a week, they declared Sonia and her vehicle 'irretrievably lost.'" He made air quotes. "The car could be anywhere by now."

The room stilled. Alana processed the information. Sonia's last moments would have been terrifying. "I'm sorry, Cash. Losing her like that must've been incredibly difficult for you."

"I guess the hardest part is the not knowing."

"I can imagine," Juliette said.

"The funeral was awful. The family had a casket." He looked

at Alana. "A casket. Can you believe that? They never found her body, but her parents insisted on a coffin. It's not like I had a say in it. We were divorced. And her brother, Darian, blamed me for her death. Shoot, I blamed myself. At the funeral, he got in my face and tried to start a fight. If Ziva hadn't stepped in and calmed him down, I don't know what would have happened.

"After the funeral, I was a mess. I couldn't focus. I couldn't go back to the field. Couldn't be there for the soldiers who needed me. I had to take some time off to be there for Penny and to just...get my head together. And when I finally got my head on straight, I knew I had to fight for my daughter. Sonia's parents wanted custody, but I couldn't let them take her away from me. It was a long, difficult battle, but in the end, I won."

"I can't believe they'd try and take Penny from you," Alana said.

"It was awful. I don't know what I would do without Penny. God opened my eyes to a second chance. A chance to be the best dad I can be."

Alana smiled. "I know what you mean. Rocco is everything to me here on earth, and he drives me to be a better person. I didn't plan to be a single mom, but I can't imagine my life without him."

"Being a parent changes everything," he said.

"Yes, it does." Alana caught the smile exchange between Noelle and Juliette. Time to bring the conversation back to business before they developed any Rocco-shaped ideas about a romance between her and Cash, because that would never happen. "After reviewing your background and what you've said here, I—we—believe Trejo isn't your only threat."

His eyes opened wide. "What do you mean?"

Alana didn't waste time sugarcoating it. "There's a distinct possibility that Sonia's parents hired someone to kidnap Penny."

———

"No. No way." Cash drew his hand over his face. Being the target of a dangerous drug lord was bad enough. He couldn't rehash a custody issue with his former in-laws. "Look, I already fought this battle in court. I have sole custody. I've offered to let them visit Penny, but they didn't want that. They moved back to Colombia and haven't so much as mailed a birthday card since. After all these years, I can't believe they'd be behind this."

Alana pulled a sheet of paper to the top of her stack. "Sonia's siblings moved back to Colombia to start a construction business before she passed away, and then her parents followed three years ago, correct?"

"Not like they notified me or anything, but sounds about right," he said.

"The business is doing well. They have the means to pull this off. To…circumvent the courts. But it's just one theory."

Noelle's fingers traced the edge of her sleeve. "We're checking into it. We'll also use our connections with Homeland to get a bead on whether Sonia's parents have traveled to the States recently."

"Juliette is working with Matt to see if we can pull phone records and credit card statements." Alana tapped her folder. "A few other threads we plan to pull. If Sonia's family isn't involved, at least we'll eliminate them as suspects."

Alana had a point. The police did it all the time. It's why they'd included him in the initial investigation. Maybe they were leaping to conclusions, but he'd rather know for sure where the enemy lines were.

There was one thought niggling in the back of his mind. "It did seem like a pretty big coincidence that Trejo would confront me at the exact moment Bizik snatched Penny."

Alana's dark eyes softened. The only way he could describe her in that moment was *beautiful*. "Don't worry. We'll figure out if it's connected. In the meantime, we'll keep you both safe."

He had to clear his throat to speak. "I have no doubt."

The thick folder in front of him beckoned. As a distraction, he opened it for the first time. A quick scan of the papers said Alana had done her homework. Full background checks on his colleagues at work, Penny's therapists and doctors, teachers, Sonia's family, police reports, and a brief bio on his parents and sister. Several papers appeared to be satellite images and water current maps of Savannah and Tybee Island.

He put the sheets on the table and turned them toward Alana. "These charts are from the Coast Guard?"

"I'm taking a second look at the investigation," Alana said. "Covering all the bases."

"Yeah, okay." He tucked the papers back into the folder. There was a part of him that didn't want to go there. Not right now.

The muscles in his neck ached. He kneaded the tendons and looked through the doorway. Penny was on her tummy, head propped in her hands, crossed legs swinging in the air. Rocco had his legs stretched out, leaning against the desk. Raven enraptured them with whatever story she was reading.

"It's been a long night. I should probably get Penny home soon. When do we start this whole bodyguard thing?"

"Right now," Alana said. "Officially, I'll take point on your case. We've discussed the rotations and come up with a reasonable plan. I'll take day shifts. Juliette and Noelle will alternate night shifts. Twelve hours. When we're in public, one of them will assist. Does that still sound good?"

Twelve hours a day with Alana. He had to fight a grin. Things with Trejo were serious. The weight of their situation did not escape him. But electricity sparked in his veins at the idea of spending more time with Alana. "Yes. That all sounds great, thanks."

"You've expressed interest in having Rocco around," Noelle said. "I'll leave it up to Alana. If she's comfortable having Rocco there, then we are too."

"There's one other thing," Noelle said. "Close personal protection at the hospital will be tricky. Besides the issues with sterile environments, doctor-patient confidentiality…"

"We're not saying it can't be done, but it would be easier if you took time off." Juliette tossed her pen on the table. "Trejo's shown he has no qualms about public attacks. It's the smart thing to do."

The Elite Guardians had no idea what they were asking. The clash between professional ambition and paternal duty dominated his thoughts and kept him up at night. The title of Chief of Surgery was his dream. His North Star, guiding him through the long nights and demanding surgeries. And it was within his reach. A breath away. This was forcing him to give it up.

EIGHT

EAST RIVER STREET

SUNDAY, 12:29 P.M.

After church services, Alana drove to lunch while Cash used his phone to check on his post-op patients. In the back seat, Penny's sleepy head jostled against Rocco's old high-backed car seat. Alana figured it was too risky to bring Rocco along if she was on the clock in public places and had sent him to church with Miss Martha.

Not the easiest thing when she considered the harrowing experience at Hillspring Church last Christmas. But she refused to let fear drive her decisions, especially when that was in the past and there was a very real threat to Cash and Penny right now.

Cash finished his text and tucked his phone under his leg. "I'd say everything's gone off without a hitch so far today...for the most part."

Alana stole a quick glance at him. "Trouble at the hospital?"

"No, I mean the mini Penny meltdown before church. I don't understand why brushing her hair is a knock-down, drag-out fight every time."

"She's probably tender-headed. I can relate. Something about having my hair pulled...I don't know. I just see red."

"See red like...?"

"Like my fist might smash into someone's face before my brain can tell my hands to stop." She flicked her gaze to him, then back to the road. He had his brows scrunched. "Okay, I'm exaggerating. But it's true that I'm tender-headed, and hair-pulling is a surefire way to get me angry."

He harrumphed. "Maybe you should try brushing her hair next time."

Alana turned off Bay Street onto the Lincoln Street Ramp, where smooth pavement gave way to bone jarring cobbled stones. She slowed to a crawl and glanced in the mirror. Penny smacked her lips, but she didn't wake. "I'd be happy to give it a shot. If you don't think I'll make it worse."

"You can't possibly make anything worse."

Alana laughed. "Are you kidding? I barely touched her yesterday and the situation went nuclear." She pulled into the prearranged parking spot outside the River Street Grill, where Cash and Penny enjoyed shrimp and grits after church on Sundays. She reached for her bag, but Cash caught her hand.

"Hang on a sec." The leather seats made a grinding sound as he twisted to face her. "I don't know if I ever really thanked you. Properly, anyway. For what you did to save Penny. You put yourself in a dangerous situation. More than dangerous. You could've been killed. Twice." His eyes searched hers. "Somehow 'thank you' doesn't seem to cut it."

His warm hand still held hers, and she gave it a gentle squeeze. "I was just doing—"

"Don't pass it off as a part of the job. You went above and beyond...literally."

"If we're being honest here, I think you should know…that was my first hot air balloon ride."

Cash laughed so hard that it set Alana off too. She leaned over, clutching her quaking abs with one arm. Cash pulled his hand away and used it to cover his mouth. Every time she got herself under control, she'd look at Cash and bust up again.

From the back seat, Alana heard Penny's little giggles. Alana twisted around to see her kicking her feet and covering her mouth with her hands. Bright blue eyes shone with pure joy. "Daddy funny."

"Not Daddy," Cash said. "Alana. Alana's funny."

Penny kicked her feet higher and pointed. "Alana funny!"

The laughter died down, and Alana wiped beneath her eyes. Oh, how she'd needed that. Cash too, she guessed. The joke wasn't even that funny, but the stress and seriousness of the last few days had needed a release.

"I hungry!" Penny chirped.

"Me too," Cash said. "Shall we?"

"Yeah, sure. But we need to do things by the book." She pulled out the earpiece that gave her hands-free communication with Juliette. "Juliette, do you copy?"

"Copy. Security sweep is complete and you're clear to proceed."

A cotton warehouse built in 1780 housed the restaurant with authentic brick and cobblestone architecture from the eighteenth century. Not Alana's favorite, as the dark and cozy atmosphere reduced visibility. Juliette had snagged a table in the smaller dining room, which meant Alana would have a full view of the room. They'd decided Juliette would eat a quick lunch in the main dining area to cover potential threats in the zones Alana couldn't see.

"We'll be right in." Alana unbuckled her seatbelt and said to Cash, "Okay, wait for me to come around. Then you can get out and get Penny."

"Got it. But hey, um...you know, I kid around about Penny's meltdowns, but...I don't know. It's just my way of blowing off steam. It can be frustrating sometimes, but—"

"Cash, I get it." She patted his forearm. "Believe me, I get it. Rocco had colic and screamed for the first few...I don't know... years?" She chuckled. "It's not easy going at it alone. At least you're blowing off steam with someone who relates."

Alana escorted Cash and Penny inside. Laughter and the clinking of glasses echoed from the bustling bar area, and the savory scent of grilled meats wafted through the air. Her stomach rumbled with hunger.

They followed the hostess to their reserved table in the back room. Alana's eyes flicked from one face to another along the way. She nodded to Juliette as they passed. "I'm starving," she said into her comms.

"Try the lowcountry shrimp and grits. I promise, it's life changing," Juliette said.

Their waitress was a tall, curvy woman wearing a sleek black-on-black outfit and her hair pulled into a ponytail. When she reached to refill their drinks, Alana noticed tattoos on her wrists and hands. The waitress smiled at Cash. "Fancy seeing ya'll here on a Sunday."

Cash chuckled. "Alana, this is Jennifer. She's our regular server."

"Yep, worked here twenty-four years. Ain't about to quit now." She winked at Alana. "Get you somethin' besides water, darlin'?"

"Water's fine, thanks." Alana liked the waitress. She was polite and cheerful, but there was something familiar about the tattoos that made Alana's skin tingle.

When the food arrived, Cash and Penny chatted and laughed while enjoying their lunch. Alana tried to listen in on their conversation, but her attention kept getting pulled toward a man sitting alone at a nearby table. His eyes darted around the room while taking sips from his drink. She didn't like it. Not one bit. She was about to radio Juliette when the man sprang to his feet and rushed out. Alana kept her eyes on him as long as she could.

"Juliette, a man in a gray suit just left. Follow him, but keep your distance," she said into the earpiece. "Make sure he's not up to something."

With Juliette on the suspect, Alana shifted her focus back to Cash and Penny.

Her heart stopped. Where was Penny?

She moved to stand but then heard a soft giggle. The little girl's bright eyes peered out from under the tablecloth. "Dropped dis." Her fingers clutched a fidget spinner.

Alana forced out a measured breath. That little jolt had probably shaved about three years off her life.

"Sometimes I let her hide under there. I think it helps her escape some of the stimuli." He motioned to Alana's plate. "Didn't like the grits?"

"What?" She looked at the untouched bowl. "Oh. I guess I'm a little distracted."

He wiped his mouth with his napkin and placed it on the table. "Cool if I run to the restroom?"

"Sure, but...keep your eyes open. Juliette's off checking on a suspicious man who just left." Alana flicked her eyes around the restaurant, then back to Cash. "And I don't know what it is, but something is...off."

"We're almost done here, so I'll make it quick and we can leave."

"I'll box this up for later." It was delicious, and she couldn't enjoy it right now anyway.

"Good, I'll be right back." Cash stood and left several bills tucked under the centerpiece. "Tell Jennifer she can keep the rest."

Alana peeked under the table. "Hey, Penny, do you know how to write your name?"

"Yeah. P-E-N-N-Y."

"That's right! Hey, I have a crayon right here. Do you think you can show me on paper?"

"Okay!" The little girl crawled out to grab the crayon.

Alana glanced up to check on Cash. He'd paused near the door to allow a waiter carrying a tray full of food to pass. The waiter stumbled and the tray tipped. Cash flinched and tried to dodge, but he was too late. Plates of food rained down, drenching him from head to toe. The tray of dishes crashed to the floor in an explosion of porcelain.

In her peripheral vision, Alana saw a figure wearing a full-face motorcycle helmet lunge toward Penny. He scooped her up and turned to run.

The little girl's piercing screams echoed through the restaurant.

Alana charged the kidnapper and slammed her shoulder into the man. He stumbled and collided with a table. The helmeted figure regained his footing and rushed forward.

Alana pulled her Taser gun and aimed but couldn't fire with all the commotion of diners jumping from their seats. "Stop! Stop right now!"

The kidnapper glanced over his shoulder. A woman screamed and sprang from her chair. The chair toppled over in front of him. He tried to spin but lost his footing and fell backward onto a table. The legs buckled under his weight. Plates and glasses shattered as the table collapsed with the man holding Penny to his chest.

Penny screamed louder, but Alana was there. She gathered Penny into her arms and backed away. The helmeted figure rolled to his feet and sprinted out of the dining room.

Alana hesitated for a moment, torn between chasing after

him and staying with Penny. Before she could decide, Cash took off after the kidnapper.

"No! Cash! Wait!"

But it was too late. Cash disappeared through the doorway.

———

Cash's heart pounded as he burst through the swinging doors of the kitchen. The sweltering heat hit him like a sledgehammer, making him gasp for air. Pots and pans clanged as the helmeted suspect darted past the horrified cooks.

Cash's eyes locked on the suspect. "Hey! Stop that man!" At least, he assumed it was a man by the square shoulders and slight knob protruding from his throat. The black motorcycle helmet hid his face, so he couldn't really tell.

The kitchen staff stood frozen in place. Eyes wide and mouths hanging open. Not a muscle moved to help. Guess he was on his own. "At least call the police!"

Helmet Guy grabbed a rolling bread rack, swung it around, and shoved it at Cash. It rolled down the stove aisle, and a chef flattened himself against the grill to keep from getting hit. It rolled to Cash. He caught it and thrust it behind him. It crashed into a prep table and fell over.

When he turned around, Cash saw flames climbing up the back of the chef. "Hang on! Hang on!" He grabbed a towel and beat the flames out.

The chef gaped at Cash. "Oh my...thank...I didn't even realize..."

He pushed the towel into the chef's hands and took off. "Just call the police," he yelled over his shoulder.

He burst through the back door and into a narrow alley. The cool air hit him like a refreshing wave, but the smell of garbage and stale cigarette smoke made him want to gag. His feet slipped on the greasy brick pavement, and he grabbed a handrail to steady himself. It was covered in something he didn't want to think about.

He looked left and right. Which way had he gone? Savannah was always full of tourists around spring break, and the fact it was a weekend meant the locals were out too. Every street was filled with slow-moving people. He spotted the black helmet bobbing through a crowd on Factors Walk and Cash bolted after him.

Helmet Guy had a head start, but Cash was fast. He had to catch him and figure out who'd paid him to kidnap Penny. This was his chance to put an end to this dangerous game once and for all. Helmet Guy weaved in and out of the crowd. His bulbous head stood out among the sea of people until the street began to slope downward.

Cash pushed himself harder and topped the hill in time to see Helmet Guy turn right on the River Street access ramp and disappear. A few seconds later, Cash rounded the corner. Eyes on the hunt for the black helmet. He sucked in a ragged breath and spotted him jogging up the steep stone steps to the street level above. Cash's calves burned as he chased up the stairs after him.

As he reached the top, Cash caught sight of the attacker running across Bay Street. A car screeched to a halt and laid on the horn. Helmet Guy pounded his gloved fist on the hood. His head turned in Cash's direction before he ran to a black motorcycle parked at the curb and threw his leg over it. The bike looked menacing. Sleek and aerodynamic, with a shiny blacked-out finish that seemed to absorb all the light around it.

Half a block away. He could do this. He could catch this guy.

Cash crossed the street behind a dump truck rumbling by, filling the air with exhaust fumes. The motorcycle engine roared to life with a deep, throaty growl that shook the air. There was no plate on the bike. No way to identify it.

No. No. No. If he couldn't get there before Helmet Guy pulled away, he'd never catch him.

The motorcycle roared, drowning out the distant sounds of sirens. Helmet Guy glanced over his shoulder and revved the bike louder. The fool was taunting him. Cash lunged at the guy, but it was too late. The bike peeled away, kicking up bits of gravel and debris that pelted Cash's legs and face. He winced and shielded his face with an arm.

His eyes locked onto Helmet Guy as he weaved the motorcycle through traffic, the wind tearing at his clothes. The sound of the engine and the single taillight disappeared into the distance.

Cash turned around to head back to the restaurant only to find a small group of curious onlookers gathered around him. A few people offered help, but he waved them off and leaned his back against a nearby wall. He just needed a minute to catch his breath. Give his pounding heart time to slow. Detective Williams had said stranger abductions were among the hardest crimes to solve, and now, because he'd been too slow, they still didn't have any idea who was behind the kidnapping attempts. The thought of him still being out, able to try again—well, it made his blood boil.

He couldn't stand here and fret about it. He had to get back to Penny and Alana. As he picked his way back down the almost vertical staircase, he replayed the events of the past few days in his mind. Three men had tried to take Penny. Two were dead after failing. If Trejo wanted a life for a life, why kidnap Penny when any of those men could have pulled a gun and...No. He wouldn't go there. Trejo wanted Cash's life, not Penny's.

But if that were true, why hadn't Helmet Guy turned and shot him—

Cash stopped dead in his tracks and rubbed his forehead. "Ah! I'm so stupid!"

What had made him think he could chase that guy down and

not get shot? He shook his head and drew a deep breath. He couldn't run off without protection. That's why he'd hired the Elite Guardians. So they could chase down bad guys, not him. They had developed strategic plans to stop attackers, and here he was running down the street like he was in an action movie.

Thanks to Alana, Penny was safe. But this...whatever this was...it wasn't over. One thing he knew for sure...Trejo wasn't going to stop.

NINE

SUNDAY EVENING

Alana was quiet on the drive back to Cash's house, having drained all the adrenaline out of her system. She'd made the right decision to leave Rocco at home. Her brain didn't even want to consider what could have happened if he'd been there today.

Penny slept in her car seat, holding her daddy's hand. The last few days had been traumatic for the little girl. Shoot, they'd been traumatic for Alana. She couldn't shake the sound of Penny screaming out of her head.

They'd almost lost her. Again.

Alana turned into Cash's driveway and drove toward the house. No, it wasn't a house. It was a sprawling estate with breathtaking views of the Herb River. The pristine white home sat at the end of a circular drive, where she parked behind Juliette. The lot was narrow, so Alana could see Cash's neighbors, but the mature landscaping created a sense of privacy and seclusion.

"We'll wait here while Juliette does a thorough security sweep of the house and grounds," Alana said.

Cash turned and looked in the back seat. "Wow, she's still asleep."

"Probably for the best. She's been through so much." She wasn't sure if napping was normal for Penny, but Rocco had given them up years ago. "Is Penny okay? What I mean is, this is her second time falling asleep in the car. Are you sure this isn't a side effect from the injection?"

"I thought about that, but still...all her bloodwork is normal. Not so much as a fever. I'm chalking it up to the fact she hasn't gotten much sleep the last few days. Neither of us." He rubbed his jaw. "So, that was pretty stupid of me today, huh?"

"Chasing that motorcycle guy?" She lifted an eyebrow, pretending to think for a moment. "Incredibly risky, but incredibly brave."

"I don't know about that last part." Smile lines formed around his eyes. "At least I wasn't dangling from a hot air balloon."

"Hey now." She bumped his shoulder. They laughed and Penny stirred but didn't wake.

Alana looked past Cash to the house. Yellow lights flicked on behind each window. She let her eyes drift to Cash. He had his head turned, staring at Penny in the back seat. There was more behind the man than she'd realized. In the short time they'd been together, she found herself wanting to know him better. Not just the handsome man who'd found ways to make her laugh even in the serious moments, but as the father who would do anything to keep his daughter safe.

"All secure," Juliette said through Alana's earpiece.

"Copy, we'll head inside now."

Cash carried Penny inside and settled her onto the couch. Alana draped a soft blanket over her. They stood there, shoulder to shoulder, watching her sleep.

Cash's pinky finger brushed her knuckles, then intertwined with hers. She looked first at their hands, then at his soft eyes searching her face. "Thank you, Alana." The words were a whisper that sent the heat rushing to the tips of her ears.

Their moment was interrupted by the sound of Juliette's footsteps pounding down the staircase. "Everything's locked up tight. Quite the security system you've got here, Cash."

Alana moved to the alcove off the kitchen and feigned interest in the marshy river behind the house. From the way her cheeks and ears burned, she was sure her entire face was beet red, and she didn't want to explain it to Juliette.

"After the break-in a few months ago, I knew it was time for an upgrade." He carried two bottles of water between his knuckles and offered one to Alana.

"Thanks," she said, taking it. "I read the police report, but tell us what happened."

Juliette accepted a bottle from Cash and sat in one of the four matching armchairs. Alana followed suit, and Cash sank into the chair beside her.

"Let me think. It was probably back in November. Libby came home with Penny and found the back door wide open." He gestured to the French doors off the living room. "They knocked out a pane on the door, reached in, and bam—they were inside."

"In broad daylight?" Juliette asked. "Bold."

"Sounds like they knew you'd be gone." Alana screwed the cap onto her water bottle. "They didn't take anything?"

"Nothing I could find. The police thought Libby interrupted them and they took off. She didn't see anyone, and I didn't have surveillance cameras at the time, so we'll never know for sure."

Alana had faced off with Jeremy Black in her own backyard. She could think of too many bad scenarios for Libby and Penny if they'd walked in to find Black in the house. "Close call, though. You think the break-in has anything to do with the attempted kidnappings?"

"I doubt Trejo was behind it. The timing isn't right. I went back and checked the records. I didn't see his brother in the OR until a few weeks ago."

"I think I'll do another exterior perimeter check and leave you two to noodle it out." Juliette rose and left through the back door. With such a large estate, they'd decided to perform outside security sweeps every thirty minutes and inside every hour.

Cash leaned in. "Do you think Rocco could come over for a while? I think it would help Penny to have him around. He eases her anxiety. If it's too dangerous, you don't have to, of course."

The fear she'd seen in the little girl's eyes earlier tore at her heartstrings. "After all she's been through, I want to do whatever I can to make Penny feel safe and secure. With two bodyguards and your security system, we should be fine. I'll call Noelle and ask if she can bring Rocco over."

Cash's eyes softened. He reached over and squeezed her hand. "Thanks, Alana."

There went her ears again. Flaming hot. She distracted herself by pulling her phone out and making the call. "Hey, Noelle. Can you do me a favor? At the shift change, can you bring Rocco with you? After what happened today, we thought Penny could use a friend."

"Not a problem," Noelle said. "Let me wrap a few things up and I'll be on my way. Shift change is in an hour anyway."

She checked her watch. "Wow. Lost track of time. Thanks for doing that. I'll see you in a bit."

"No worries."

Alana disconnected the call. "Noelle will be here with Rocco in an hour. She'll take over for Juliette then."

"I better wake Penny. I don't want her to sleep too late."

"Good idea." Alana smiled, remembering she'd learned that lesson with Rocco the hard way. "While you do that, I'm going to check the windows and doors on the lower level."

After a thorough interior security check, Alana returned to the living room. She smiled at the sight of Penny and Cash together underneath the grand piano in his expansive living room. They'd built a cozy fort out of pillows and blankets that enclosed the space on three sides to make the perfect hiding spot. Fairy lights draped under the piano glowed a soft yellow. With a door made from sheer curtains, it looked like a secret world hidden away from the rest of the house.

As she was admiring their handiwork, the doorbell rang. For some reason she said, "I got it," even though she'd already said only an Elite Guardian would answer the door.

Through the peephole, she saw Noelle and Rocco waiting. The door was half open when Rocco rushed inside and threw himself at her waist. She caught her son in a hug and squeezed him. "I really missed you today, bud."

Noelle closed the door and turned the deadbolt. "Tell your mom what you told me in the car."

"We practiced Bible quiz in Sunday school, and my team got first place. I got to pick a prize from the treasure chest, and look what I got for Penny!" He held up a sparkly reflective pinwheel. "And Miss Martha let me have soda at lunch."

Alana raised an eyebrow.

"Diet soda," he said. "Can we stay late since it's not a school night? Please!"

Oh, it wasn't a school night, was it? With everything happening, she'd forgotten all about spring break. "We'll see, bud."

Penny and Rocco's greeting seemed more fitting for a soldier returning from months at war than two kids who'd met a few days ago. Penny tugged Rocco's hand. "Come!"

"Hey, Rocco," Cash called from beneath the piano. "Come check out our fort. It's pretty comfy in here."

Rocco's eyes lit up. "No, way! You guys made that?"

The kids crawled through the opening. With a growl, Cash

LYNETTE EASON & KATE ANGELO

grabbed Penny and lifted her over his chest. "You forgot to tell Rocco about the tickle monster!"

If Alana had had any doubts about bringing Rocco over, the squeals and giggles coming from the fort put them to bed.

Noelle laughed. "Oh, to be that carefree again."

"Thanks for bringing Rocco with you. I know it's not really our usual way of handling things."

"Hey, I'm all about unusual. I think it's great for him to spend time with Penny." She leaned close to Alana's ear. "It's like one big happy family."

Alana's elbow jutted out, but Noelle dodged her strike. She grinned and showed her palms. "Hey...I'm just sayin'..."

"Maybe you should shut it." There went all the blood to her ears again. She turned away. "Let's let them play, and I'll give you a tour."

"Fine, let's take a look. But you know I'm only teasin', right?"

"Yeah, yeah."

Noelle was half kidding, but she knew Alana had always wanted a normal life. The picture-perfect family with a loving husband and as many children as God would give her to raise. Her heart longed to create moments and memories like these, but for whatever reason, it hadn't been in God's plan. And somewhere between raising her son as a single parent, trying to make ends meet, and working toward her goal of setting up the outreach, she'd decided to set those dreams aside.

But maybe...just maybe it was time to bring them back.

———

Cash was a man who knew his limitations, which was why he hadn't bothered trying to impress Alana with his woeful cooking skills. Instead, he'd ordered what he considered to be the best pizza in town.

Juliette and Noelle joined them for dinner, and he found himself lost in their playful banter and child-appropriate stories of crazy clients. He'd almost forgotten what it was like to have adult conversation that wasn't centered around medical jargon. They stayed away from any talk about his current situation with the kids around. Hard to believe he'd been chasing a criminal across the streets of Savannah earlier today.

Juliette pushed back from the table. "Thanks for dinner. I'm gonna get out of here and leave you in the excellent hands of these two."

"And I should do rounds just to keep things tight. I can make some calls and see if we have any updates while I'm...you know...outside." Noelle cut her eyes toward Rocco, then back to Cash.

"Can we go back to the piano fort?" Rocco asked. "We want to keep reading *The Hobbit*. They were just captured by the wood elves, and we need to see how Bilbo escapes."

"Yeah, sure." Cash never would've thought it possible for two kids to be content reading a book when a house full of toys and electronics awaited. Rocco carried a phone, but he'd never seen the boy look at it for more than a few seconds.

Once dinner was cleared, Cash sank into the couch beside Alana. "I'm curious...how old was Rocco when you gave him a cell phone?"

"Um, probably around eight."

"And he's, what...nine now?"

"Actually, he's eleven. Why?"

"Just wondering about the appropriate age for electronics."

Alana laughed. "Oh...believe me, he wouldn't have a phone if he didn't need one. Rocco is diabetic. Type 1. He's a little small for his age."

That made sense about the phone. "Pretty common for children with diabetes, but he'll catch up. So, the phone is for his continuous glucose monitoring system?"

"The CGM and his insulin pump. I'm a bit of a helicopter mom." She glanced at her hands. "But I can't be there all the time...so the system works great for us."

Other parents probably gave her grief for giving her young son a phone. For some reason, complete strangers were compelled to offer advice on raising an autistic child. More often than not, it was criticism masked as helpful tips. As far as he was concerned, Alana could manage her son's medical issues in the way that worked best for their lifestyle.

"I think it's a great choice for active children and families. And I'm sorry about the pizza. I'll try to keep that in mind for future meals."

"We've learned to splurge now and again, but thank you, Cash. That means a lot to me."

They sat in comfortable silence. The mere presence of Alana in his home pushed back the danger and kept it at bay. And their connection went even deeper. She got being a single parent. He could see it etched in her features. The constant pull between a career and parenting—the one job that never ended. Alana knew the weight of tending to Penny's emotional state like a mother would. And it was sweet to see her interact with Penny as a mom, not just a bodyguard.

He leaned back and stretched his arms across the back of the couch. "I've made up my mind to keep Penny home as much as possible. After what happened today, it's too risky to have her in public."

"That's probably a good plan." Alana angled herself to face him. "How will she handle it?"

Cash caught the soft scent of lavender. Was that her shampoo, or perfume? Maybe a soap or lotion. Whatever it was, he liked it.

"I mean, you said changes in the routine are hard for her to process, right?"

"Oh, right." He pulled himself back into the conversation.

"It's spring break, and with work, I hadn't made any plans other than keeping her therapy appointment. Libby was making plans to take Penny on one of the trolley tours. You know, the kind where the actors get on at random stops?"

"Yeah, we've been meaning to do one of those since we moved here."

"Maybe we can all go sometime."

"Yeah. I'd like that." Alana flashed a small smile and brushed her bangs aside. He liked the way they sometimes fell into her eyes and she'd toss her head to get them back in place.

"I have to admit, Alana," he said with a sigh. "When Jonah suggested hiring you—the Elite Guardians, I mean—well, I couldn't wrap my head around it. Maybe I still can't. But all I know is if it weren't for you..." Well, he didn't need to spell it out for her. "I just can't believe this is happening. I spent years as a combat surgeon, working in war zones, and now I can't even keep my daughter safe in our own hometown."

"It's not your fault. You're doing everything you can. Sometimes, no matter how prepared we are, bad things happen."

"I just wish I knew what was going on. Why someone would want to take Penny."

Alana's expression softened. "I have a theory, but it's a long shot."

"I'm listening." He leaned in.

She glanced in the direction of the piano fort, then scooted closer. "It's not so much a theory as a door I'd like to close." Alana spoke in a quiet voice but paused and pressed her lips together. "Okay, so here's the long shot part. Ever since you told me about Sonia, I can't get over how difficult it must be. The not knowing, I mean. I thought I could study these current maps and the weather patterns and maybe get an idea about where her car could be."

Cash's heart skipped a beat. "Alana, that's great, but I've

spent years trying to find her car. The Chatham County dive team tried, and the Coast Guard said they'll look during training exercises, but nothing. I don't mean this to sound hurtful, but what makes you think you'd do any better?"

"Don't get me wrong, the underwater search and recovery team is great. When they offered a job, I thought about taking it. It's just that they aren't actively searching. They don't have the time to pore over data when so many other cases keep them occupied. I have a friend who does this type of search for a living. He has the right equipment to scan some of the probable areas for anomalies."

"Side-scan sonar?"

Alana nodded.

"Why would he do that for us?"

"He owes me a favor."

He wasn't sure he wanted to know why some guy owed her a favor. It seemed like it would be a pretty big favor to conduct a search on that scale. Especially when others had failed. "What happens if this friend finds an anomaly?" His words had a hint of sarcasm, but he hadn't meant it that way.

If Alana noticed, she ignored it. "He'll mark it and we'll determine if it's safe to dive."

It seemed like a lot of work for...for what? Another disappointment? "You can investigate it, sure. But I don't know how this will help us stop Trejo's men from trying to kidnap Penny."

Alana waffled her head side to side. "Maybe it won't help at all, but if we found Sonia's car, at least you could have closure."

"This is all a lot to think about, and it's been a rough couple of days." He rubbed his forehead. "Do you mind...I mean, can we talk about you for a little while?"

Her eyes widened. "Me? You want to talk about me?"

"Yeah. It wouldn't hurt to know a bit more about the woman

protecting my daughter. It'll take my mind off things, you know?"

"Fair enough." She pulled her legs up underneath her. "Well, what do you want to know?"

"Williams told me you were a dive detective, so let's start there. What made you switch to the exciting world of personal protection?"

"That's a way longer story than we have time for right now, but I can give you the Reader's Digest version."

"Reader's Digest? Aren't you too young for that?"

"Rocco's doctor isn't."

Cash chuckled. "I'll have to get you an e-reader. Those waiting room magazines are brutal."

"Good idea. I've been reading S. M. Warren's latest book, but when I have time to read, I don't have it with me. Never liked reading on my cell phone." She did the head shake again to get her bangs to lie correctly. "Anyway, Williams is correct. Before I moved here, I was an underwater dive detective for LAPD. My unit was a part of SWAT, so I have tactical training. My sister, Christina Sherman—well, Christina Parker now that she's married—works at the Elite Guardians Agency headquarters in Columbia, South Carolina. So here I am."

"That's not the Reader's Digest version. That's more like a byline. A tweet at most. You gotta give me more than that."

"Fiiine..." She rolled her eyes. "Christina and I were reconnected after years of being apart. When she told me about the new branch opening in Savannah, I knew it was where I needed to be. Close to her, but not so close we'd smother each other, you know?"

Cash nodded, taking in the way her eyes held a glimmer of something deeper, something she wasn't saying. He leaned even closer. He wanted to know everything about her. Every secret, every hope and dream. "Alana, I have a feeling there's more to you than you're letting on."

For a moment, her guard slipped, and he saw the flicker of vulnerability in her eyes. "Isn't there always?"

And just like that, Cash was hooked. Pulled right into her orbit.

"Can I ask you something?" She looked down at her nails. "Do you...or have you...ever considered...dating again?"

His head cocked to the side. Of course he'd considered it. He just hadn't expected that question from *her*. "What do you mean?"

She shrugged. Glanced at the piano fort, then back to her hands. "I don't know. It's just...you're a good-looking guy, and you seem like a great dad. I'm sure there are plenty of women out there who would be interested."

So, she'd noticed. Okay, time to play it cool. "I...I haven't really thought about it."

"You know what? Sorry. That's too personal. I didn't mean to pry."

"No no no." He touched her hand. "I just...well, it's difficult to trust people with Penny. Between work and spending time with her, who has time to think about finding someone who would fit?" As if someone could just...fit.

"I know exactly what you mean." She gave him a sympathetic smile. "It's not easy to let someone else into your daily life. They could rock your little dinghy. Know what I mean? Throw the whole thing off balance."

Yeah, he could picture it. His work-life balance was a delicate dance. Funny, he'd always thought someone else would help anchor them. "What made you ask?" Please say him. Or Penny.

"I dunno..." She pinched her lips and wrinkled her nose. Cutest thing he'd ever seen. "I guess I'm curious. But you know what? It's none of my business. I'm just the bodyguard."

Cash nodded, studying Alana's features in the dimming light. He'd thought she might have been trying to put herself out there, but then she'd just shut it down. It wasn't where he'd hoped this conversation would go. Had he read her wrong?

Well, he sure didn't think the timing was right, but maybe... just maybe Alana was the right woman.

Too bad she was only here because he'd hired her to protect his daughter.

TEN

Yep, she still wasn't a morning person. Alana rubbed her tired eyes and checked the time on her phone.

At the crack of dawn, Alana had relieved Noelle from her post so that the other bodyguard could catch some sleep. While everyone else was sound asleep, Alana had taken the opportunity to brew a pot of coffee and delve into studying maps of currents and tides around the area where Sonia's car had plunged into the water. After what Cash had said last night, she couldn't get it out of her head that maybe...just maybe Sonia was still alive and behind the attempts to kidnap Penny.

She sipped her coffee as her thoughts lingered on Sonia's fate. If she had died, her last moments would've been terrifying. Trapped in a sinking car with no one to help her. Alana didn't have to imagine the fear and panic that would have consumed Sonia, because she had firsthand experience. During a SWAT underwater training exercise, she'd been trapped in a sinking car and had to escape.

With a deep sigh, Alana pushed the memories aside. She

needed to confirm her theory about where Sonia's car could be, and that meant going on a dive. It was a risky move, but she was determined to find answers. She couldn't let Sonia's death go unresolved. Not when there was a chance she could give Penny and Cash closure. And not when there was a chance that something was off.

Alana poured herself a cup of coffee and glanced up when she heard footsteps. Cash padded down the stairs barefoot in his blue scrub pants and fitted white T-shirt. A small smile tugged at the corner of her lips, and her heart fluttered. She couldn't believe how much she wanted to be near him. His presence alone made her feel alive.

When he saw her, he grinned. Somehow he managed to make sleep-tousled hair look good. "Good morning."

"Morning." She took a sip of her coffee and tried not to stare. "Did you sleep okay?"

He nodded, walking to the coffee maker and pouring himself a cup. "Yeah, I slept great. I must've been exhausted. Are they still asleep in the fort?"

"Yep. Noelle said they barely stirred all night."

"Amazing. Kids can sleep anywhere." Cash gestured to Alana's laptop and notes on the table. "What's all that?"

"The current maps I mentioned. I got up early to do some research."

Cash leaned back and folded his arms. "Really? You did that?"

"I hope it's okay. We don't have to pursue this—"

He reached out and took her hand. "No, you're amazing, Alana. I didn't expect you to go to such lengths."

"I'm glad to hear you say that, because I think I know where the car could be." Alana said. "But I want to dive to confirm it."

He released her hand and sipped his coffee. "Show me."

"Based on the maps of ocean currents during Hurricane Irma, I think we should start searching in the areas with strong eastward currents." Alana pointed to the map on her laptop screen.

"Why eastward currents?" Cash leaned in to get a closer look, and her heart rate quickened.

She tried to focus on the maps and notes on the screen, but her mind kept wandering to the man beside her and the way he made her feel when he was close.

"Well, during the storm, the winds were pushing water toward the shore from the east. As the water moves toward the shore, it accumulates and creates a current that moves parallel to the coastline. That means the car, if it was swept out to sea, would likely have been carried eastward by the current."

Cash nodded. "Makes sense. So where do we start diving?"

She drew back and looked at him. "We? Are you saying you want to come with me?"

"Of course I do. It's always been unsettling, the way she disappeared." He rubbed the back of his neck. "I know it's not logical, but some small part of me thought she could be alive. Like that old movie where the woman falls overboard and everyone thinks she's dead, but really, she's living a new life wholly unaware. I know it doesn't make sense. She'd never leave Penny on purpose. I didn't realize it until we talked last night, but I need closure."

"It could be dangerous."

"Right, because deep-sea diving with you is way more dangerous than traveling with the SEAL team as a combat surgeon." His mouth twitched into a smile.

Alana rolled her eyes and smirked. "Okay, fine. Smarty pants."

She pulled up another map that showed the ocean currents in the area after the storm and traced her finger along the lines on the map. "This is where the strongest eastward currents were during the height of the storm. It's possible the car could have been carried in this direction and eventually washed up on shore somewhere in this area here."

Cash studied the map and nodded. "All right, how soon can we go?"

"I've checked the weather and the currents. We'll need to dive today because conditions won't be as favorable tomorrow. My friend will take us out. He's got all the gear and everything we'll need."

"Perfect," he said.

After spending the morning with Rocco and Penny, Cash and Alana entrusted the kids to Noelle and Juliette and headed out in Cash's truck. Alana settled into the passenger seat and tried to shake off the ominous feeling that crawled up her spine.

She stared out the window, trying to distract herself by studying the blur of green as they rumbled toward Tybee Island Marina. The afternoon sky was painted deep blue without a cloud in the sky. A serene contrast to the unease that knotted up her stomach.

She turned to look at Cash, who was focused on the road ahead. Maybe she shouldn't have let him come along. What if they found Sonia? If Sonia's car had been submerged underwater for four years, the chances of finding a recognizable body were slim. The thought of Cash seeing his ex-wife's body after it had been underwater for such a long time made her chest tighten. Sure, he was a doctor, but it was different with loved ones.

Alana took a deep breath and tried to push the gruesome thoughts out of her mind. She had to remain focused and keep her emotions in check. This was about more than Cash and Penny. Sonia's entire family deserved closure too. It might not be her job anymore, but she would do everything in her power to provide it. Even if it meant braving the unknown and facing the harsh realities of her fate.

"It's going to take about twenty minutes to get to the

marina." Cash glanced over at her. "Do you want to go over the plan again?"

"No, I've got it." She snapped back into focus. "I just hope we can find something down there."

"I hope so too," Cash said. "But even if we don't, I'm thankful you're willing to try."

They rode in silence for a few minutes, the weight of their mission hanging heavy in the air.

"You know, I used to come out here with Sonia and Penny all the time. We'd fish, swim, and have picnics on the beach."

"I'm sorry, Cash. I know it must be hard to come back here."

"It is," Cash admitted. "But I need to do this. For Penny, and for myself."

Alana reached over and squeezed his hand. He held on and smiled at her.

"Okay, so I'm dying to know. How in the world did you end up on the LAPD SWAT team?" He glanced at her and grinned. "And a dive detective at that!"

"It's a long story, but I ended up working at a gym run by a man who had a mission to save street kids. He gave me a job as a cleaner, and then he helped me get on my feet and get a job with the police department."

"Really? That's impressive." Cash raised an eyebrow. "Wow, you really have been through a lot, haven't you?"

Okay, she was not ready to go there. She needed to divert this conversation. "Life wasn't always easy, but it made me who I am today."

"Yeah. Okay. Well, I'm glad you're here with me now," he said. "So how do you know our dive captain?"

"Oh, Oak and I go way back." She grinned and watched his face for his reaction. "We both fought in the youth mixed martial arts world championship."

———

When Cash realized his mouth had fallen open, he closed it. Jonah had mentioned Alana had expert martial arts skills. He hadn't said she was a champion fighter.

He parked the truck at the marina and turned to face her. "Excuse me. I think I heard you wrong. Did you say *World MMA Championship?*"

Alana laughed, clearly taking in the stupefied expression on his face. "Yes, I trained and competed for a few years. It helped me deal with some of the issues from my childhood. But that's all behind me now."

His gaze lingered on her eyes for a moment. Boy, she was stronger and more resilient than he'd imagined. He'd seen her in action, and she was a force to be reckoned with, for sure. But hearing some of her past...well, he couldn't imagine what she'd been through to become the woman she was today. "Whatever pain you've gone through...I'm sorry for it."

"I've been through some stuff, but it's all in the past. Come on. Let's focus on finding Sonia's car."

More than anything, Cash wanted to know what had shaped Alana so profoundly, but he was too close to sensitive territory. It was time to back off. He hadn't earned the right to pry, but in time, he hoped to earn enough trust to know her deeper, because the more he did, the more she amazed him.

"Right." Cash clapped his hands. "Let's do this."

They stepped out of the truck, and Cash breathed in the salty smell of the ocean. The boat dock wobbled beneath his feet, swaying with the movement of the water. The wood creaked and groaned with each step.

At the end of the dock, Cash took in the expansive view of the marina. Boats of all shapes and sizes bobbed gently in the water. Seagulls flew overhead. Their cries mingled with the sound of distant boat engines and the soft lapping of the water against hulls.

It was a peaceful scene, but they were there to search for

Sonia's car. Looking out at the vast expanse of the ocean before him, he wondered what secrets it held. Impossible to discover them all, and finding Sonia's car would be like finding a needle in a haystack.

"Over here," Alana called.

She stood beside a soft blue Boston Whaler gleaming under the bright sun. His eyes followed the smooth lines and crisp white accents of the boat's trim. He whistled. "Now that's what I call a boat."

"What, better than the SEAL team?"

Cash laughed. "Well, the Navy's boats were designed for stealth and speed, not comfort. But this Whaler is the boat of my dreams."

"Dream boat, huh? What is it with men and boats?"

He clutched his chest as if she'd shot him in the heart.

She laughed. "Well, it's pretty, that's for sure. Looks like it can handle some rough waters."

"Absolutely. I'm looking forward to taking her out and seeing what she can do."

A man sporting two large scuba tanks on his broad shoulders strode toward them. He wore a sleeveless shirt and a pair of cargo shorts that revealed muscles that corded with every movement. He had a clean-shaved head with a series of intricate tattoos etched into his scalp that seemed to come alive in the sun.

As he approached, his smile revealed a set of pearly white teeth that contrasted with skin the color of polished mahogany. "Well, well, well, look who's here! Alana Flores, is that you?" His booming voice carried over the water.

Alana's face lit up. "Oak Landry, it's been too long!"

He put the tanks in the boat and picked Alana up in a bear hug. Oak set Alana on the dock and turned to Cash. "Is this your diving partner?"

"You know it." Alana grinned. "Let me introduce you to Dr. Cash Thomas."

"Hey, bro." Oak stuck out a meaty hand and crushed Cash's in a firm handshake. "Nice to meet ya. Any friend of Alana's is a friend of mine."

"Thanks, man." Cash would have to ask Alana if the name Oak was his given name or a nickname for the giant man. He nodded to the boat. "I've got a little crush on your Whaler. She's a beauty."

Oak's eyes lit up. "My pride and joy. Worked hard for this girl. Shoulda seen the old one."

Alana climbed into the boat and stood with her arms folded. "You boys gonna dive today or stand around drooling on the dock?"

Oak's boisterous laugh was contagious and Cash joined in.

"Well, you haven't changed much," Oak said. "I suppose we'll join you since I can't think of a better way to spend the day than on the water."

Cash untied the boat while Oak fired up the engine. Cash guided the vessel out of the slip. When the bow cleared the dock, he hopped aboard and took a seat beside Alana. The boat picked up speed, and a familiar thrill of freedom and adventure raced through him. He loved being on the water. The sun on his skin, the smell of the sea, the wind in his hair. All of it. The first thing he'd do when he made chief was go boat shopping.

The ride was far from smooth. The boat pitched and rolled beneath them as they cut through the choppy water. Each wave sent the vessel soaring into the air only to come crashing down with a bone-rattling impact that hit them with a salty spray.

Beside him, Alana's hair whipped in the wind, fanning him with the scent of lavender that mingled with the salty sea air. He slid an arm around her shoulders, his other hand grasping the railing. "I think I'm in love."

Her eyes snapped to his, and she wrinkled her eyebrows.

"With the boat." He smiled. "I'm in love with the boat."

Alana shook her head and looked out across the water.

As the boat crested yet another massive wave, lifting them into the air, Oak cast a knowing grin at Cash. As if he knew this wild and tumultuous ride was exactly what Cash needed. A moment of escape. A break from the pressures of life on land.

An hour later, they reached the dive spot, and Oak slowed the boat to a stop. The sound of the engine died away, leaving only the gentle lapping of water against the hull. Oak set the anchor, and the boat came to a gentle sway as it settled in place. He clapped his hands. "All right, let's get this show on the road. I'll get the dive lines ready, and you two gear up."

Cash helped Alana sort the equipment in the bow of the boat, where they'd be out of Oak's way. Cash unzipped the dive bag and froze. He looked up at Alana. "This gear is military grade."

Alana glanced toward the stern, where Oak was setting dive lines, then back to him. "I told you Oak would hook us up with everything we needed."

"I...I guess I thought..." He shook his head. "I don't know what I thought."

"We're set up for a SAR operation. The search part anyway. We'll need heavy duty search and rescue equipment to have enough time underwater to explore the site where Oak located multiple aberrations. The wetsuit should be a good fit for you, and we have FFMs with wireless underwater comms."

Cash picked up the black full-face dive mask. "Oh, I love these."

"Me too. Can you hand me my wetsuit?"

He found the smaller and held it up. When she didn't take it, he looked up. His breath caught at the sight of Alana in a modest royal blue one-piece swimsuit. The sunlight caught her sleek black hair as she gathered it into a high ponytail and secured it with a band from her wrist.

"Um, here you go." He swallowed.

"Can I ask you something?" Alana pulled her wetsuit up over her toned arms.

He worked to get his feet through the tight ankle holes. "Yeah, of course."

"Are you sure you want to do this?"

He furrowed his brow. "Why wouldn't I?"

"Aren't you worried about the possibility of finding your ex-wife's body in the car?"

Cash's face tightened. He took a deep breath. "Honestly, I don't know. It's been so long, I guess it's hard to imagine we'll find anything at all."

Alana nodded and tugged the back zipper of her suit. "Whatever happens down there, I'm here for you."

"Thanks. It means a lot that you and Oak would be willing to try."

He finished suiting up. The cool neoprene wetsuit clung to his body. Now if only the snug suit could hold his roiling emotions inside.

No way they'd find Sonia's car. Not after all this time. But then, what would he do if they did?

ELEVEN

Once again, Alana found herself on the hunt for a dead body.

Only this time, she didn't have the full force of the LAPD dive unit behind her. She hadn't expected body recoveries to be a part of working for the Elite Guardians. Generally, if a dead body was involved, then the bodyguard hadn't been a very good one.

But hey, she'd take the cool embrace of the Atlantic Ocean over swimming in that icky Forsyth Park fountain any day.

Alana's heart raced as she took her first freefall step into the crystal-clear water and swam down. At the end of the dive line, she turned and looked up. Cash was silhouetted against the backdrop of the deep blue ocean. The filtered sunlight outlined his body and highlighted his strong physique.

He stepped in and swam down. Scuba bubbles floated around him like tiny, delicate clouds, rising lazily to the surface. As she took in the sight of him, a flood of heat jetted through her body.

Stop that. Now was not the time for a physical reaction to what was nothing more than a girlish crush. Her *first* girlish crush, because she was *so* not like that. Her stomach did not do flip-flops around a guy. There were no insects flying around her belly. She would not gush over Cash just because he was a loving, caring, kind, strong, intelligent, handsome father. Did she just say handsome?

Well, that was beside the point. Her heart only betrayed her because Cash was the first man who fit her so well. Both single parents with exceptional children. Both experienced divers. Both former law enforcement. Well, in Cash's case, he was military, but still very similar. Did he still have his service dress whites?

Oh wow. Why were these thoughts drifting through her head right now? She had to stop. Had to focus on her breathing and the task at hand. They weren't on a recreational dive. They were looking for Sonia's remains.

Alana paused near Cash and spoke into her wireless device. "Can you hear me okay, Cash?"

"Loud and clear. How about me?"

"I hear you perfectly."

"This is some high-tech equipment for a boat charter."

"Oak has connections," she said. "We can talk later. We have limited time, so we should keep moving."

Cash gave her the thumbs-up, and they ran through equipment and hand signal checks in case the comms went out. As they descended deeper, the sunlight filtered through the water casting a blue-green hue all around them. The visibility was good, but not as clear as she had hoped. They swam side by side with their dive lights illuminating the murky depths.

They swam closer to the seafloor and came across a sandy area dotted with patches of sea grass. A southern stingray materialized from beneath the sand and zipped off. Its wide wings flapped as it disappeared into the distance.

When they reached the bottom at around sixty feet, they began scanning the area around the coordinates she had mapped out. They swam toward a rocky outcrop covered in a kaleidoscope of coral formations. Vibrant, colorful marine life darted through the reef and around her head. "Let's spread out but keep a visual."

"Copy."

She searched each crevice for any signs of the car. Parts that broke off or personal items that found a place to rest here. Something glinted in a small opening between two rocks. Her heart quickened, but she found nothing but a few rusted beer cans and some fishing line.

She turned and came face to face with a moray eel peeking out from its hiding place and gasped.

"You okay?"

"Got an up-close view of this eel's sharp teeth on full display." Interesting creature. Lovely, yet terrifying. "I'm just glad he wasn't hiding in the hole where I stuck my hand."

"Alana, come check this out."

She glanced around and saw that he was pointing at a massive object buried in the sand a few yards away. It was outside her search coordinates, but not by much. "Let's check it out."

They swam closer, sweeping their dive lights over the object. As they got within a few feet, she realized it was a rock.

"False alarm," he said. "Sorry."

"No worries. We'll keep looking as long as we can."

They continued searching and checked in with each other through the comms to make sure they were still on track.

She paused to check her gauges. They were running out of time. They'd searched for half an hour, scouring the ocean floor for any signs of Sonia's car. Nothing. Whatever Oak had picked up with his metal detectors, they weren't finding it.

What had made her think she could locate Sonia's vehicle when teams of divers with better gear hadn't been able to do it? Now she had Cash's hopes up, thinking he'd be able to lay Penny's mom to rest.

A group of blue runners darted past Alana. Her eyes followed them, admiring their elongated bodies, sleek and streamlined. Beyond them, a sand tiger shark hovered near a mysterious formation rising up from the ocean floor.

She swam toward it with her dive light shining on layers of sediment. It was bigger than Sonia's car, but years of debris and sediment buildup would add to the vehicle's bulk. Could this be it?

She approached the odd hill-shaped formation. Its contours were smooth in some places and jagged in others, hinting at the powerful forces of nature that had shaped it over time. Coral and sea creatures clung to the surface, creating their very own ecosystem in the depths.

The shark swished away, leaving Alana to her discovery. She descended the slope. The water became darker. More still. The eerie atmosphere and the close proximity of the shark sent shivers down her spine.

"Cash, I think you'll want to see this."

"Where are you?" Cash's voice crackled in response.

Alana shined her dive light in his direction. "See me?"

"Yep. On my way." Cash swam up beside her. "What is that thing?"

"I don't know, but we're going to find out."

He reached out to touch the muddy, pockmarked hill. As he ran his hand over it, pieces crumbled away, revealing a glint of metal beneath the rust.

The oxygen monitor on her wrist beeped. "We're at thirty percent. We need to start ascending in three minutes." Time was not on their side, but they'd come too far to turn back without answers.

"Mark the spot."

"Done. Now hurry," she said.

They clawed the mud. Pieces of sediment and rusted metal crumbled away from beneath her fingers. She didn't want to leave without knowing if they'd found Sonia's car or not. A cloud of dirt and debris swirled around them. They dug deeper, uncovering more of the object's form.

The shape made Alana's blood run cold.

Cash yanked his hand back at the same time she did. They stared at each other in disbelief.

"That's not Sonia's car," she said. "It's a bomb."

———

Cash leaned against his truck, hands in his pockets. "Of all the things I expected to find at the bottom of the ocean, a bomb wasn't one of them."

Alana sat on the tailgate, swinging her feet. She'd changed out of her swimsuit and into a fitted black T-shirt, tactical pants, and combat boots. Her hair had dried in the salty wind and now cascaded down her back in beachy waves. "Like diving isn't already dangerous enough with the risk of equipment failure, decompression sickness, strong currents—"

"And don't forget the dreaded shark attack."

Alana rolled her eyes. "Please."

"Okay, fine. But you must admit. An unexploded military device was a whole new level of danger you hadn't even considered."

"True. I guess Oak's equipment needs an upgrade. At least our digging didn't trigger an explosion."

Alana had noted the coordinates of the bomb before they broke the surface with a rush of bubbles. Oak had radioed the Coast Guard, who'd told them to evacuate immediately. By the time they made it back, several agencies had overrun the place, including the Savannah PD bomb squad and U.S. Marine Corps explosive ordinance disposal unit.

Cash glanced at the horizon. "I have this nagging feeling we were so close to finding Sonia. So close to knowing what happened to her that day the storm swept her car off the road."

Alana hopped off the tailgate. She wrapped her arms around him and rested her cheek against his chest.

He enveloped her in his arms and pulled her closer.

"I'm so sorry, Cash. I wanted to find her for you. For Penny."

He breathed in and exhaled slowly. "Every part of my logic says Sonia is dead, but a teeny tiny space in my heart held out hope that Penny could one day see her mother again."

Alana didn't respond. Didn't move. He rested his chin on her head and looked out to the ocean. The sun dipped below the horizon, leaving behind a fiery trail that reflected on the water. The sky turned shades of orange, pink, and purple, casting a warm glow over the entire marina.

When Alana pulled away, he loosened his grip a fraction at a time. As she stood there with the wind playing with her hair, the sun seemed to dance on her skin, making her glow with an ethereal beauty. She looked up at him. "You know what?"

Even in the midst of the chaos surrounding them, Cash was captivated by her. "What's that?"

"Sharks aren't all that dangerous."

Cash threw his head back and laughed. "Tell that to Bethany Hamilton."

"I'll give you that one." She released her hold and stepped back. "I'm gonna run ask that officer how much longer we need to wait around."

After talking to the officer for several minutes, Alana returned and propped her elbow on the hood of his truck. "Well, it's definitely a military UXO. The Marine EOD unit is securing it for transport now. The officer asked if we could hang tight until the Marine lieutenant can have a word with us."

"I'd say he wants more than a word with us. It's not every day you find something like that."

Alana chuckled. "Oh, I've found a lot of things on a dive, but I've never uncovered an active military bomb. But we did our part. Got the coordinates and got out of there. Now it's up to them to take care of it."

Cash nodded, taking in her words. He admired her calm demeanor even in the face of danger. "Hey, what happened to Oak? He disappeared."

Alana's eyes swept the marina, looking everywhere but at Cash. "Oh. Yeah. He does that."

That was an odd response. There was something more to Oak than a former MMA fighter turned fishing and dive charter captain. He opened his mouth to ask a follow-up question, but his attention shifted to a man in a crisp Marine uniform, striding toward them. He approached and introduced himself as Lieutenant Ryan from the Marine Corps Air Station in Beaufort.

"I understand you two were diving in the area and stumbled upon the unexploded ordinance." Lieutenant Ryan's voice was firm. His face granite. The kind of man who didn't need to assert his authority. It was simply a given.

Cash responded with a crisp "Yes, sir."

"What exactly were you doing in the area?"

"We were searching for my ex-wife's car."

Ryan's eyes swept to Alana, then to Cash.

"Not my car," Alana said.

"My ex-wife is deceased. A storm surge from Hurricane Irma swept her car off the road. It's never been recovered."

Ryan lifted his chin. "And what made you two think you could recover a vehicle in the middle of the ocean?"

"That would be me, Lieutenant. I served on the LAPD dive unit." Alana clasped her hands together. "I read the reports and studied the currents to come up with a search grid."

"You accessed the reports?" Ryan's eyes narrowed a twinge.

"Yes, sir. I'm currently working for the Elite Guardians Agency in private security."

"Ah. I read about the incident in Forsyth Park last week. It was in the papers. That you?"

Alana shifted her weight. "Yes, sir. I haven't seen the article, but we managed to stop a woman who'd been stalking S. M. Warren for months."

"Good on you," Ryan said. "Now, on behalf of the United States Military, thank you for recovering the unexploded ordinance. As you may or may not know, ocean disposal of munitions was formerly an accepted practice. We do not have accurate information on the number of military UXOs on the sea floor, nor their locations. However, when one is located, we work swiftly and diligently to retrieve and secure the device."

It sounded to Cash like Ryan had memorized the speech. How many times had he delivered it?

Ryan continued. "I was informed that during retrieval of the UXO, divers did uncover a vehicle obscured by debris and vegetation, which is making it difficult to remove. It's too early to tell the make and model or if there is an occupant. We're working with local detective Matt Williams, who says he will keep you two posted."

Cash exchanged a look with Alana. The woman who had not only awakened his heart but also had the skills and tenacity to help him find what had been lost for all these years. "You did it. You found Sonia's car."

Alana slipped her hand into his. The gesture spoke more than words ever could. A banner of hope unfurled itself inside his chest. All the guilt, all the regret, all the wondering...could it really be over, just like that? And all because he'd met Alana. Could it be that God had orchestrated the events that'd brought them together? That His guidance had led Penny to Alana to bring them to this very moment?

Questions rattled around in his head, but he said, "I'd like to be there when you bring the car up. I need to see it with my own eyes."

Ryan's jaw tightened. "That's not possible. It will take time to bring up the UXO and secure it. We'll need to keep a two-hundred-yard safety zone at all times. I know you don't want to hear this, but the vehicle is our secondary concern. We're losing daylight, so we likely won't extract it until sometime tomorrow."

"Is there anything we can do to help?" Alana asked.

"No, ma'am," Ryan said. "It's too dangerous for civilians to be involved in a situation like this. We appreciate your assistance in locating the UXO and the car, but we'll take it from here. In fact, we'll need you to vacate the premises as soon as possible."

Cash didn't like it, but he understood the seriousness of the situation. This was a dangerous military operation, and they were the same civilians the military were sworn to protect. They couldn't be standing around if the bomb detonated. "Thanks, Lieutenant. We'll head out, but I'd appreciate it if you could give me an update. You have the info?"

"Yes, sir." With that, Ryan did an about-face and headed toward the dock.

Cash released Alana's hand and drew her into a tight embrace. "Thank you," he whispered. His lips brushed her earlobe.

"You're welcome."

Cash wanted to stay there forever, holding her close and breathing the intoxicating aroma of her salty skin. In that moment, time slowed and nothing else existed but the two of them.

But they should really leave before someone came along and escorted them out. He released his grip and let his hands slide down her arms before stepping back. "We should get out of here."

"I guess you're right." Her eyes scanned the area. "Although, I'm dying to stay here and help. This is the exact thing I'm trained to do. Well, maybe not the bomb thing. We have bomb techs for that. But retrieving evidence like Sonia's car."

"So, what's the next step?"

She lifted her palms. "I guess we wait."

Alana's eyes darted over his shoulder. She whirled around and stepped behind him. When Cash turned around, a weary man in a dark off-the-rack suit stood in front of her.

"Dr. Thomas?"

"That's me." He stepped beside Alana. Job or not, he wasn't about to let her take the brunt of an attack on his watch.

"I was asked to give you this." The man held a white business card between his first two fingers and offered it to Cash.

Cash took the card, and the man walked away without another word.

He turned the card over and saw a single word, printed in bold, black letters.

SPAGHETTI.

"Great, now what?" Alana asked.

Cash pocketed the card with the secret phrase before Alana could read it. He forced a thin smile. "Looks like someone wants to see us."

TWELVE

Despite the day's events roiling and clashing in a swirling storm of thoughts, Alana always came back to a single word.

Spaghetti.

She tried to shake it loose. Tried to focus on the fact they may have found Sonia's car. Maybe her body. But it was like trying to ignore a low battery on a smoke detector in the middle of the night.

And then there was the Suit. The one who'd approached Cash at the marina. Definitely government. The wrinkled suit, bleary eyes, and seven-dollar haircut all screamed FBI to Alana. The way Cash had tucked the card away so fast set alarm bells ringing in her mind. Clearly it was something he hadn't wanted her to see.

But she had seen it.

She hadn't asked about it. If Cash wanted her to know, he'd have told her. Just because they'd grown comfortable with each other didn't mean he owed her an explanation for everything.

So they drove from Tybee Island to the south side of Savannah in silence. The only sound was the rumble of the engine and the rush of wind against the windows. Cash spoke only once, to point out the hospital where he worked.

He drove through the darkened streets of an area of Savannah she hadn't visited before. Storefront lights cast a neon glow across the pavement. He turned a corner and pulled into a gravel parking lot. They parked in front of a weather-beaten building with peeling white paint against a dull gray background. A faded sign above the entrance, Atlas Gym, looked as though it'd seen better days.

Cash cut the engine.

"This is where we're meeting whoever it is that gave you that card? At a gym?"

"Yup." His bright smile lit the darkened parking lot.

Helpful. If his smile weren't so bone-rattlingly adorable, she'd be annoyed.

He hopped out of the truck and slammed the door with a crunch. "C'mon."

Alana looked around as they entered the gym. The familiar sounds of punching bags and the smell of sweat hit her all at once. This was no sleek, upscale fitness center.

Nope. This place was designed for fighters. For those who came to sweat and bleed. The warriors who trained and honed their skills in the brutal art of combat.

It reminded Alana of her own days when the sound of bone hitting bone and the taste of coppery blood in her mouth were familiar companions.

Alana halted Cash's stride with a hand on his chest. "Hold up a minute. Are we here because of what I told you about my MMA days?"

"You give me too much credit." Cash chuckled and shook his head. "No, I used to box in the Navy. A buddy of mine owns this place. I come here from time to time, that's all. But I'm starting to think you and I have more in common than I first thought." His grin could melt the paint off the walls.

A funny twinge in the tips of her ears told her they were ablaze again. Great. "Let's hope we don't have to use any of those skills tonight." She eyed the two boxing rings in the center of the gym.

"I dunno. I thought we could go for a round or two while we wait." He gestured to a wall of gloves and headgear.

"I'm not really dressed for it." She gestured to her pants and boots.

"Is that a hint of fear I hear in your voice?"

Alana raised an eyebrow and surveyed the boxing ring. It'd been years since she'd been in one, but she trusted that muscle memory would kick in no matter how she was dressed. "You're on."

They left their socks and shoes in the cubbies and grabbed gloves and headgear. Cash motioned toward the center ring. "Ladies first."

Alana climbed up onto the apron of the ring and ducked through the ropes. A bit of the old Alana came alive the moment she stepped onto the mat. The former scrappy sixteen-year-old homeless girl who'd lived to fight.

Cash joined her on the mat and adjusted his chin strap. He grinned. "You ready for this?"

"Born ready." The familiar rush of adrenaline coursed through her veins. She bounced on the balls of her feet to get the blood pumping to other parts of her body than her ears for once.

They circled each other, throwing light jabs and hooks they could dodge with ease.

"You're quick," Cash said.

"Thanks, but don't go easy on me."

He laughed. "I wouldn't dream of it."

Alana threw a kick, and Cash blocked it. "Is that how a world champion kicks?"

Alana laughed. "I was just warming up. I'll show you a real kick."

Cash grinned. "Bring it on, champ."

They exchanged blows, each trying to anticipate the other's next move. Alana was surprised at how evenly matched they were. She threw a series of kicks and punches, and he continued to block each strike. Cash had a natural agility that made him a formidable opponent.

"Not bad, but you'll have to do better than that if you want to take me down."

Alana rolled her eyes. "You wish, cowboy. I'll have you on the mat in no time."

Except, watching his smile and his movements had her mind drifting and her focus waning. Someone must've turned the heat up, because the room was about twenty degrees hotter. A bead of sweat trickled down her temple. She swiped it with her glove.

Cash saw his opening and faked a left jab, then swung a right hook, catching her off guard. She stumbled backward, losing her footing. She landed hard on the mat.

"Sheesh, are you okay?" Cash leaned in to help her up.

She caught him by surprise and took him down with a swift leg sweep. She rolled over him and pinned him to the mat. Hovering over him, she smiled. His warm breath on her neck sent a shiver down her spine. They were so close. Their faces only inches apart. She could lean in and kiss him...

In a flash, she was on her feet backing away. That was too close. What was she thinking? She'd almost kissed Cash. Her client. This whole thing was so unprofessional of her. She wiped her brow with her glove and headed for the ropes.

"Oh no you don't." Cash spun her around. He wrapped his arms around her waist and pulled her close. "Nice move...champ."

"Thanks. You're not too bad yourself."

They stood face-to-face. So close their breaths mingled in the sliver of space between them. The heat radiated off Cash's body. Her own heart thundered in response.

"So what are you going to do? Quit on me?"

She shook her head. "Never."

His gaze dropped to her lips. "Good, 'cause I don't think I could let you go."

They leaned closer. Drawn by an invisible force neither could resist. As their lips met, the outside world disappeared. Nothing else existed. It was just the two of them, caught in each other's gravity.

The sensation was electric. A shockwave spread through her body the likes of which she'd never known before.

"Ahem." A feminine voice sounded nearby.

The moment shattered like glass. They broke apart, and Alana leaped back, pulling herself out of Cash's arms, but the electricity between them still crackled in the air. Her cheeks burned as she averted her gaze over Cash's shoulder.

A woman stood beside the boxing ring, hands planted on her hips, a stern expression on her face. Her luscious strawberry-blonde hair flowed down her back, but she wore a baseball cap pulled low on her forehead. The brim cast a shadow over blue eyes that seemed to be throwing daggers in Alana's direction. She wore a black leather jacket over a cropped white tank top, and tight black leather pants that hugged her curves. Her makeup was flawless, with long lashes framing her eyes and a nude lipstick that accentuated her plump pout.

The woman was beautiful. Alana couldn't shake the feeling that this woman knew Cash, and Alana was an outsider.

"Am I interrupting something?"

"Of course you are, Bailey," Cash said. "Why are little sisters always so pesky?"

This knockout of a woman was Cash's little sister? Great. Perfect way to meet the family. Oh, hi. I'm the complete stranger kissing your brother even though my agency is providing personal protection for your niece.

Oh boy. What was that anyway? She couldn't go around kissing a client. What had gotten into her? Her cheeks burned. In fact, heat radiated from her entire body. She could play it off as overexertion, right? She removed her headgear and ran her fingers through her dampened hair, trying to tame the sweaty locks.

Cash stripped off his gear and tossed both of theirs into a nearby bucket in a clatter of plastic on plastic. His hand was warm on the small of her back as he led her out of the ring. Electricity still sparked at his touch.

Bailey strode over to them and planted a kiss on Cash's cheek. "Looks like we've got someone else to keep you in line, Cash." Her eyes flicked over to Alana, and she offered a polite smile. "This must be the woman I've heard so much about."

Cash's smile faltered for a second. A flash of confusion rippled across his face. "Um, yeah. This is Alana." His hand lingered on the small of Alana's back. "Alana, this is Bailey."

Bailey extended her hand. "Nice to finally put a face to the name, Alana. I'm Bailey, the baby sister who usually keeps him in line. But by the looks of it, I think you're doing a pretty good job. Nice sweep."

She shook Bailey's hand and searched her eyes for any hint of disapproval or suspicion. "It's nice to meet you too, Bailey."

"Listen, I have some information. But we can't talk here."

"Let's go in the office." Cash led the way, and Bailey fell into step beside Alana. They weaved their way through the crowded gym. The air was thick with the sounds of grunts and the clanging of weights.

"I hope my brother wasn't too hard on you in the ring," Bailey said.

"He gave me a good challenge, but I held my own."

"That's what I like to hear. It's good to see him enjoying life."

They came to a stop beside a tall, dark-skinned man wiping his brow with a towel. When he finished, he glanced at Cash and flashed a smile. "Hey, if it isn't the Thomas twins." He locked a grip with Cash and pulled him in for a man hug with a hearty thump on the back.

Twins. That's right. She remembered reading the shared birthdate in the file.

Cash returned the hug. "Atlas, good to see you, my friend."

"Bailey, it's been a while." Atlas gave her a gentle hug, and Bailey kissed his cheek. "Look at you, girl. You look incredible."

"Thanks," Bailey said. "All in a day's work." The brief look they shared said Atlas knew something Alana didn't.

Atlas turned to Alana. "And who is this fury?"

"Easy now," Cash said with a chuckle. "Alana, this is my buddy, Atlas Shaw. He owns this place."

Atlas wasn't a large guy, but he was muscular. With his chiseled features and rugged jawline, he was the kind of handsome she'd rarely seen outside movies and magazines. Warmth and kindness burned behind his intense gaze, and a controlled power emanated from his stance—like a coiled spring ready to unleash.

"I saw you in the ring with this guy." He nodded to Cash. "You're agile. Very fluid motions."

"Thanks, I had fun." She didn't want to talk about her past life as a fighter. Her eyes roamed the busy room and noticed four teenagers working the heavy bags. "You've got a great gym. Get a lot of kids in here?"

Atlas exchanged a look with Cash. "I bring in kids from the rougher neighborhoods and give 'em free classes. Teach 'em some discipline and give 'em somethin' to strive toward besides gang life."

Alana raised an impressed eyebrow. "I knew a guy out in

California who did something similar. I've seen firsthand how one person can make a difference in a young person's life."

"He's basically saving lives," Bailey said.

Atlas smiled and patted Alana's shoulder. "You're always welcome here if you want to join me in the life-changing, life-saving business of mixed martial arts."

Cash cut in. "Hey, man. Can we use your office to chat for a bit?" He nodded. "Privately."

"Sure thing. You know where you're goin'. I've got a class starting, so just lock up when you're done."

Atlas was one messy dude. Piles of papers and notebooks covered every surface. The walls displayed posters of past fights, the vibrant colors muted by the dim light of a single lamp on Atlas's desk. A small window with dusty blinds let in a sliver of natural light, casting long shadows on the cluttered room.

She took a seat beside Cash on the beat-up leather couch in the corner and caught a whiff of musky sweat mixed with dust and the faint aroma of coffee. It was strangely comforting. Reminded her of the gyms and locker rooms she'd visited over the years.

Bailey moved the computer keyboard and sat in its place, leaving her feet dangling. She gripped the edge of the desk with both hands, and her expression turned serious. "Thanks for coming so quickly. I'm sorry to pull you away from Penny."

"You know I'll always come if I can," Cash said. "But what's so serious you had to play the cloak-and-dagger game?"

It clicked for Alana. "The card? That's what *spaghetti* meant?"

Cash rubbed his jaw. "You saw that, did you?"

"He handed you the card right in front of me."

"It's a covert way to get Cash to meet at the gym," Bailey said.

"A secret word we had as kids to let each other know things were…"

"Messy," Bailey finished.

Twin language. "Clever."

"And by the way, I don't normally dress like this." Bailey gestured to her leather pants. "I'm undercover. Part of the cloak and dagger."

Alana nodded. "Detective?"

"FBI. And what I'm about to tell you is classified. It cannot leave this room, not even in a whisper. This is life or death stuff." Bailey leaned in. Her blue eyes blazed with intensity. "What you two are doing is going to get me killed."

THIRTEEN

As if they hadn't already been facing life or death the past few days, now his sister too? His kiss with Alana had been pure bliss that'd left him floating on cloud nine, but Bailey's words sent him crashing back down to earth.

Cash leaned forward, elbows on his knees. "Look, Bailey, don't tell us anything that could get you fired or put your life on the line."

"I can step out if you need," Alana offered.

"No, it's fine." Bailey offered a soft smile to Alana. "You can both hear this. I've already cleared it with my SAC."

"Was that your supervisory special agent who handed me the card?"

Bailey nodded. "The case I'm on...they have people everywhere. I can't risk the wrong person seeing me talking to a cop, so he's the only one who has access to me."

"Probably for the best," Alana said. "Safer that way."

His sister was good at her job. She hadn't set out to be undercover, but after they'd pulled her in to assist a few times, it'd become apparent she was great at it. This was the first time a case had brought her so close to home. At least…that he knew of. "Yeah. Well, knowing my baby sister is hobnobbing with dangerous criminals for weeks and not hearing from her is frustrating. Stressful."

"I know. I try to check in, but it's not like I'm keeping normal working hours. Criminals do their thing while the rest of the world sleeps."

"I know." He blew out a breath. "But do you really have to dress like some sort of Kardashian wannabe?"

"Gotta dress the part, bro."

Alana shifted on the couch beside him. "Tell us how we're wrapped up in your case. If you can."

Bailey stopped swinging her legs and crossed her ankles. "I'm working undercover as an illegal arms dealer. I've infiltrated the Madrina cartel—"

"You're posing as an illegal arms dealer for the Madrina cartel?" His big-brother hackles were up. "Bailey, that's dangerous. You could get hurt. Or worse—"

"I know the risks," Bailey said. "This is important work. You know how many people die every day from illegal guns?"

Actually, he did know. Still, he didn't like his sister putting herself in harm's way. "I know. And I know you've got backup. Be careful, okay?"

"Always am." Bailey gave him a small smile. "As I was saying, I already have enough evidence to put a major hurt on their business. But this one guy can't stop running his mouth. He's telling me exactly how they're getting guns, drugs, and truckloads of cash in and out of the US. I've worked up the ranks and finally scored a big meeting. If things go well, we have the potential to take down all the major players."

Alana scooted to the edge of the couch. "I understand if you can't tell us, but we've heard about a player named Luis Trejo who has it out for Cash. Any truth to that?"

Bailey held up a finger. "See, that's the problem. After Trejo made bail, Detective Williams pulled a warrant to search his house. But Trejo isn't some low-level dealer in the Madrina cartel. He's a distributor. He deals directly with the head of the cartel, and he's the one who set up the meeting. Trejo is supposed to take me to meet the leader, but if he gets picked up it will blow my whole operation. Possibly my cover, which could get me killed."

Cash jumped to his feet. "You do realize Trejo has been trying to kidnap Penny and kill me, right? The nightmare of the past few days could be over and now, what? You're willing to let a potential killer go free?"

Alana stood. "Hey, that's what I'm here for." Her hand trailed along his shoulder and settled on his back. "You have protection."

A crease formed in Bailey's brow. "You really think Trejo is after Penny?"

Cash exchanged a look with Alana. Her detective skills were more in line with Bailey's, so maybe she could talk some sense into his thickheaded sister.

"It's all circumstantial," Alana said. "Each man who tried to kidnap Penny had ties to the Madrina cartel. Trejo attacked Cash and pulled a gun. Williams thinks Trejo wants to kidnap Penny for revenge, but my gut says there's something else going on here."

"Yeah?" Bailey crossed her arms and leaned back. "Tell me."

"So, I'm from LA, right? I've lived it. I've worked it. If a gangbanger wants you dead, you're dead. End of story. They're all about organized violent blitz attacks. We're talking jumped in the street by a group of thugs. A drive by. Trejo could've shot Cash at the hot air balloon festival, but he didn't." Alana shook her head. "No, he's had ample opportunities to take Cash out, but he hasn't. Revenge might be part of it, but there's some other reason they're after Penny."

"I see." Bailey chewed her lip and gave a slow nod. "Is it possible Penny has something Trejo wants?"

He darted his gaze between Alana and Bailey. Both women stared at him. "Are you kidding me? What could Penny possibly have that a gang member wants?"

"Maybe it's not something she has but something she saw or heard," Alana suggested. "Something that could incriminate them."

"How?" Cash threw out his hands "She's just a little girl. When would she possibly have seen or heard something to incriminate an arms dealer?"

Bailey looked at her feet. Her features pinched. Despite her undercover training, Bailey couldn't hide anything from him. They were twins. They had a special connection, and he knew her better than anyone else. "What's that look, Bailey? What's going on?"

"I...I can't—"

"Bailey!" He crossed the room. "This is my daughter we're talking about! Your niece! You have to tell me!"

She held up her hands. "Cash, I can't. I don't have authorization."

His pulse throbbed in his temples, but he forced a calm, even tone. "Bay, whatever you tell me, it won't go anywhere. You can trust me. You can trust Alana. This is Penny we're talking about. Someone is after her. You know I won't say or do anything to jeopardize her life or yours."

Alana hiked her thumb over her shoulder. "I can step out if that helps. Give you some privacy."

Bailey released a heavy sigh and held up a hand. "No, just... sit back down. Both of you. I know my brother, and whatever I say to him he's going to tell you anyway. But that's it. You hear me? It stops with the two of you." Bailey's laser stare was dead serious.

Alana tugged his hand and pulled him onto the couch.

Cash sat on the edge of the cushion and stared up at Bailey. "Okay, yeah. We promise. My heart can't take this, so just tell me already."

"Cash, you gotta promise you won't run off and do something stupid. We need to play this smart. Remember, this is all classified, and you'll need to step back and let the FBI do its job."

Whatever Bailey was sitting on must be big. He wasn't the type to let his emotions get the best of him. If he were, he would find Trejo and deliver his own brand of justice. "C'mon, Bay, you know me better than that."

Bailey's eyes bored into his, and he steeled himself for whatever bombshell she was about to drop.

"You're gonna find out about this sooner or later. Especially now that they've found her car." Bailey sighed. "Sonia was under FBI surveillance for money laundering for the Madrina cartel. It's possible Penny has information they want."

———

Alana watched the color drain from Cash. Shock and disbelief rolled like waves over his face. Penny's mother, the woman Cash married, had been under FBI surveillance?

The weight of Bailey's revelation hung heavy in the air. Cash's silence was deafening. Outside the room, sounds of fighters hitting the heavy bags and sparring were distant and muted. The gym seemed less welcoming. Less safe.

The Madrina drug cartel was one of the most dangerous and elusive organizations in the country. Now Cash and Penny were tied to them, and Bailey was wrapped up in the investigation. "Wait. If Sonia was laundering money for the cartel, isn't your undercover work a conflict of interests?"

"No, they closed that part of the investigation when Sonia

was declared dead." Bailey cast a sympathetic glance at her brother.

"I don't understand this." Cash stood and paced the room. "Why would Sonia be involved with the cartel? And why would the FBI think she was laundering money?"

Bailey took a deep breath. "I'm so sorry, Cash. I never wanted you to—"

Cash held up a finger. "Don't. Don't sugarcoat this."

She nodded. "Sonia was having an affair with the leader of the cartel."

"That's ridiculous. Sonia would never do that." He stopped pacing. "Okay, maybe she was lonely. I was gone and she was a new parent. But she'd never get involved with someone dangerous like that."

"I know," Bailey said. "I didn't want to believe it either. But the FBI have evidence. I saw the photographs. The bank statements. They were building a strong case."

"I can't believe this. I had no idea." Cash rubbed his forehead. "And now Trejo is trying to kill me and kidnap Penny because of something Sonia may have done?"

Alana's pulse quickened. That gut feeling she had made a whole lot more sense now. If Sonia had been involved in money laundering, then it was possible she'd had information the cartel couldn't let leak. Which would have made Sonia a liability. "Bailey, do you think Sonia was murdered?"

Cash's sister wiggled out of her jacket and left it rumpled on the desk beside her. Red splotches covered her neck, and Alana noticed the room was thick with hot air.

Bailey gathered her hair off her neck and twisted it into a low ponytail that she tucked under her ball cap. "Well, murder is one theory."

"One?" Cash stilled. "What's the other?"

"No sugarcoating?"

"Right," Cash said, sitting on the arm of the couch.

"The agents working that side of the case believe Sonia faked her death."

Alana hadn't verbalized it, but the same thought had been rattling around her head. It was one reason she'd wanted to search for the car. "I thought if Cash and I could find Sonia's car or her remains, it'd bring some closure and settle any doubts that she could be involved in the attempted abductions, but the feds won't let us near the dive spot," Alana said. "Somehow we need to find out if Sonia is really alive or if the attempts to kidnap Penny connect to this...this spaghetti mess."

Bailey nodded. "That's why I need to keep working with Trejo. He's my best shot at getting to the cartel leader. Car or no car, once I'm in the top tier, we'll know more about what is going on here."

Alana leaned forward. Her mind raced with possibilities. "But how can you believe Trejo? He's tried to kill Cash and kidnap Penny multiple times. He's not exactly trustworthy."

Bailey chewed on her lower lip. "I know. But I've built a relationship with him. He trusts me. And I've got backup, Alana. I'm not going at this alone."

"Wait, wait, wait." Cash held up both hands. "What you're talking about is crazy. What if he finds out we're related?"

"He won't. My cover has been tested and it's solid."

Cash shook his head. "I still think this is nuts. Sonia wasn't some money launderer for a cartel. How would she even know how to do that?"

Bailey sighed, then hopped off the desk and crossed the room. She placed both hands on Cash's shoulders. "I know it's hard to believe, Cash. But the FBI has reason to suspect it. They found several inconsistencies in her financials and connections to the cartel. One of our suspects lives in a house she decorated."

Alana thought of the estate where Cash and Penny lived. He could afford it on his salary now, but back then when he was deployed? It wasn't a big leap to consider the Madrina cartel had been paying Sonia to launder money through her interior design business. "What do you think, Bailey?"

"Honestly?" She stepped back and crossed her arms. "If it's true Sonia was having an affair with the leader of the cartel—whose identity we still don't have—then I could see the cartel helping her. They could've faked her death to protect her or so she could run off into the sunset with her lover."

Alana could see the disbelief etched on Cash's face. It was a lot to take in.

"Why would she leave Penny behind?" Cash leaned forward, hands gripping his knees.

"I don't know, Cash," Bailey said softly. "Maybe she had no choice but to leave Penny but now she wants her back."

"Why would she want to come back now after all these years?" Cash asked—of himself, it seemed, more than anyone else. "I can't even wrap my head around this. I can't believe that Sonia is still alive. I can't imagine leaving Penny behind like that, especially with her autism."

Alana could see the pain and confusion in Cash's eyes. He was hunched over, elbows on his knees. "I know this is a lot to take in, but maybe she did it *for* Penny. To keep her safe from the cartel." She wrapped an arm around Cash's shoulders. "Maybe Sonia didn't run off with anyone. She could be in hiding. Afraid of what the cartel will do if they find out she's alive."

"Or the FBI is wrong and she really died during the hurricane," he said.

"It's just a theory," Bailey reminded them. "We don't have any proof that Sonia is alive."

Alana had to put an end to the suppositions. Nothing mattered until they had facts. "If that's really Sonia's car, then we should have answers tomorrow when the divers pull it up."

Cash nodded. "Until then, I guess if there's even a chance

that Sonia is alive and involved in all of this, I can't afford to ignore it."

Alana glanced at Bailey. "What can we do?"

"The FBI is asking Savannah PD to back off Trejo for now, which means I need you to keep Cash and Penny safe while I get my meeting. It's our only chance to bring down the entire organization and end this. Can you do that? Can you protect them?"

The weight of Bailey's request settled on Alana's shoulders. This wasn't just about protecting one little girl anymore. This was about taking down a criminal enterprise. One with tentacles reaching into every corner of the country. "Of course. My agency and I will do whatever it takes to keep them safe."

Cash stood and blew out a breath. "I don't like this. I don't like any of it."

"Neither do I, Cash." Bailey's voice was gentle. "But this is our only lead right now."

"And what if Sonia is alive? What if she's involved in this? What does that mean for Penny?"

Bailey patted Cash's cheek. "I'm working on it, big brother. Trejo is the key to everything, and we can't let him get arrested before my meeting." She grabbed her jacket off the desk. "I've got to go. I've got a meeting in an hour."

Cash held Bailey in a tight hug. "Be careful out there. Don't get yourself killed trying to save the world."

"I'll do my best, big brother." When Cash released her, Bailey hugged Alana. "Take care of my family. We'll see each other again soon, I hope."

"Me too," Alana said.

After Bailey left, Cash leaned back on the desk and shook his head. "After everything we've been through, now we're facing the wrath of the entire Madrina cartel."

Alana crossed the room and stood close. His hands slipped

around her waist. "Glad you hired the Elite Guardians, aren't you?"

He gave her a lopsided grin that caused her heart to stutter. "For more reasons than one. But unfortunately, I've gotta deal with the possibility that my ex-wife is still alive and coming for our daughter."

FOURTEEN

The one-two punch of Monday still had Alana a bit off her game. Actually, it was more like a triple whammy that'd left her mind spinning with a torrent of questions about the case as she waited with Rocco in the doctor's tiny exam room.

What was Bailey doing at the moment? Had Trejo given her any valuable information? Were they any closer to finding out the truth about Sonia? Whatever was happening, at least there hadn't been any more attempts to kidnap Penny, but that was due to the fact they were lying low.

"Mom, are you okay?" Rocco's voice interrupted her thought spiral.

"Yeah, sorry." She smiled at her son and ruffled his hair. "Just a bit distracted."

"Can I ask you something about your job?" The white sanitary paper crinkled under his legs.

"Sure, hon." She braced herself. Rocco never wanted to talk about her work. She'd assumed it was out of sight, out of mind for him.

"Is it wrong if I like going to work with you?"

"Going to work...oh, you mean because you like hanging out with Penny?"

"Yeah. And Dr. Cash. I really like them both. I mean, Penny can be annoying sometimes. Like when her words get stuck and she screams about stuff. But then I think about how hard she works at something I do all the time without even thinking."

Alana sat on the doctor's rolling stool and scooted herself in front of the exam table. "Like what?"

"You know...talking is so normal for me. But it's not for her. Like sports aren't easy for me. I get mad when I can't make a basket in P.E. Imagine if you want to talk but can't."

"You're right. That would be hard." She patted his knee. "We each have our challenges in life and special skills. I think it's cool how good you are at helping Penny relax when she's getting upset."

"I tell her just to wait until the words come and she stops. Then the words come." He raised both hands in a shrug, like what he'd said was the most obvious thing in the whole world.

Her son had become so intuitive and selfless. "You're probably helping her more than you realize."

"How?"

"Being such a great friend for starters. Penny needs that."

"I also like Dr. Cash. He's nice to me. And fun. I think it would be cool to be a doctor like him when I grow up." Rocco tore a small piece of the sanitary paper and rolled it into a ball between his fingers. "And...and I wish he could be my dad."

Dr. Cohen burst into the room with her usual contagious energy. Alana wanted to have that conversation with Rocco, but she was so not prepared.

"Hey, Rocco! I'm so glad to see you!" The pediatric endocrinologist gave Rocco a high five. Alana began to vacate the stool, but she patted her shoulder. "No, no. You sit there. It's more fun to roll around."

"It's okay," Alana said, standing. "I'd rather stand."

"Suit yourself. How's Mom doing lately?"

She nodded. "Good. It's been a quiet week for once."

"Not too quiet, though. I saw something about you in the paper, didn't I?" Dr. Cohen sat on the stool and used the toes of her hot pink Crocs to pull herself to the exam table.

"It's possible." She changed the subject. "How'd the test results go?"

Dr. Cohen eyed the medical chart. "Blood work is looking good. Real good. Way to go, champ." She gave Rocco a fist bump.

They spent the next ten minutes answering questions about Rocco's diet and blood sugar levels while Dr. Cohen performed the routine check-up. Alana let Rocco answer most of the questions, only stepping in as needed.

Diagnosed with type 1 diabetes at age nine, Rocco would live with the disease the rest of his life. It was important he took ownership of his health as much as possible.

Besides, her mind kept drifting back to Cash. She'd tried to keep a professional distance from him over the last few days. They hadn't talked about their kiss at the gym, but it simmered just below the surface.

When Dr. Cohen finished her exam, she gave them the all-clear and reminded Rocco to be mindful of his symptoms. They checked out at the front desk and waited for the receptionist to print Rocco's insulin prescription. Alana turned and looked through the plate-glass windows. Who was standing beside her Jeep?

"Hang on, Rocco. Stay there." She walked across the lobby, trying to see a face. Before she reached the window, whoever it was got into their car and left.

Paranoid much? She couldn't believe how fast her heart was beating. She took the prescription and confirmed Rocco's next appointment in three months. Just in case, she checked the underside of the Jeep before allowing Rocco to climb in.

"What are you doing?"

"Just checking things out. Go ahead and get in. Belt up while I take one last look at the tires."

She circled the Jeep, running her hands around the wheel wells and under the bumper. Everything seemed good. No weird packages or slashes in her tires. It could be paranoia, but better safe than sorry.

They headed for Cash's house with Rocco chatting in the back seat. He told her all about the improvements he'd made recently on the robot and his plans to enter it into a robotics competition in the fall. She loved the idea and shared his excitement, but she couldn't forget his words about Cash earlier.

It was the same conversation she'd had with Noelle last night when she'd confessed to their impulsive kiss at the gym.

"I don't know what got into me," she'd said. "And now I'm both excited and confused."

Noelle had had a hard time keeping the smirk off her face. "Other than the fact he's our client, I don't see why you're so resistant to him. Cash is a good man and a good father."

"That's true, and Rocco is smitten with Cash and Penny both. When we're together, he's a fun guy, but being a father is more than that. It's about being there for hard stuff and the mundane moments. The everyday things that make up a child's life. A good father would be a constant presence and a leader for the family."

"Yeah, so? Cash doesn't seem to have a problem with that. Why do you?"

She'd sighed, knowing Noelle didn't want to hear the ugly truth about how men only wanted to be the leader for the easy stuff. "Look, Cash is in the middle of a dangerous situation with the Madrina cartel. His life is in danger. Penny's life is in danger.

The last thing he needs right now is the added responsibility of a relationship."

Noelle had shrugged. "Then again, maybe it's exactly what he needs. Someone he can come home to each night. An adult who can share in the ups and downs of parenting and those mundane moments you mentioned."

"Well, I don't know if that someone is me."

"Oh, c'mon, Alana. You have so much in common, right down to your experience parenting children with special needs."

She'd given that one to Noelle. "It's an emotional roller coaster all on its own. Over the last few days I've seen our connection goes beyond our parenting roles. We have a shared faith. We both believe a marriage should be built on the firm foundation that is God. That's the only way a marriage could weather the storms."

"See? You guys owe it to yourselves to at least consider it," Noelle had said.

Alana had shaken her head and chastised herself for even considering it. "It's too complicated. Too risky. Maybe Rocco isn't missing a father figure in his life. Maybe he's been missing *me*. We've been out of our routine. Spending too much time playing house with Penny and Cash is giving Rocco mixed signals. I should probably steer him away from the idea of me and Cash."

Alana pulled her mind back to the moment. She'd been checking her mirrors, and so far, she wasn't being followed.

When a natural pause in her conversation with Rocco presented itself, she pounced. "Hey, bud. What you said earlier about Cash." She flicked her eyes to him in the mirror. "You wanna talk about that a bit more?"

Rocco looked up with a sort of deer-in-the-headlights look. They weren't really the *feelings* type of people. Neither was used to talking about their emotions. "It's important to have these conversations, even if we're a little uncomfortable."

Rocco fidgeted with the seatbelt. "Um, I guess so."

"I know we've spent a lot of time at Penny's house, and it hasn't been a very fun spring break for you. I'm sorry about that."

"No, it's been the best spring break ever! Really, Mom."

"I'm glad to hear you're having fun. Normally I wouldn't bring you to work with me, but you've had a special bond with Penny right from the start."

"Yeah, it's like...she's the sister I've always wanted."

Alana stiffened. That wasn't the direction she wanted this conversation to go. "This is the first I'm hearing about a sister."

"It's not like you ever dated anyone long enough for it to be an option," he said.

"Wait a second, mister. I am *not* dating Cash. He's a client."

"Oh, sure, Mom. I see the way he looks at you," Rocco teased.

Alana suppressed a smile. "Don't change the subject, young man. You blindsided me with that bit about wanting Cash to be your dad."

"I know, I just...I really like Dr. Cash. He's always nice to me, and he never treats me like a kid. And he's always there for Penny, and you too, Mom. I guess it would be nice to have a dad."

Alana's heart ached at her son's words. How long had he needed a father figure and never voiced it? Cash would be a great guy for Rocco to look up to and depend on. But even though she found herself wanting to spend more time with Cash, she didn't know if she was ready for him to take on that kind of role in their lives.

"I know, sweetie. But you realize we don't know Penny and Cash that well. It takes time to get to know people, and it's only been a week."

She flicked her eyes to the mirror. Rocco nodded, but she could see the disappointment in his eyes. "I know it hasn't been long, Mom, but I haven't had a dad for eleven years. How much longer am I supposed to wait?"

"Wow...um...that's pretty heavy, Rocco. I don't have an exact answer." She gripped the steering wheel, trying to think of something that could make sense to someone so young. "These things are...complicated."

"You're just worried Dr. Cash will leave you the same way my dad did."

———

THURSDAY, 5:31 P.M.

For the first time in a week, Cash could breathe.

Bailey had called and now began speaking rapid-fire before he could utter a greeting.

"Listen up, Cash. I got an update on Trejo." Bailey's tone was low but firm. "I scored my meeting, and the FBI gave Williams the green light to execute their warrant. Expect them to arrest Trejo and some of his crew tonight or tomorrow morning. They have a thing for six a.m. wake-up calls."

A weight lifted off his chest. "That's great news, Bailey. Sounds like we could be closer to figuring out what he wants. Any update about Sonia?"

"Cash, I can't talk long. Williams has news and he'll call—"

"Please don't make me wait, Bay. I need to know about Sonia."

Sounds of a bustling restaurant filled the silence as he waited for Bailey's reply. "The Coasties confirmed it's her car. You guys weren't far off in your search, and they're pulling it up as we speak."

Cash groaned. "And no one thought to tell me? I wanted to be there."

"No way. They won't let a civilian on the barge. Besides,

they're taking it straight to a secure evidence storage facility to process it. But I'll see if my SAC can get our evidence response team involved since we believe it could be tied to the cartel's illegal activity."

Cash sighed. "I guess that works. Just...be careful when you go to meet this leader. I don't like thinking about my little sister tied up in all this."

"First, you're only two minutes older than me. Second, I have the weight of the agency behind me. We're going to get some answers and put an end to this." Cash could hear dishes clattering in the background.

"I know. Don't take any risks, Bailey. I don't want to lose you too."

Bailey scoffed. "You're not getting rid of me that easily. We'll talk more later."

The call disconnected and Cash glanced up to see Noelle eyeing him from her spot on the floor beside Penny. "You all good?"

"Yeah. Sounds like things are moving, but nothing concrete." He liked Noelle and trusted her, but he couldn't divulge much more than that. Only he and Alana had been authorized to be briefed on the details of Bailey's undercover case.

It didn't matter. In a day or two this would all be over and he could return to normal life with his daughter.

Noelle sat beside Penny, who was sprawled out on the living room floor and surrounded by crayons and pages of colorful drawings. Penny's little hand scrawled across the page, filling in the white space with a vibrant green.

Noelle lined the crayons up in tidy lines according to their shade each time Penny switched colors. "She has a natural ability for art."

"Yeah, I think she could spend hours dedicated to a single drawing. Although, be sure to give her ample time to detach from her work. She doesn't like it when you try and pull her off abruptly."

"Good to know," Noelle said. "I heard you talking to Libby earlier. How's she doing?"

"Tired, but chipper. She was released to recover at home this morning and asked if I could bring...You Know Who...over to see her. I said we'd visit soon, but kept it vague."

"I take it she doesn't know what's been going on?"

He shook his head. "No, and I'd like to keep it that way. She needs to rest, not worry about us."

"That's smart." Noelle took the green crayon Penny had abandoned and lined it up with the rest. "Alana's on her way with Rocco. She said Rocco checked out fine."

"Great. I think I'll start dinner. Penny, you wanna help Dad in the kitchen?"

"No! I color!" Penny shouted, not bothering to look up.

Noelle smiled and Cash shrugged. "I think she knows I'm useless in the kitchen."

"I'd help, but..." She dipped her head to Penny. "Busy."

Cash chuckled and opened his tablet. "Surely I can follow a simple recipe, right?" He'd decided to try burrito bowls, which mostly required transferring ingredients from their original containers into a larger one. He only had to cook the chicken and cut a few vegetables.

He washed his hands and began pulling ingredients out of the fridge. Alana had offered to make dinner every night. It could be her way of ensuring Rocco ate diabetic-friendly meals, but if she didn't trust his cooking, he wouldn't blame her. One thing was for sure, they couldn't keep eating takeout every night.

Alana intrigued him. And yeah, that kiss at the gym had caught him by surprise, but everything about it had said she'd wanted it too. All the time they spent together was great for getting to know her and Rocco, but it wasn't helping his heart.

Instead of listening to her when she talked, he'd catch himself watching her mouth. What would it be like to kiss her any time he wanted?

Shaking his head, he focused on slicing the tomatoes, not his fingers. He really had to quit daydreaming about kissing her. He'd hired her to protect his daughter, not to get involved with him romantically. But something about the way she moved and looked at him made him want to forget all that and just give in to the attraction between them.

The doorbell rang and Penny sprang to her feet. "Rocco!"

Noelle moved fast and beat Penny to the door. "Hang on, sweets. Remember what I taught you about the door?"

Penny nodded and cupped her hands around her mouth. "Who dere!"

"It's Rocco and Mom," came Rocco's voice through the door.

"Good job, Penny," Noelle said, opening the door.

After greeting Penny, Rocco ran to the kitchen and threw his arms around Cash's waist. His elbows went up to allow Rocco's head to nestle into his chest.

What was this? His eyes shot up across the island to where Alana stood smiling. Cash dropped his arms and squeezed Rocco. The warmth of the little man's embrace was different than Penny's. His small arms were strong. Confident.

Rocco looked up. "Thanks for letting us come over, Dr. Cash." He slipped out of the embrace and hurried to the living room.

Alana strolled over and peered at his handiwork and smiled. "Wow, what's all this?"

"Thought I'd try my hand at dinner tonight." Oh, how he wanted to kiss the corners of her beautiful smile. He averted his eyes. "Burrito bowls sound good?"

"Perfect. I'm starved."

Noelle slipped her purse over her shoulder. "Well, sorry to

miss this little experiment, but I've got dinner plans with Jonah tonight."

Cash raised his eyebrows. "Jonah, huh?"

"Please." Noelle rolled her eyes. "We're just friends. You good here?"

"Yep. We're staying a little late since it's still spring break."

"Can we have a sleepover?" Rocco pleaded.

Alana put a hand on her hip. "No begging, and no sleepovers. But we can have a movie night if Cash is okay with it."

"Works for me." There might have been a twinge of disappointment at Alana's declaration. A sleepover meant they could stay up all night talking. Every night he learned a little more about Alana, and there never seemed to be enough time.

"Juliette will check in at eleven," Noelle said on her way out the door. "And I'm always a call or text away."

Dinner wasn't half bad if Cash did say so himself. They ate over a game of Uno that he was sure Rocco helped Penny win by playing cards she needed. Their close bond reminded him of growing up with Bailey.

Funny, this was the first time it'd occurred to him how much it meant to have a sister to share life with. Penny needed a brother like Rocco. One who loved her and protected her at all costs. And Penny would so benefit from a sibling to lean on as adults. Same way Cash and Bailey leaned on each other now.

After dinner, Cash settled onto the couch beside Rocco. "Oh, that popcorn smells good. What're we watching?"

"I picked this one." Rocco had picked an action-packed superhero flick.

"Nice pick." Cash grinned. Having a boy in the house had the additional benefit of fewer princess movies.

The movie started, and Rocco leaned over and whispered something to Alana, making her laugh. Alana stroked Penny's hair as Penny laid her head in Alana's lap. He'd been so focused on his work for the past few years that he'd forgotten how much he was missing in life.

As the movie went on, Penny and Rocco drifted off to sleep, and by the end, both kids were zonked out.

"Let's make a break for it," he whispered.

"Yeah, I think my leg is asleep." Alana lifted herself from under the weight of a sleeping Penny and covered her with a warm blanket.

They tiptoed to the kitchen.

"Now for the best part." Cash opened the freezer. The cold air swirled around them. "Madam has two choices of the finest gelato for dessert."

"Raspberry, please."

"A wise choice. My personal favorite as well." He scooped two generous bowls and turned toward the sitting room.

Alana caught the hem of his T-shirt and tugged. "I've been dying to try the fort."

"Your wish is my command," he said with a slight bow. Those dark eyes could get him to agree with almost anything.

Alana handed her bowl to him and crawled into the shadowy fort. She propped herself against the cushions and took the bowls so Cash could climb in. He settled beside her. Their bodies pressed close in the small space. His senses jolted awake at the scent of her.

They ate in comfortable silence except for the occasional clink of spoons hitting the bowls.

Alana breathed in. "Is it just me or does this taste better in the fort?"

"I think you're right. Good idea." He nudged her shoulder with his. "Oh, I had some news today. The Coast Guard confirmed the car is Sonia's car, and they were pulling it up as of a few hours ago."

Her eyes went wide. "Way to bury the lead. Tell me everything."

He lifted a shoulder. "Not much to tell. Bailey called a few minutes before you got here and let me know. They'll take the vehicle to a secure facility to process it. She also scored her meeting and gave Williams the green light to arrest Trejo."

"So, we could have some answers soon?"

"That's the hope. Bailey said one of the detectives would call, but I figure that won't happen until they have something solid to tell me."

Alana found something interesting in the bottom of her bowl. "Can I change the subject for a bit?"

"Yeah, sure."

"When did you first realize Penny was autistic?"

He swallowed a spoonful and wiped his lower lip. Not the question he'd expected. "She was about two and a half. She wasn't hitting her milestones, wasn't making much eye contact, and had trouble communicating. I thought it was shyness or maybe losing her mom. But then she started having meltdowns and sensory issues, and I knew she needed help. It was tough for her."

"And for you too?"

"This is going to make me sound awful, but when the specialist diagnosed her with autism, I didn't want to believe it. I didn't want her to be different. To go through life with challenges. I told the doctor she was wrong." How arrogant he'd been that day. "I wanted to believe it was something she could grow out of. At worst, maybe she'd need more therapy to deal with losing Sonia."

Alana put her bowl on the floor and wiped her mouth with her napkin. "It's not easy to grow up without a mother."

He studied her. "You?"

"Yeah, but my mom abandoned me on purpose. Penny's mom didn't have a choice in the matter."

"That we know of."

"Yeah, well...either way, it's not easy on Penny. Believe me."

His heart ached at the thought of a young Alana abandoned by her mom. He stacked his bowl in hers and took Alana's hand, feeling the warmth and softness of her skin against his. "You're a strong woman, Alana. A great mother and quite the athlete from what I've seen."

"Thanks, Cash." She smiled at him. A genuine, warm expression that made his heart race.

He studied her in the soft glow of the string lights. Her dark eyes a tantalizing reminder of the woman who had captivated him from the moment they'd met. He fought to keep his composure, knowing that she was here to protect his daughter and he was a distraction. But the pull of her was impossible to resist. In that moment, every nerve ending tingled with the thrill of the possibility of knowing her and connecting more deeply.

Cash had no idea what was happening between them, but somehow, he'd fallen head over heels in love with Alana Flores.

Too bad he'd have to fire her if he wanted to date her.

FIFTEEN

Oh boy, maybe being in the piano fort with Cash wasn't such a great idea after all. They were sitting close. Too close.

The blankets enclosing them in the confined space seemed to amplify their body heat. Or maybe that was just her, flushed from the way Cash was looking at her. This man did things to her insides. Things she'd never experienced before. She tried to tell herself this was nothing more than an infatuation, but a still, small voice told her Cash was a missing piece to her soul.

She'd tried to rebuke the voice. Tried to pray it away and ask God to help her resist falling for this man. Somehow the opposite was happening.

Rocco's little announcement earlier hadn't helped things either. It was for his own sake she hadn't dated. Relationships never worked, and she didn't want to parade men through Rocco's life.

And she couldn't fall into a relationship with Cash if he was a client. The kiss at the gym still lingered in the back of her mind, but if she wanted to pursue something after Trejo was arrested and Penny was safe, she had to get to know Cash on a deeper level.

She grabbed an orange throw pillow and hugged it to her chest. "Tell me why you joined the Navy."

"My dad was in the Navy. He was my hero. He would come home from deployments with stories about all the places he'd been, the people he had met, and the adventures he had saving lives every day. He always made it sound so exciting, like being in the Navy was the greatest thing in the world."

She brushed her bangs out of her eyes. "The veterans I worked with on SWAT had some cool stories. They took turns showing scars from their fire fights." Some of their stories made Alana's life surviving foster care look like a walk in the park. "When did you finally enlist?"

"I'd been offered a scholarship to play ball in college, and I was so excited to come home and tell my mom. With twins, paying for college was a huge weight on my parents. I was so proud to take that burden away. But when I got home, my mom was on the couch with Bailey. They were hugging each other and crying. My dad had been killed in combat."

"Oh, Cash. I'm so sorry." She lowered the pillow and touched his arm.

He twisted the fringe along the edge of the pillow. "Oh man, the guilt hit me in the gut. Here I was doing a happy dance all the way home thinking about myself and my scholarship. All the while, Bailey and Mom were sobbing, completely crushed by the news."

Alana wasn't sure what to say, so she didn't say anything.

He squeezed her hand and flashed a thin smile. "I didn't take the scholarship. I joined the Navy to honor my dad. I wanted to make him and my mom proud. I thought it would be a way to make a difference and to live up to his legacy."

"But it hasn't been easy for you, has it?"

"No," he admitted. "It seems like every time something good happens in my life, everyone else's falls apart."

Cash's story broke Alana's heart as she realized the depth of pain he carried. How wrong she was to assume his life had been perfect because of his success. Nice house, nice cars. Great job. She should know better than most that outward appearances are often contrary to the inner turmoil. In many ways, his childhood had been more difficult than hers. "You know, sometimes I think of life as being like a mountain range. There are peaks where everything is wonderful, and there are valleys where everything seems to go wrong. But in the end, it's the combination of the peaks and valleys that makes the view so beautiful."

She shifted to face him. "See, when we're in the valleys, we don't usually notice the beauty all around us. We can only see the struggles and difficulties. But when we reach the top of the mountain, we get a different perspective. We can see the entire range, and it's breathtaking. Sometimes we need the valley to appreciate the beauty of the mountains."

Cash was quiet for a moment. "I never thought of it that way," he admitted. "I've been too focused on trying to stay on the mountaintop even when those around me are in the valley. I've been selfish. Thinking only of myself, I guess. But maybe it's time for me to stop thinking it's my fault for being on the mountaintop and turn to help others climb back up."

Alana admired his willingness to reflect on his actions and take responsibility for his attitude. "You put that beautifully. The valley may be challenging, but it's where we grow and learn the most. Helping others climb back up to the mountaintop can be the greatest gift we can give."

Cash took a deep breath. "You know, the day I was promoted was the day I got the news that Sonia had passed away. You've helped me realize that I've been carrying this weight for so long. Believing that every success in my life always meant that someone else has to suffer. But you're right, maybe the valley is where we can find true strength and purpose."

He lifted her chin. His gaze lingered. "Thank you for

reminding me of that." His hand traced a gentle path along her cheek.

Her heart fluttered at the tenderness in his touch. He gazed at her with deep affection, sending a rush of warmth through her body. She smiled at the joy of being so close to him.

Then Alana heard it. The slight click on the home alarm system that indicated someone had tripped a motion sensor.

————

A tiny war waged inside Cash. The side of him that wanted to kiss Alana was about to win when she tensed and pushed herself away. Without a word, she scrambled out of the fort and reached for her gun. His mind raced to piece together what was happening as he crawled out behind her.

"Motion sensor outside," she whispered. "We need to move the kids to the fort without waking them."

He nodded. Tried to focus on the children when all he wanted to do was run outside and check it out for himself. But Alana had planned for this and he trusted her. He picked up Rocco, cradled the boy in his arms, and motioned for Alana to take Penny. Together, they moved them into the safety of the fort.

Once they were secured, he turned to Alana. She had her phone out, checking the security cameras.

So stupid. He'd left his own phone in the kitchen. He whispered, "What's going on?"

"Someone's outside. Close enough to the house to trip the motion sensor."

"Is it Juliette? Maybe she's early."

Alana shook her head. "No. Juliette would call. Stay put and let me check it out."

"Hold up a sec." He crossed the room and grabbed the

baseball bat from under the couch. If Trejo was making a move, he *would* defend his family.

Alana moved to the front door. Raised her weapon and pressed the muzzle against the wood. She leaned in and peered through the peephole.

His heart raced as the bright flashing lights of the police cruiser illuminated the room through the sidelight windows. The harsh red and blue colors cast eerie shadows on the walls.

Alana's phone rang. He could hear her side of the conversation, which was a lot of "uh-huh" and "I understand." Her shoulders dropped and she holstered her weapon. She hung up and gave him a small smile. "The police were doing a drive-by and saw someone running away from the house."

He tightened his grip on the baseball bat. "What? Who was it?"

"The neighbor. Looks like her cat escaped. She was searching in the bushes by your porch."

"Oh man." He leaned against the wall and put his hand on his chest. "Are you kidding?"

"Don't worry. The officer gave her an earful about staying off private property. They're going to hang out for a while, but I need to do a security sweep. Someone could have used that as a distraction." She gestured to the living room. "Sit. Give your heart a few minutes to slow. I'll be right back."

Cash was too amped to sit. He checked on the kids. Still sound asleep. He retrieved their ice-cream bowls and carried them to the sink. He'd just finished washing and drying them when Alana came back.

"We're all good. Nothing out of order. What about the kids?" Alana walked to the living room.

"Slept right through it, thankfully." He settled into the soft cushions beside her.

Warmth emanated from the crackling fire in the fireplace. The flickering light cast a soft glow on Alana's face and highlighted the delicate features that he found so captivating. Where had they been headed before the alarm blared?

"Boy, that false alarm got my heart racing," he said.

"Tell me about it," Alana said. "I'm not sure if I should be mad at that cat or not."

Cash let out a small laugh. "I never knew a cat could cause so much trouble. Next thing you know, we'll be putting the house on lockdown for a squirrel."

Alana chuckled and leaned back against the couch. "It's funny how the smallest things can cause the biggest scares."

"I'm glad you were here. We did good together." He took her hand and traced invisible lines on her palm with his finger.

She held his gaze. "Are you okay?"

"Yeah, I'm fine. In the moment, I was reminded how much I have to lose. And since my heart nearly exploded over an old lady and a cat, you owe me."

"Owe you?" Her eyebrow arched. "What do you mean?"

"Here I was spilling my guts about my childhood—in a pillow fort with fairy lights, no less—and now it's your turn."

"Oh? Is that how this is supposed to work?" She smiled. "A little quid pro quo, then?"

"A story for a story. Unless you can think of something else you'd like to exchange?" He wagged his eyebrows. "A kiss, maybe?"

"Men!" She slapped his chest.

He caught her hand and kissed it. "I might be a red-blooded American soldier boy, but I hope you know I'd never do anything to hurt you."

Alana's expression softened. "I think I do know you, Cash Thomas."

He wrapped an arm around her shoulder and pulled her close, snuggling in to hear the story. "So, tell me what happened after you moved to California."

Alana placed a hand on his chest and blew out a breath.

"Well, I moved in with my aunt and uncle in a bad area of Los Angeles. The neighborhood was tough, but my home life wasn't a good situation either. My uncle would get drunk and beat my aunt up."

Cash's protectiveness surged within him. No child should have to witness violence. His parents had had a few good arguments that turned into shouting, but never anything physical. "Your parents weren't around at all?"

"No, my mom struggled with addiction and finally gave me up to foster care. I never knew my dad." She took a deep breath before continuing. "My aunt couldn't—or wouldn't—leave, and I didn't want to be around to watch him hit her. I stayed out of the house as much as I could. Started running with the wrong crowd. I thought it was my only option. I got involved with a gang, thinking it would give me protection and security. A family."

Cash listened. His heart cracked with every word. He held her tight, wanting to protect her from the world. "But you got out."

"Well, first, I got into some trouble and ended up getting arrested. That's when I realized I was pregnant with Rocco." She sat up and shifted so she could see him. "Getting out of a gang was no walk in the park, but I had to do it, or I'd end up like my mom.

"This is where the money from Rocco's father came in?"

"Partly. I was in court facing some pretty hefty charges when a man stepped up to the judge and asked if he could talk to me in private. The judge agreed and we went into a little room where he told me he owned an MMA gym and group home to help teens get on their feet. I was skeptical, but my attorney said I could either go to jail or be released into the program." She sniffed a laugh. "I mean, the choice was easy at that point."

"Not everyone would make that choice," he said. "Sounds like God was looking out for you."

"Yep. He wasn't supposed to be in court that day. He had lunch plans with the bailiff and court ran over. There he was, waiting for his friend, and he felt prompted to help me." She shook her head. "His program wasn't a normal halfway house or group-home situation. He was a missionary who took in street kids and taught us how to fight. Not just physically but to fight for ourselves. For our futures. He showed us that we had value. That we were worth something."

"Wow, having someone believe in you is life changing."

"It was hard work. We had strict schedules and we trained. Hard. It was difficult, but I kept fighting. Kept pushing forward. He became like a father to me. A father I never knew I needed." Her eyes drifted to the fire.

Cash held her in silence. Gave her space to process the memories and keep going if she wanted.

She turned back to him, and he brushed her bangs back to better see her eyes. "What I didn't know when I went to live at the gym was the connections with law enforcement. SWAT, FBI, DEA—the whole alphabet soup. Lots of the guys trained at his gym and gave us advice. It was because of the gym that I set my sights on the police academy."

"Wow, you're an incredible woman, Alana," he said. "I love that you still have this fire in you. It's inspiring."

Alana smiled. "Thanks, that means a lot."

"Do you still keep in touch with your mentor?"

"Yep, we email and text. He keeps me updated on the students I support."

"You support? What do you mean?"

"The gym operates on donations, and you can also sponsor a student. It's amazing what a small amount of money can provide. I sponsor two or three girls a year, and through the process I get to know them. I can give them the encouragement they need to keep going forward. Here, look." She pulled out her phone and thumbed to a photo of a young African American teen with a referee holding her gloved hand in the air. "That's Tasha after she won her first tournament at age fourteen."

Cash shook his head in amazement. "Just when I think you can't be any more amazing." He pointed at her phone. "Alana, that's incredible! I want to be a part of something like that. I wonder if Atlas would be interested in starting something similar."

His mind drifted to Dante, the boy who'd died on his table. He had seen too many young lives cut short by violence, by a lack of hope and opportunity. But Alana gave him hope, reminded him that there were people out there fighting for a better future, for a better world. He squeezed her shoulder, grateful she'd brought so much clarity to his life.

Alana turned toward Cash, their faces just inches apart. "That's a great idea. After this is all over, let's put them in touch."

"Speaking of the gym..." His eyes dropped to her lips. He recalled their adrenaline-filled kiss at the gym. The taste of her. The warm comfort of finally giving in to what he wanted. But he wanted more than a chemical romance.

He wanted...*her*.

The air between them crackled with intensity. Was this the right moment to show her? To tell her that he'd fallen in love with her? The warrior bodyguard, the loving mother, the broken teenager. All of her.

Alana's hands cupped his jaw and drew him in. She pressed her forehead to his. "Cash..." His name came out on a hot breath that mingled in the air between them. "I really want to kiss you, but as your bodyguard I shouldn't do this."

"Yeah," he breathed.

"You probably need to fire me."

"I definitely need to fire you."

"Or I could quit."

"Or you could quit."

"Yeah, okay." She slid her hands around his neck. "I'll do that."

Alana kissed him then.

He pulled her closer and kissed her back. His fingers in her hair, he massaged her head. If there had been any doubt before, any room for wondering, it had evaporated. He was completely hers.

Cash wasn't sure how long they kissed before they parted with one last soft kiss to her temple. Alana's eyes shone with a myriad of emotions. His thumb traced the curves of her face as he looked into her eyes. "Wow, I think I could do that forever."

Alana leaned closer, her breath warm against his cheek. "Well, maybe that could be arranged." Her lips feathered his ear.

"Is that right?"

"Mm-hmm."

He leaned to kiss Alana again, but a small voice interrupted him. "Daddy? I thirsty."

He stared at Alana, wide-eyed. "You think she saw us?"

"We both saw you," Rocco said. "And you were kissing! Does this mean you're getting married?"

SIXTEEN

Okay, so kissing Cash? Not her smartest move. Kissing Cash with the kids asleep a few feet away? That ranked right up there with hanging from the hot air balloon. Now she'd gotten herself in to a real mess.

Yep. Spaghetti all over the place.

Still, as Alana packed extra supplies for Rocco's insulin pump, she listened for sounds of him stirring in his room. How was she going to explain why kissing Cash didn't mean they were getting married, or even dating, without sending the message that it meant nothing? The last thing she wanted was to raise a son to believe physical intimacy should be expressed outside the bounds of marriage.

She zipped Rocco's backpack and looked up. Her sleepy son staggered out of his room.

"Morning, bud."

He waved with one hand and rubbed his eye with the other. "What time are we leaving?"

"Soon as you eat." She nodded to the plate of scrambled

177

eggs, bacon, and strawberries waiting on the breakfast table. "I packed some extra supplies and snacks in your backpack for the robotics competition. Noelle will pick you up from Cash's house and bring you back when it's over."

"Cool." He sat and snagged a piece of bacon. "Is Jonah going with us?"

Noelle and Jonah took Rocco on nights when Alana worked late. Noelle insisted there wasn't anything romantic between them, but sometimes Alana thought Rocco was their idea of a chaperone. "I'm not sure, but won't your friend Ivy be there?"

"Yeah, but she's not really my friend. She's in high school now."

Alana paused. "Wait, aren't you about the same age?"

"Mom, she's *really* smart," he said, as if that explained everything. "So, was last night kinda like your first date with Cash?"

Alana looked up from Rocco's phone, where she'd been thumbing through his monitoring app. Oh, he was going there already? Okay, then. "We need to talk about what you saw last night. I do like Cash a lot, and if things were *different*, we'd probably date each other. But it's dangerous to have feelings for a client. It's my job to keep him and Penny safe, not go on dates. The last thing I want to do is jeopardize their lives because I'm too wrapped up in my feelings."

"No way. You're like, the best bodyguard ever. You can do both."

He wasn't getting it. She put a hand on his shoulder. "No, I can't. Not at the same time. It's unprofessional."

He pushed his eggs around the plate with his fork. "Yeah, but I like spending time with you and Cash and Penny. I like feeling like we're all in this together. I don't want to go back to...to just us."

"I know what you mean. This last week has been pretty

great." She pulled out a chair and sat beside Rocco, forearms on the table. "Can we make a deal?"

His head snapped to full attention.

"We both like Cash and Penny, and we'd like to see them in our lives. But how 'bout we keep that between you and me for now, and I promise when he doesn't need the Elite Guardians anymore, we will talk about it."

Rocco's grin stretched ear to ear. "Yeah, okay, Mom. It's a deal."

Alana stood and kissed the top of his head. "All right, eat so we can go. We don't want to keep them waiting."

She finished packing Rocco's bag and slung it over her shoulder. Out of the corner of her eye, she noticed the shed in her backyard. Who knew finding Penny that day would've turned their entire world upside down?

Alana parked in the circle drive of Cash's house. Its pristine white exterior contrasted with the dark, ominous clouds looming overhead. They stepped out of her Jeep and approached the front door, her senses on high alert. She'd taken counterintelligence measures to ensure she wasn't followed on the drive over, but her skin still crawled with the inexplicable sensation of being watched.

Noelle opened the door and greeted Alana with a smile. She was dressed in dark jeans, a slim-fitting long sleeve button-up, and black flats. Her purse was already on her shoulder. "Morning. Sorry I can't stay. I told Jonah we'd pick him up by eight thirty." Noelle glanced at her watch, then to Rocco. "All set to go?"

Rocco still held Penny's hand after greeting her with a hug. "I'm super ready! I'm just sad Penny can't go with us."

"I know, but it's not safe for her to go in a big crowd until we catch the bad guys," Alana said. "But don't worry, Penny and I will have our own little adventure while you guys are gone."

Noelle fished her keys from her purse and checked her watch again. "We better get going or we'll be late."

Alana waved goodbye and closed the door. Penny began to fidget and whine. Tears welled in her eyes. "No, Rocco! No go!"

"It's okay to be sad." She knelt beside Penny. "Rocco will come back, and you'll have so much fun with him. Is there a game we can play while he's gone? Or we could read together."

Penny shook her head and continued to cry. Her reaction didn't look pretty, but she was doing an amazing job containing herself. Some days when Rocco left, she did nothing but scream. At least now she only sobbed.

Watching Penny cry made Alana itch to console the child. "Is it okay if I give you a hug?"

Penny held her arms out, and Alana held her tight, rocking and whispering comforting words and prayers.

Penny's breathing slowed, and she looked up at Alana with a tear-streaked face. "Alana brush hair?" She grabbed the ends of her long strands and folded them in half.

"Oh, you'd like me to braid your hair again?"

Penny's face lit up and she nodded. She sniffled and ran her arm under her nose.

"I'd love to do that." Alana stood. "Can I carry you upstairs to find your hairbrush?"

Penny held her arms out, eager to be lifted up. Alana hoisted her onto her hip, and Penny wrapped her arms around Alana's neck. For a moment, Alana stood there with Penny's head against her shoulder. She'd always dreamed of having more children but had never thought it would be in her future.

Cash jogged down the stairs in his scrubs. "Morning, girls." He crossed the room to the kitchen and grabbed his keys off the counter.

Ten different questions flew through her head, but she said, "Morning. What's going on?"

"I just got paged. They need me at the hospital for an MCI, and ER is short-staffed. I'm going in."

"MCI?"

"Mass casualty incident. Multiple officer-involved shootings. The hospital is already overwhelmed, and there's another dozen patients on the way."

Alana could hear the stress in his voice, but there was something else there too. A distance between them. Did he regret what had happened last night? Realize he'd made a mistake after Rocco mentioned the M-word?

No, she was jumping to conclusions. There was a medical emergency, and he was in doctor mode. She adjusted Penny on her hip. "I'll call Juliette and ask her to meet you at the hospital."

He waved a hand. "No, don't bother. I'm going right into surgery. It's a secure area. I'll be fine."

"Okay..." She dragged out the word. "But you do realize you shouldn't go alone, right?" She darted her eyes between Cash and Penny, hoping she didn't have to spell it out for him.

His gaze drifted to Penny. He put his phone on the counter, whipped a penlight out of his breast pocket, and clicked it on. "Penny, wouldn't you like to play with Daddy's shiny flashlight?"

Penny nodded and took the flashlight with a smile.

Cash lifted her out of Alana's arms and carried her to the piano fort. "You can use the flashlight as long as you're in here, okay?"

"Okay, Daddy." Penny opened a book and shone light on the pages.

Cash motioned for Alana to follow him into the kitchen. He pulled her into a tight hug and kissed the top of her head. Her arms went around his waist.

"Listen, I appreciate the concern, but I'll be fine." He kissed her head again before loosening his hold. "When one cop goes to the hospital, they all go. The boys in blue are there, and they won't go home until they know their fellow officers are stable."

She didn't like it, but he was right. If anything, Cash might be safer there than at home. "Did you say multiple officers were shot?"

"I'm not sure of the details, but they are overrun. They need me."

"Just...watch your back, okay? I know you're capable, but you're not invincible. There's plenty of danger between home and the hospital. Your daughter needs you to come back to her." She ran a finger over his chin. "And I need you to come back to me."

He leaned in and kissed her. Soft and sweet but passionate. A promise to come back for more. "I'll be back before you know it."

Alana closed her eyes and leaned in for another kiss, then her eyes snapped open. "Wait, doesn't Penny have a speech therapy appointment today?"

Cash smacked his palm against his forehead. "You're right, I completely forgot. Would you mind—"

"Not at all." She kissed him on the cheek, then patted his chest. "Now go save our boys in blue."

He kissed her again and headed for the door.

Alana flicked her eyes over to Penny playing with the flashlight in the fort. Braiding Penny's hair would be Alana's pleasure, but there was one thing she had to do first. She swiped her phone and pressed the speed dial. "Hey, Juliette. Can you do me a favor? Cash got called to the hospital, and he's on his way without security detail."

"Say no more. I'm in the car, so I'll reroute."

"Thanks. I don't know why, but I can't shake the feeling something bad is about to happen."

———

FRIDAY, 9:00 A.M.

By the time Cash made it to the hospital, he'd determined he needed to get his head in the game. It would be a crazy day in the ER, and he couldn't have his mind in two places. Who was he kidding? His mind was all over the place. Torn between Penny, work, Trejo, and Alana.

He'd wanted to talk to her about the kissing and the kids, but she'd bolted as soon as Juliette arrived for her shift last night. This morning, he was the one who'd rushed off, for a different reason.

One thing was for sure, he wanted Alana and Rocco in his life. And he planned to tell her. Right after he fixed his patients.

The cold, sterile air of the trauma unit hit him as he walked in. The familiar smell of disinfectant and antiseptic filled his senses. Crackling radios echoed through the halls. Uniformed and plain clothes officers paced the waiting room, every one of their faces etched with the same look Cash had seen time and time again.

He walked toward the scrub room and caught up with Brooke. "Hey, what's going on? I didn't expect so many..."

Deep creases lined Brooke's brow. "It's bad, Dr. Thomas. We have three officers in critical. One serious. Not to mention the four civilians. From what I gathered, there was a shootout early this morning. Some officers serving a warrant, and things went haywire."

No. It couldn't be...Was this the aftermath of Trejo's arrest? If so, then his sister had secured her meeting and Trejo was captured. Or killed. Which would mean Penny was safe, and he could get his life back.

Brooke followed him to the scrub sink and rattled off the patient information. After he removed his watch, he rolled up his sleeves and began lathering his hands with surgical soap. He scrubbed under his nails, up his arms to his elbows, and all the way to his shoulders. The adrenaline began its push through his veins. He could hear the chaos of the ER outside, the shouts of the trauma team, and the cries of the injured. This was what he lived for, what he was trained for.

Brooke had a fresh surgical gown and held it up for him to step into. Cash turned off the water and dried his hands on a sterile towel before slipping into it. He held up his arms, and Brooke tied it in the back, making sure it was snug and secure.

"Thanks, Brooke. Who's first?"

"Trauma five."

The first patient was a young Hispanic man in his late teens. He had multiple gunshot wounds, and his blood pressure had bottomed out. Cash barked orders to the team. "Get me a central line, stat! Two units of O negative! Where's my thoracotomy tray!"

The team worked in perfect unison. They moved quickly to stabilize the patient. Cash was focused, his mind working at lightning speed as he made incisions and worked to repair the damage done by the bullets.

They finished, and Cash was handed the chart of their next case. His eyes fell on the patient's name. An icy cold knot formed in his chest. "Luis Trejo." The chart burned in his hands. Or maybe that was his imagination.

"Is everything okay, Doctor?"

"No, it's not." He thrust the chart at Brooke. "I can't operate on him. Get another surgeon in here, now."

"But Dr. Thomas, you're the only one—"

"I can't do it, Brooke. I...I...he tried to...no. You have to get someone else."

Brooke nodded and ran from the room to find another surgeon.

Cash walked into the OR where a team prepped Trejo for surgery. He stood at a distance and stared at the man lying on the operating table in front of him.

Luis Trejo. The man behind the attempted kidnapping of Penny. The man responsible for gun and drug trafficking. If he was here, where was Bailey? He had to find out if she was okay.

Despite his years of experience as a trauma surgeon, Cash struggled to process the situation. This was the second time in his career that he couldn't operate on a patient due to emotional ties. The impact of the decision weighed heavily on his shoulders. Calling in another surgeon could have dire consequences if Trejo took a turn for the worse. But Cash wouldn't touch the man unless he crashed. Then he'd do everything in his power to save Trejo's life.

He might not tell Alana she was right about the danger that lurked everywhere, but he understood it better. Right now, that danger was right in front of him, lying on his operating table.

Cash handed the surgery off to another doctor and took over a patient with multiple GSWs. After an hour, Cash emerged from the OR and sucked in a deep breath of sterile air. Juliette was waiting in the lounge. "I thought I told Alana I didn't need a bodyguard today."

"I'm just taking orders."

"Never leave a sailor behind?"

She tilted her head. "Something like that."

"In our case, that doesn't apply to the men's room. I'll be right back." In the locker room, he pulled out his phone and called Alana. "Hey, how's it going there?"

"We're coloring. You sound tired. Are you okay?"

"Yeah, it's crazy here. A lot has happened, but I can't talk long. I was thinking about what you said last night, and I had an idea."

"I'm all ears."

Cash started pacing. "I'm gonna have another patient any minute, so I'm laying it all out there unfiltered, okay?"

"Okay." He could hear the hesitation in her voice. Maybe he

should do this in person, but something in him didn't want to wait.

"The gang violence in Savannah is out of control, and I'm sick of seeing so many kids in my OR because of it. I'm thinkin' about investing in Atlas's gym. Starting a program like the one you attended. Creating a safe haven for high-risk youth. A place to learn discipline and a way to channel their anger into something positive." He heard his name over the intercom and groaned. "Look, I gotta run. Sorry to dump that on you, but pray about it and let's talk tonight."

"Yeah. Of course. I'll do that."

"Good. Oh, and Alana?"

"Yes?"

"I can't *wait* to see you." They said goodbye and disconnected.

He bounced on the balls of his feet and pumped a fist in the air. The program wouldn't be an easy task. The gang violence was much bigger than just one gym, and there were countless obstacles to overcome. But he could make a real difference in his community. He could save lives beyond the walls of the OR.

Four hours and three operations later, Cash was finally ready to go home. The shift had been brutal, but at least all three wounded officers would recover from their injuries.

As he walked down the hallway with Juliette, Brooke stopped him. "Hey, that patient. The one you handed off. I'm sorry, but he...didn't make it."

Juliette sank back to give them the privacy needed to discuss patients.

Cash's mouth went dry. "Are you talking about Trejo? Luis Trejo?"

She nodded. "He died on the table."

The news hit him like a defibrillator. It took a few minutes to process.

Everything was finished. He and Penny were safe. They could

put the nonsense with Trejo behind them and move on with their lives.

Only one more door to close.

Sonia.

"Thank you, Brooke. I'm going home."

He still hadn't heard from Williams. Probably dealing with the fallout of the arrest going horribly wrong. The FBI was smart to make them wait until Bailey had her meeting.

Cash stepped out of the elevator behind Juliette. He focused on the sound of their footsteps echoing against the concrete walls of the parking garage. His thoughts spiraled from Trejo to Sonia to Penny to Alana. It would take time to process everything. Time he didn't want to waste right now. With Trejo out of the picture, he didn't need protection from the Elite Guardians anymore. He could live his life again. Take that sunset ferry ride with Penny. Take Alana and Rocco to dinner with Penny. Ask Alana on a real date.

A black SUV screeched to a stop behind them. A team of black-clad men poured out. Juliette shoved him between two cars.

A shadow behind him caught him off guard. He spun to see a man with a gun aimed at his chest. Then he heard it. The sharp crackle of a Taser. Two probes shot out and embedded in his chest with sharp pinches. Electricity raced through his muscles. His entire body seized and he went down. Face first.

Footsteps rushed toward him. A hood was thrown over his head, his arms wrenched behind his back.

Rough hands dragged him across the concrete floor. He tried to resist, but his limbs wouldn't cooperate. Muffled sounds came from somewhere off to his left. Another scuffle.

A pinch in his neck. Then silence as everything went black.

SEVENTEEN

From her chair in the corner, Alana observed Penny's speech therapy session. The small room, painted in calm shades of blue and green, housed a variety of books and puzzles. Penny drummed her fingers on the child-sized table and read flashcards. The way the woman redirected Penny seconds before her frustration boiled over impressed Alana. She'd tuck that technique away for later.

Alana had dressed Penny in the sunshine-yellow shirt and found matching yellow hair ties to hold her braided pigtails. It was true what people said. Picking outfits for little girls was more fun than dressing little boys.

When Penny finished her therapy session, she ran down across the room with her arms out for an unexpected hug. "I did good, see?" She pointed to the round unicorn sticker on her shirt.

"That's amazing, Penny! Way to go!" Alana held her and whispered, "I'm so proud of you."

On the way out, Alana held Penny's hand in her left, leaving her gun hand free for the most dangerous part of their trek. Getting into the car.

Alana could not shake an unsettling sense of being watched. In the parking lot, her vision sharpened. She scanned the area with laser-like precision, taking in every detail. The glint of sunlight off a car's windshield. The rustle of leaves in the breeze. The distant hum of traffic. It all registered in her mind as normal. Yet the hairs on the back of her neck stood at attention.

Alana helped Penny into her booster seat and waited as Penny buckled herself.

"Wow, you did the buckle all by yourself." She handed Penny a book and closed the car door.

She caught a flicker of movement near the building. A shadow that shouldn't be there. Her muscles coiled and her hand went to her holster and rested on the butt of her gun. She concentrated on the target area a full minute. Nothing happened. The shadow remained still.

Alana hurried to get in the car. She plugged her phone into the USB port and left it in the console tray. When she turned the key in the ignition, the engine roared to life. The GPS map application appeared on the infotainment system, and she searched for a choke point. A bridge or narrow road she could use to channel the traffic to see if any cars followed.

Through her rearview mirror, she kept an eye out for the shadow to move as she navigated her way out of the parking lot and pulled into traffic. Her gaze flickered back and forth, keeping a close eye on the cars around them. Nothing seemed out of the ordinary.

She blew out a heavy breath and glanced in the rearview. Penny looked at her book and swung her feet. She chattered to herself and didn't seem worried or tense at all. Maybe Alana was paranoid.

Maybe, but her instincts told her something wasn't right.

She took a sharp turn onto a narrow street that led to a bridge over the Savannah River. The road was flanked by tall buildings and dense foliage, making it difficult to see far ahead. The slow-moving traffic gave Alana time to study each car. Had that blue sedan been parked at the therapist's office?

Alana jumped in her seat when her phone trilled through the car speakers. The name on the display read Det. Matt Williams. She answered the call through her earpiece to keep little ears in the back seat from hearing something they shouldn't.

"Hey, Matt, what's going on?"

"Alana, we found Juliette in the parking garage. She's unconscious and Dr. Thomas is missing."

"Missing?" Alana's heart slammed into her chest. Her mind raced with a barrage of questions about Juliette and Cash, but Matt started talking.

"We executed a warrant at Trejo's house this morning. Things didn't go well. There was a standoff, and someone inside started shooting. Multiple officers and civilians were wounded."

"The mass casualty incident Cash left to help with..." Alana said it more to herself than to Matt. Cash was missing, and her partner, her sweet friend Juliette, was hurt. "You found Juliette? Is she okay?"

"She'll be fine. Video surveillance showed Cash and Juliette attacked in the parking garage. They were caught off guard and outnumbered. Juliette did the right thing—pushed Cash between two cars—but they anticipated it and had someone hiding. They incapacitated them with Tasers and a fast-acting drug. Diazepam, probably. They left Juliette but loaded Cash into a black SUV. We've got the plates and put out a BOLO so officers will be on the lookout."

"Was this Trejo?"

"I just don't know, Alana." She could hear frustration in his voice. "If this was ordered by Trejo, then we have a bigger problem than we thought."

"Why?" Traffic on the bridge slowed. The green line on her map program turned red and alerted to an accident ahead.

"Because he's dead. Died on the operating table."

"Dea—" Alana caught herself before she repeated the word. Alana was even more convinced this wasn't Trejo, but she didn't have permission to tell Williams about Sonia and her money laundering. At least, not yet. Not when it could blow an entire undercover operation. Could she possibly get in contact with Bailey through the special agent in charge?

She looked in the mirror at Penny. She seemed engrossed in her book, oblivious to the world around her. Still, Alana knew children were always listening and was careful to choose her words. "They pulled up the car this morning. Did they find anyone inside?"

"You mean, did they find a body?"

"Yeah. I'm stuck in traffic with Penny right now. Gridlocked due to an accident up ahead. Can't really go into details on my end."

Matt was silent so long she checked to see if the call had dropped. It hadn't. Probably he was deciding how much he could tell her. Finally, he said, "No. No human remains in the car. It was empty."

A cold knot tightened in the pit of her stomach. "I expected as much, but a small part of me wanted to be wrong."

Her phone bleeped. The screen showed the call had disconnected. The icons on her display showed zero bars of service. "Great," she muttered.

"Great!" Penny echoed.

Yep. Kids were always listening.

Alana glanced in the mirror. The same blue sedan was four cars behind. She tightened her grip on the steering wheel. They had a bigger problem than a dropped call. They were being followed.

———

Cash's head throbbed. His entire body felt weighted like sandbags. He slitted his eyes and blinked. Tried to focus on his surroundings. Why was his vision so blurry? He tried to move, but his limbs wouldn't respond. Thick, rough ropes bound his arms and legs to the chair.

"What is this?" he muttered.

He tugged at the ropes, gritting his teeth as the fibers dug into his skin. His muscles grew taut as he strained against the bindings. He flexed his arms, trying to summon every ounce of strength in his body, but the ropes didn't budge.

It was then that he noticed the stinging pain in his chest. He lifted his shirt to see two round puncture wounds, the skin red with purple bruises forming around the marks. "Stun gun," he groaned.

What had happened? Think. He had to think.

The ER had been overrun with injuries today, and they'd paged Cash to assist. Yes, he'd operated on patients injured in the shootout at Trejo's house. But how had he gotten here? And where exactly was *here*?

He closed his eyes and searched for memories. Okay, yes. Now he remembered. The officer had come out of surgery alive but critical. Once the ER was under control, he'd finished his charts and headed home.

Oh, Brooke had stopped him. Said Trejo died in the OR from his injuries. And Juliette had been there when he left the hospital. He'd been distracted, though. Unable to believe that Trejo was finally dead and that he and Penny were out of danger.

But if Trejo was dead...why...

Memories tumbled back. He was in the parking garage with Juliette. She pushed him. The crackle of the stun gun. A jolt of electricity. A hood. A needle. And everything went black.

What had they drugged him with? Prop...propo... The word

wouldn't take shape in his sluggish brain. He shook his head, trying to clear the fog. The word came to him. Propofol. They'd probably injected him with propofol or another sedative like benzo...benzodiazepine. That explained his brain fog and weighted limbs.

How long had he been here? He still didn't know where he was. He tugged against his restraints, trying to get a better view of his surroundings. The room was small, with only a twin-sized bed and the chair he was in. But the walls were strange. Made of gleaming teakwood instead of painted sheetrock. There was a strong chemical odor in the air, and the only light came from a dim glow beneath the cabinets.

He was on a boat.

That smell was wood polish, and beyond that, the air was thick with the smell of salt and dampness. He could make out the faint sound of water lapping against the hull.

What was he doing on a boat, and where were they taking him?

Penny!

Cash prayed that Alana had Penny. That she was safe. And if this was some sort of ransom exchange, Alana would refuse to let anyone near his daughter. He didn't care what happened to him so long as Penny wasn't harmed.

He pulled against the ropes again and again, but they held firm. His chest heaved with effort. Okay, he had to calm down. Slow his breathing and think if he wanted to get out of this alive. But first, he needed to figure out where he was and who had put him there.

His ears perked up as he forced himself to listen for sounds beyond the thick silence of the cabin. He focused all his attention on his surroundings, desperate for any clue that might reveal his location or captors.

Then he heard it. Faint, muffled voices coming from beyond the walls of the cabin. Heavy footsteps thudded outside the room. The hair on the back of his neck prickled. He couldn't see who was approaching, but considering his situation, it couldn't be good.

The footsteps stopped and the cabin door creaked open. A man with dark hair and dark eyes stood in the doorway. Acne scars marred his skin in a constellation across his face. His short hair receded at the temples, and his thick eyebrows hung low over his eyes. He had a silver gun resting at his thigh. "Good, you're awake." He had a heavy Latin accent.

Cash struggled against the ropes binding him to the chair. His eyes darted around, searching for an escape. "Who are you? What's going on? Where am I?"

"My name is Ramón, and you're on a boat, my friend." He stepped into the room. "And you're a long way from home."

"What do you want?" Cash demanded.

"You'll find out soon enough." Ramón's throaty laugh resonated through the cabin and sent shivers down Cash's spine. "I'm going to give you a little freedom, but don't even think about trying to get away. Trust me, it won't end well for you." He tapped the gun on his leg.

Cash nodded. At this point he'd do almost anything to be untied. His muscles ached from being bound for so long. Ramón untied his hands and feet and grabbed him by the arm. He jerked Cash up and dragged him toward the cabin door.

In the hallway, Cash's eyes went wide in awe at the sight before him. This was no fishing boat or cargo ship. This was a luxurious superyacht.

"Move." Ramón jammed the gun into his back.

Cash followed the narrow hallway at least forty feet before it opened into a lounge that flowed into the aft deck. The cream-colored walls contrasted with the dark wood floors. A white semicircular sofa sat in the center of the room, adorned with plush cushions. The coffee table in front of the sofa was made of gleaming stainless steel, with intricate designs etched into the surface.

Along the walls, floor-to-ceiling windows offered a breathtaking view of the expansive ocean. The bright blue water stretched out as far as he could see.

Ramón walked to the center of the room and picked up a remote control. With the press of a button, the glass wrapping the aft end of the deck slid away. He shoved Cash's shoulder. "Outside."

Cash walked through the open transom and marveled at the endless expanse of sea and sky that stretched out before him. Smooth white lounge furniture was arranged around a stunning swimming pool that ran the length of the deck. The pool's clear blue water appeared to merge with the boundless ocean.

"Hello, Cash." A feminine voice broke his thoughts.

His heart skipped a beat as he recognized the voice. He whirled.

"Long time no see," she said.

EIGHTEEN

Gridlock on the bridge was the last place Alana wanted to be in a situation like this, but the traffic began to move again. Through the rearview, she stared at the blue sedan. Still there. She drummed her thumbs on the steering wheel and glanced at the speedometer. They were crawling at fourteen miles an hour. Really? "Hurry up. Hurry up."

"Hurry up!" Penny echoed.

Ahead, the traffic began to move, and Alana merged into the right lane. She checked her mirror. The blue sedan clicked its blinker on and merged into the lane six cars behind Alana. At least there was a bit more distance between them now.

Her little detour had worked to flush out the vehicle tailing her, but it'd also cost an extra twenty minutes. But they were nearing the end of the bridge, and then Alana could lose the tail for good.

From her lifted Jeep, she could see over the traffic to the three-car pileup in the left lane. The first car in the accident had taken the brunt of the impact, its rear end twisted and mangled clear up to the back seat. The rear window had shattered into a thousand tiny pieces that glittered across the pavement.

A third car had tried to avoid the crash at the last second but hadn't quite made it. The damage was minor, but the cars blocked the right lane. Three people stood on the side of the road, talking and gesturing to the wreck.

The distant sound of a motorcycle cut through the hum of Alana's engine. In her mirror, she saw a leather-clad rider weaving dangerously through the slow-moving traffic. The rider, hunched over the bike, sped between the cars, coming up behind her car at breakneck speed. One wrong move, one lane correction from the cars, and it wouldn't end well for the rider. Why did motorcycle drivers always seem to have a death wish?

Alana followed the traffic onto the narrow shoulder and passed the accident. The roar of the motorcycle engine grew louder until the vibrations rattled inside her chest.

Penny put her hands over her ears and squeezed her eyes shut. "Too loud!"

"Hold your ears longer. The sound will be gone in just a minute." She glanced in the mirror again. Something about the glint in the motorcycle helmet made Alana's blood run cold.

It was the man from the restaurant, picking up her tail on a motorcycle that could outmaneuver traffic.

Alana started to hit the gas, but then a man stepped around the accident and walked into her lane. He lifted a gun and took aim at her vehicle. The motorcycle raced up behind her and revved the engine louder. Penny shrieked in the backseat.

Alana tightened her grip on the steering wheel and weighed her options. Could she outmaneuver him? Could she ram him with the car? Her eyes darted back and forth between the man with the gun and the road ahead.

She might not be able to help Cash, but she could save Penny. She slammed her foot on the gas. The gunman jumped clear of her Jeep at the last second, and Alana sped off the bridge, taking the shoulder to pass a line of traffic at the light.

She took a hard right that sent her cell phone flying into the passenger floorboard.

It was out of reach—nothing she could do about it now. She barreled through the next intersection and took the next left and another left. Her thumb fumbled for the button on her steering wheel to activate the voice dialing feature. After the beep she said, "Call Detective Matt Williams."

The voice activated system responded, "I'm sorry, I did not understand your request. Please repeat."

With Penny screaming bloody murder in the background, the speaker probably couldn't understand her, but she couldn't risk reaching for her phone while driving. She hit the button again. "Call Detective Williams!"

"I'm sorry, I did not understand your request. Please repeat." The robotic voice was really grating on her nerves.

A motorcycle raced up beside Alana's Jeep and held a gun aimed at Penny's window.

"Loud!" Penny had her eyes squeezed shut and her ears covered.

"I'm sorry, baby. Hang on." Alana swerved left, but the rider dodged her attempt to run him off the road. In the distance, two black dots appeared.

Oh no.

Two motorcycles identical to the one beside her sped toward her—right for them.

At the next intersection, Alana turned left. She had no idea where she was going and prayed it didn't lead to a dead end. She tried the voice dialing again, this time speaking slower and more enunciated. "Call. Detective. Matt Williams."

The system beeped. Alana held her breath. Had it finally understood her? "I'm sorry, please repeat your request."

Alana let out a growl of frustration and slammed the butt of her hand on the steering wheel. Forget it.

All three motorcycles swarmed around her Jeep. They closed

in on all sides, trying to force her off the road. Fine. If they wanted to go off-road, she'd take them off-road. Alana steered right, taking the shoulder and running one of the bikers into the ditch.

The Jeep teetered with two tires on the road and two in the grass. The rugged tires ate up the soft ground and kicked up mud that splattered the windows.

A gunshot echoed through the air like thunder. The wheel jerked out of her hands, and her Jeep skidded to the right. She tried to regain control of the vehicle but couldn't.

They careened off the road. The tires hit the dirt and bumped over the ditch. Alana bounced and hit the top of her head on the roof. Through the mud-splattered windshield, she saw that they were headed for a tree.

"Hang on, Penny!" Alana put her arms up and mashed the brakes too late. They crashed into the tree. Her body jerked hard against the seatbelt. The airbag exploded into her face with such force she almost blacked out.

For a second, she just lay there breathing. Then she twisted to see over her shoulder. "Penny!"

———

The woman standing near the bar looked like a complete stranger. Almost everything about her had changed. Everything except her eyes. Cash would know those eyes anywhere.

The sunlight bathed her pale skin in the yellow-orange glow of the afternoon. She stood with her hip cocked. The hem of her short green dress flowing in the slight breeze. Long delicate fingers snaked around a champagne flute filled with amber liquid. Her thin frame was all sharp edges. A far cry from the curves he remembered.

Cash twisted his face into a scowl. The mere sight of her had his heart thrumming through the roof. After all she'd put him through over the years, she had the nerve to stand there with a tight smile on her face like they were friends.

Well, they weren't friends. And now, he doubted they'd ever been.

She set her drink on the bar and lifted herself onto the padded deck stool, crossing her slim legs and smoothing the silky material of her dress down over her thighs. "Well, aren't you going to kiss me hello?"

Cash gritted his teeth. "What do you want, Ziva?"

Ziva made a *tsk, tsk, tsk* noise and shook her head. "Now, now. Just because you divorced my sister doesn't mean we can't still be friends."

"I didn't divorce her. She divorced me." He tapped his chest. "And where is she, Ziva? Where is Sonia?"

She ran a lazy finger around the rim of her glass. "At the bottom of the ocean, I suspect."

Cash stormed toward her. "They found her car, you know."

Ramón stepped in front of Cash, but Ziva waved him off. "It's okay, Ramón. Cash here is a softy. He wouldn't hurt a fly."

"Don't bet on that," Cash said.

Ziva smiled.

"I don't understand. Why did you bring me here? Why like this?" He held up his hands, gesturing to the yacht. "And why Penny? Is this about custody? I would've let you see her."

"I doubt that." She tossed back the remainder of her drink and stood. "Come. We'll talk."

With no other option, Cash followed Ziva up a narrow staircase to the deck above.

"Three years ago, I was diagnosed with Hodgkins lymphoma. After undergoing a grueling round of chemotherapy and radiation, I had a relapse. Do you know how rare that is?"

"I'm not an oncologist, but I think somewhere around thirty percent experience disease relapse."

"That's right. Seventy percent are usually cured after their treatment, but I relapsed."

"I'm sorry, Ziva. Can you try autologous bone marrow rescue? It's where they take your stem cells—"

"I know what it is because I did it. They removed my stem cells from my blood, and after yet another horrible round of chemo, they returned my stem cells back into my body."

They passed through what Cash assumed was the owner's suite overlooking the pool. A massive bed was positioned in the center of the room beneath an enormous skylight. He imagined the effect was like sleeping under a blanket of stars.

Ziva continued to talk as they walked. "My only option now is ALLO. That's where Penny comes in. We'll need to take stem cells from her blood and infuse them into mine."

Cash placed an arm on her elbow and stopped her. "Ziva." He softened his tone. "If you needed a donor, you could've just asked."

She laughed a soft laugh. "Oh, you're cute." She opened a door and gestured for Cash to enter.

He scanned the makeshift medical facility set up in the spacious cabin. The bright white lights overhead cast a sterile glow on everything in the room. He'd seen his fair share of oceanic trauma rooms and operating theaters, but this was something else. The cramped quarters were filled with all manner of medical equipment, from IV stands to surgical tools, arranged with precision on tables and trays. In the center of the room was a plush leather recliner surrounded by a cluster of IV stands.

Cash looked at Ziva. "You expect me to perform the procedure here?"

"It's simple, darling. You collect healthy cells from my niece through the IV, then transfuse them to me through a central line." She smirked. "You *can* place a central line, can't you?"

"You can't be serious. This...this won't work. You don't even know if Penny is a match."

"Oh, but I do. She's a perfect match."

"How do you—the break-in a few months ago. That was you?"

Ziva arched an eyebrow.

"But Penny hasn't been prepped. She needs a filgrastim injection to increase her blood stem cells."

"Already done."

"The injection at the hot air balloon festival." Cash shook his head. "No. No, I won't do it. Not here. Not like this."

"Oh, but you will." She stepped closer and lowered her voice. "You don't have a choice."

He squared his stance. "No, if we do this, it will be in a hospital. Surrounded by trained medical staff. I'm not a monster, Ziva. We can go to the hospital—"

Ziva spun on her heel and marched off. He hesitated, then followed her into another spacious living area.

"Sit." The single word was a command, not an offer.

Cash wanted to spit out a retort about not being her lap dog, but he bit his tongue and took a seat on the couch opposite her.

"We won't be going anywhere. We're just outside the coastal jurisdiction of state and local law enforcement. I'd like to keep it that way. Besides, I wouldn't need you if my own doctor hadn't been so stupid."

"What do you mean?"

"He delivered the benzodiazepine sedative we used on you to one of my lieutenants in Savannah this morning and got himself killed."

Cash swallowed a lump in his throat. "Trejo? He...he was working for you?"

"Of course." She picked up a remote control and pressed a button. Nothing happened that Cash could see. "He's always been reliable in the past. But this time...well, let's just say his men got what they deserved. Unfortunately, my private physician got caught in the crossfire."

Death. Each of the men who'd tried to kidnap Penny had wound up dead one way or another.

Ziva's callousness surprised him. Then something clicked. She'd called Trejo one of *her* lieutenants. His heart began to pound as his mind put the pieces together. "You're involved with the Madrina cartel?"

"Honey, I *am* the Madrina cartel."

A stewardess carrying a silver tray appeared. Ziva took the gleaming knife off the tray and studied its sharp edge with a look of satisfaction. "Thank you, dear."

The stewardess bowed and vanished.

In a flash, Ziva was across the room. The blade pressed into his throat. Her face held inches from his. The sweet scent of the champagne on her breath filled the air between them. "You *will* perform my stem cell rescue, or you'll watch as I gut your daughter and your precious undercover FBI sister right before your eyes."

NINETEEN

Alana's vision flashed white. She was disoriented and in pain, but she unbuckled her seatbelt and shoved the airbag out of the way. Penny was screaming and crying in the backseat.

"Penny, are you okay? I'm going to get you right now."

Her heart broke at the sight of the little girl's face red and streaked with tears. Her entire body quaked. Alana struggled to keep her voice calm as she spoke. "It's going to be okay, baby. We just had a little accident, that's all. I need you to be brave for me, okay?"

A helmeted rider yanked on Penny's door handle.

Alana grabbed her gun and opened her door, but the man shoved the door closed and held it with his weight. With one swift blow from the butt of his gun, the man shattered Penny's window. Glass sprayed everywhere, some of it cutting into Alana's skin. Penny's screams went frantic.

The helmeted man reached into the car and yanked the door handle. Alana scrambled into the back seat and threw herself over Penny. She raised her gun, but he wrenched it from her hands.

Alana grabbed his wrist and pinched a pressure point,

causing him to drop her gun. It hit the frame of the Jeep with a clang and fell outside.

The man aimed his gun at Penny. "Get out of the car. Now. Or the kid dies."

"Not without Penny," she screamed.

Hands grabbed Alana by the ankles and dragged her out of the passenger side. The second biker threw her on the ground, but she scrambled to her feet and lunged at him. She landed a punch in his hard stomach and sent him staggering backward. He recovered and swung his gun at her head. Alana ducked, but not fast enough.

The butt of his gun grazed her eyebrow and the skin popped open. Blood trickled down her face, and she swiped it with her sleeve. She aimed a kick at his gun hand. The biker swung his arm in an upward arc and caught her foot. He shoved her boot back and knocked her off-balance.

Her back hit the ground, and in an instant, he had his gun aimed at her head. Alana rolled out of the way a second before the biker fired a shot. She scrambled to her feet again and darted around her Jeep, searching for her gun, but as she rounded her vehicle, her breath caught.

Every nerve in her body seemed to explode at the sight of the other man trekking up the hill with Penny in his arms. She forgot the gun and charged up the hill after him. "Let her go! Stop!"

The man ignored her and mounted his motorcycle, still holding a screaming Penny in front of him. No, no, no. She couldn't let him take her. She sprinted after him. The bike's engine revved up. The sound reverberated through the air like thunder.

The rubber of the back tire burned against the asphalt as it spun in place, generating a cloud of smoke. It lurched forward and shot off.

Alana raced up the ditch and ran flat out after the bike. It picked up speed, and she slowed to a stop, watching Penny disappear into the distance. She clenched her fists and pounded them on her thighs. "Nooooo!" She screamed as loudly as she could. "Penny!"

Behind her, tires screeched to a stop. A good Samaritan stopping to help. Before she could turn, a sharp pain exploded in the back of her head, sending her to her knees. Dazed, she fell onto all fours, then collapsed.

She rolled over to see the second rider standing over her. The full-face helmet reflected his gun aimed at her face.

Her eyes burned and she struggled to keep consciousness. Was this how it was going to end? Was this how she was going to die? Black clouds crept in from the corners of her eyes. She heard a crackle noise, then nothing.

———

A bump in the road jostled Alana awake. Her eyes drifted open. Everything was spinning, and she closed her eyes again. Her forehead rested against the cool window. She pressed the button and rolled the window down. The cold air bathed her face and eased the nausea. She breathed through her mouth and opened her eyes again.

Outside, the ocean zipped by in a blur. The tires hummed on the road.

Alana summoned all her strength to sit up. The last thing she remembered—Penny!

She turned and instantly regretted the fast movement. She blinked, trying to gather her bearings. A woman she recognized gripped the steering wheel with both hands, eyes glued to the road ahead.

What was she looking at? This was a dream. It had to be.

She closed her eyes. Took a deep breath and looked again. It wasn't a dream. It was the stalker who'd kidnapped S. M.

Warren and forced the author to leap from a moving vehicle to escape her captor.

Bethany Gould.

An icy cold shiver ran down her spine. Bethany had kidnapped her. Alana reached for her gun, but it was gone. Her phone too. Was this woman behind everything with Penny? It didn't make sense.

"Bethany...what...what are you doing?" Alana's words came slower than her racing thoughts.

"Sorry, toots. I know you'd rather see anyone but me. But here I am. Your own personal savior. I saw what those men did to you." Bethany stole a quick glance at Alana. "They ran you off the road and took your baby girl. And I ain't about to stand by and let nothin' like that happen. No siree. Not on my watch."

She saw what happened? No way that was a coincidence. Alana glanced at the side mirror. Blue sedan. "You were following me?"

Bethany's head danced side to side. "Kinda. I put one of them GPS tags under the vent by your windshield. At first it was a'cuz you'd done made me angry. I got a beef with Warren, and you got in the middle. Now, I'll admit"—Bethany wagged her finger—"I's tracking you outta anger. But then the judge made me go see this counselor lady who done helped me realize my anger's been misplaced all this time. But that's neither here nor there. My point is, I wanted to talk to you. Convince you to drop dem charges so I can go home and mind my own business from 'ere on out."

Alana furrowed her brow. A shooting pain zipped down her face, and she winced. She checked her face in the visor mirror. The flesh above her eyebrow was split open. The blood had clotted inside the inch-long wound but threatened to start bleeding again. "You got a first aid kit in here?"

"No, shug. It's a rental. I got a few napkins in the console here." She tapped it with her elbow. "Maybe a li'l tape in the back."

Alana pulled a stack of napkins out and looked in the back. A roll of silver duct tape was on the floor. She held it up. "Really?"

"I got it before. Promise."

Alana tore a bit of tape with her teeth and fixed a folded napkin over the cut. "How'd I get in the car? Last thing I remember, that biker had a gun in my face."

"Stun gun." Bethany cocked a sideways smile. "I distracted him playin' all helpless old woman, then *zap*."

"He could have shot you, Bethany."

"I dunno." Her lips twisted. "I guess I might deserve it after all I done."

Alana considered the best way to deal with a woman who seemed so unstable she'd stalk someone she thought had done her wrong. Bethany had risked her own life to save her, so the least she could do was give her a little trust. "Where we going?"

"Wherever them bikers are taking yer little girl. I've been followin' em these ten minutes. Looks like we're goin' to the ocean." Bethany nodded to the map on the infotainment system.

"Tybee Island." Was it possible Sonia was alive and had ordered Penny's kidnapping? "Do you have a phone I can use?"

"Sure, hon." Bethany handed Alana her cell phone.

Alana stared at it, trying to conjure up phone numbers from memory. There was one she knew by heart, but she wouldn't type it into Bethany's phone. The woman might be helping right now, but with her history of violence, giving her Rocco's cell number was not anywhere near worth the risk. Instead, she dialed 911 and asked the dispatcher to put her through to Detective Matt Williams.

Bethany pulled into a marina and pointed. "There! They're on that boat."

On the horizon, Alana saw a boat skipping across the waves and headed out to the open ocean. Her heart raced as she squinted, trying to make out any figures on the boat. "Are you sure that's them?"

"There's the bike right there." Bethany pointed to a black motorcycle parked between two pickup trucks, a familiar black helmet on the seat and Penny's yellow hair tie on the ground.

"I sure as sunshine don't see your baby girl anywhere around here, so she must be on that boat, right?"

Alana's heart thudded harder. "You're right. But if that boat disappears, even with the help of the Coast Guard, we might never find Penny. Here. Take the phone. When the detective is on the line, tell him Alana Flores said Sonia is still alive and she's kidnapped Penny and Cash. Do you got all that?"

She nodded. "Why don't you tell 'im?"

"Because I'm going after them."

Bethany's eyes went wide. "But shouldn't you wait for backup or somethin'?"

"There's no time. Just tell him." Alana jumped out of the car and raced across the dock. Her feet pounded against the wooden planks. She scanned the boats for any possible assistance. Her gaze landed on an older woman with sun-kissed skin and short blonde hair in a center console boat. Alana raced to her boat.

The woman was leaned over, packing up her dive equipment. "Please, ma'am, can you help me? They've kidnapped my...my little girl, and she's on that boat." Alana didn't take the time to explain that Penny wasn't her biological daughter but pleaded with her eyes as she gestured toward the boat on the horizon.

"Oh, honey, what happened to your eye?"

Alana touched the tape. "I told you, they took my daughter! Please, can you take me to them?"

The woman darted her gaze between Alana and the disappearing boat. "That's a big ask, honey. I don't know you from Adam, and I've got my own life to worry about."

"I understand, but please, she's just a child. The police are on their way. I'll pay you whatever you want—just, please help me." Alana's voice cracked with emotion. Tears threatened to spill over.

The woman glanced out at the water. "Well, I do know these waters. You picked the right person to ask. I'm retired Coast Guard. I'll help, but first I need to radio this in."

"Whatever it takes." Alana climbed into the boat. "Just, please let's catch up to them first. You can call it in on the way."

"You better hold on tight, honey. If we're going to catch that boat, it's going to be a wild ride. Name's Joan, by the way."

"Alana Flores." She climbed into the boat. "I'm a former dive detective, but right now, I'm just a concerned mom who wants to save her little girl."

Joan gunned the engine and propelled the boat forward, slicing through the waves with impressive skill. Alana stood beside her, her knuckles white as she gripped the grab bars and prayed they wouldn't lose the boat.

Alana squinted against the salt spray and the glare of the sun on the water. "Look!" she shouted over the roar of the engines. "They're heading for that massive yacht over there."

Joan's eyebrows shot up. "Goodness gracious, that thing is enormous. Looks like they're heading for the tender garage at the stern."

"Get us closer, then turn to starboard. And can I borrow your snorkel gear? I've got a plan."

Joan cut her a sharp glance. "What kind of plan?"

"I'll slip out of the boat and swim over to the yacht while you keep an eye on them and wait for backup."

Joan's expression turned dark. "It's too risky, Alana. You don't know who's on that boat. They could have guards, weapons...anything."

Alana's jaw clenched. "I don't have a choice. I have to do something. I wasn't kidding about being a dive detective. I can handle it."

Joan nodded and brought the boat closer to the sleek gray

yacht. Alana donned the snorkel gear. As Joan's boat turned, Alana took a deep breath and slipped into the water. A rush of cold saltwater seeped through her clothes. She took another deep breath and went under.

Kicking hard, she propelled herself toward the yacht's stern. As she swam, she worked to come up with a plan. Stay alert. Be careful. Avoid any guards. Rescue Penny.

And Cash, if they had him.

TWENTY

Alana allowed her head to bob out of the water long enough to see the boat carrying Penny disappearing into the superyacht's tender garage. It appeared to be a float-in design that took up the entire cross-section of the hull, allowing the boat to enter through the port side of the superyacht and exit on the starboard side.

She scanned the deck for signs of security and noticed an armed guard on the roof near the navigation equipment. He was dressed in black tactical gear and dark sunglasses. The rifle held across his chest looked military grade. If they belonged to the Madrina cartel, then there was no telling what types of weapons they had access to. And if there was one armed guard visible, there were more on board.

Staying low in the water, Alana swam to the swim platform at the rear of the ship. She pulled herself up, using her arms to hoist her body out of the water. She took a few deep breaths and wiped the water from her face. Looking up, Alana saw four steps leading up to a landing, then another four steps leading to the deck with a rectangular infinity pool. She hesitated, considering her options. She had to find Penny, but she also had to be careful not to be caught by any guards.

With a deep breath, Alana began to ascend the steps, leaving wet footprints and a trail of water behind. At the landing, she paused to look around and forced her breaths to slow. The pool deck was silent except for the gentle lapping of water against the hull.

She continued up the final four steps and darted behind the lounge furniture out of the view of the guard on the roof. Her heart was in her throat. She kicked herself for not asking Joan for a knife. Without a weapon, she'd have to rely on the element of surprise.

She stashed her snorkeling gear under the chair and waited for the guard to turn his back, then dashed to the stairs. Her wet clothes made a slight squishing sound with each step. There were steps leading to the deck above and another set leading below deck. She paused and listened for voices. It was silent except for a *tap, tap, tap* sound coming from below.

Alana recognized the pattern. Three short taps, followed by three long taps, and another three short taps. Morse code. Someone was tapping SOS.

She took the stairs one at a time, listening for sounds other than the tapping. When she reached the lower-level deck, she scanned the hallway for any signs of life. Outside the first cabin door, Alana paused to listen. The SOS tapping was coming from inside the room.

Using her fingernail, she tapped on the door. Three short taps, followed by three long taps, and another three short taps. A woman's muffled cry escaped from somewhere in the room. It wasn't Cash, but someone in there needed help.

Alana turned the handle and pushed the door open. Her eyes widened and her lips parted as she stared at Cash's sister tied up and gagged. "Bailey? What are you doing here?" Bailey thrashed against her restraints and screamed words muffled by her gag. "Hang on, I'll untie you."

A door creaked, and two strong arms wrapped around Alana in a bear hug, pinning her arms to her side.

Alana simultaneously arched her back and thrust her head into a reverse headbutt. Her skull connected hard. She heard the crunch of cartilage at the same time as she swung herself around and landed a jab into the assailant's solar plexus. The man grunted and doubled over as she brought the heel of her hand up into his jaw. His teeth clattered together, and she kicked the side of his knee. His leg crumpled. He landed against the edge of the bed and bounced to the floor.

Alana wrapped her legs around his neck and squeezed him in a chokehold. He struggled for a few moments, trying to break free, but she held on until he went limp.

Breathing hard, Alana untied Bailey's restraints. "That was some greeting." When she removed Bailey's gag, Bailey jumped up and hugged her. "I'll say. Are you okay?"

When Bailey loosened her grip, Alana pulled back and studied the woman's face. "I'm fine, but you?"

"Yeah, thanks." Bailey rubbed her wrists. "Man, my eyes about fell out when I saw you open that door. What're you doing here? And what happened to your head?"

Alana bound the man while he was still unconscious. "Oh, your basic motorcycle gang fight." Alana searched the man for weapons and found a small pistol concealed in an ankle holster. She did a quick check to ensure it was loaded and tucked it in her waistband.

"Seriously, though. Some thugs on their bikes ran me off the road and kidnapped Penny. I followed them to this ship. She's here somewhere, I know it. I think they kidnapped Cash too. He might be on board. Have you seen either of them?"

Alana found a pocketknife in the man's jeans and tossed it to Bailey. She caught the knife and slipped it into her back pocket.

"They kidnapped Cash *and* Penny? Oh, when I get my hands on that woman...She's gonna regret this," Bailey said through clenched teeth.

"So, it *is* Sonia? She's alive?"

Bailey shook her head. "Not Sonia, Ziva."

Cash had mentioned Sonia's older sister. Ziva was the one who'd helped Sonia get her business off the ground. She'd prevented a fight at Sonia's funeral. "I'm assuming you didn't know Ziva was here before you boarded?"

Bailey snorted. "No clue. Our surveillance team never caught a glimpse of her." Her head dropped down. "You know, the moment I saw her, all the pieces fell together. She was the one who talked Sonia into laundering money for the leader of the Madrina cartel. A few years ago, the man we knew as the leader of the cartel was found dead. Throat slit. We had no idea who'd taken over, but things were running as hard and fast as ever. It's why I went undercover. The FBI needed a woman to try and infiltrate using..." Bailey's eyes met hers and she shrugged. "Using my skills in persuasion."

Alana pictured Bailey at the gym, her curves poured into the body-hugging outfit. "Where's your backup?"

"I came in silent. No weapon. No communications. They did a full sweep at the dock. It doesn't matter. Ziva had surveillance photos of me talking to Trejo weeks ago. He let me set up the meeting. The whole thing was a trap. I wanted to meet the cartel leader." Bailey shook her head. "Never once thought it was her. Our intel said she was in Colombia with her parents."

"You think Ziva and her parents decided to go around the courts to get custody of Penny?"

"Maybe. But that doesn't explain why they took Cash."

"Not to sound macabre, but why are you still alive?"

They exchanged a look that turned Alana's blood cold. They both knew the Madrina cartel was ruthless and, so far, hadn't left any witnesses alive. "Bargaining chip. If things go south, having a federal agent in custody could go a long way. As for Cash, it makes no sense."

"It doesn't matter why they took them. Right now, we have to find them and get off this boat before she kills Cash and disappears with Penny forever."

———

Waking up in a drug-induced haze was getting old fast. Cash forced himself to bring his head up. The world swam before him, and he fought to focus. Blinking a few times, he tried to remember what had happened. He didn't know how much time had passed. The last thing he could recall was Ziva's knife at his throat. A pinch on the back of his neck and the world had gone dark again. Looking around, he saw that he was still in the living room on the leather couch.

His head throbbed, and he tried to sit up. Slow. The room was silent. Through the wall-to-wall windows, he could see the sun sinking into the Atlantic. Where had Ziva disappeared to? He struggled to understand why she'd gone to such lengths to kidnap Penny when she could have asked for a donation. There had to be something more going on behind her crazy scheme. Penny could've been hurt or killed during the kidnapping attempts.

Cash couldn't see anyone else in the room but sensed a presence. Like someone watched him.

"Who's there?" he called out.

Soft footsteps thudded toward him from behind. He turned his head to see Penny in her sunshine-yellow shirt, running toward him. "Daddy!"

A tremor quaked through his body, and a silent gasp escaped his lips. "Penny..." He struggled to stand, but his legs were water. Penny jumped into his arms, and he leaned back on the couch, burying his head in her neck. "Oh no. Oh baby, why are you here? You shouldn't be here. You should be with...Alana."

"We're on a boat," Penny said into his neck. "Big boat, Daddy."

"I know honey." He pulled back to take her in. A black smudge streaked across her cheek, and he rubbed it with his thumb. She had one braided pigtail, but the other must've fallen out and had left her hair on one side a tangled mess.

Penny had every right to be frightened out of her skull, but her inability to process the gravity of the situation protected her tender little heart. Her ASD was her superpower. Maybe it was God's special gift to Penny to protect her from all life's painful moments. His special daughter lived on the mountaintops more than most.

Still, red-hot lava coursed through his veins as he considered what she'd been put through to bring her here. Alana would've never let her go. Never let them take Penny without a fight. Which meant...

No. He refused to believe they'd killed her.

He looked past Penny to see Ramón standing beside Ziva. His hands were crossed in front of him, concealing his gun. Ziva had changed into a white button-down shirt with the sleeves rolled up, tucked into flowing cream-colored linen pants.

He tightened his grip on his daughter and glared at the woman who had taken everything from him. First Sonia and now Alana. He wanted to do something to wipe that smug look off Ziva's face. Instead, he clung to Penny.

He'd always carried the guilt over not being there when people really needed him because he was doing something to better himself. Not this time. It wasn't his fault Sonia had died while he was deployed, just like it wasn't his fault he'd been offered a scholarship on the day his father died. And it was *not* his fault a sociopath had kidnapped him and his daughter while he was saving lives at the hospital.

"You should know by now that I always get what I want." Ziva stepped closer, and Cash tensed. "And now that Penny is here, we'll get this done quickly."

"You're insane. I'm not doing this."

Ziva's smug smile faded and her eyes turned cold. She sat on the coffee table in front of him and leaned in. "Oh, I don't think you have much of a choice. You see, I have something you want." She stroked Penny's hair. "Or should I say, someone?"

"We can go to the hospital. No one has to know who you are—"

"One way or another, I'll get what I want. Even if I have to take it myself." Ziva looked over her shoulder.

Cash followed her gaze to see Ramón. He raised his gun and waved it at Cash before lowering it again.

Cash's gut twisted. He'd have to play along for now. Bide his time until he could find a way to get Penny and himself out of this mess. He forced a calm tone. "What do you want me to do?"

Ziva's lips curved back into a menacing grin that turned his stomach. "That's better. I want you to perform the apheresis session to extract the stem cells from Penny. Once that's done, you'll place the required central line in my chest and administer the stem cell transplant."

Cash's heart rate quickened. What she was asking him to do was ludicrous. He only had a vague idea of what was required for a peripheral blood stem cell transplant. But he'd keep her talking, keep her believing he would help her, and in the meantime, he'd figure out how to get a message to Detective Williams or Bailey. "And if I do this procedure, then what?"

"Well, you'll keep your mouth shut about anything you see or hear while you're here, and we'll let you both return home." Ziva's eyes narrowed. "And if you don't...well, let's just say you won't be seeing your daughter again."

Cash swallowed. "The donation process will take days—"

"You'll do it in one." Ziva rose to her feet and began to walk away.

Taking Penny off his lap, Cash stood. He crossed the room and caught Ziva by the elbow, spinning her to face him. "She's too little," he said in a low voice. "She doesn't have enough blood. Especially if you want enough for a follow-up procedure in the future."

Ziva's eyes studied him. "Fine." She jerked her elbow away. "You have two days."

"You know I'm not an oncologist, right? This isn't my area of expertise. I've never done this procedure before."

"Two days," she hissed.

His jaw muscles tensed. As much as he wanted to lash out at the evil woman running a cartel, Cash had to keep his cool and buy time. Someone had to know he and Penny were missing. They'd come looking soon enough. As long as Ziva needed his daughter's blood for a transplant, Ziva wouldn't hurt her. Cash, on the other hand...well, she could kill him and find another doctor.

He stepped back and lifted his chin. "Bring me all your charts and medical history. I need to see everything before we begin. Penny needs bloodwork too. One filgrastim injection may not have boosted her white blood cells enough. And she needs to eat before we even think about starting the donation, so whatever she wants, she gets, you hear me?"

"I'm not your waitress," Ziva spat.

"But you have one, so get her in here," Cash bit back. "Oh, and I'm not leaving Penny cooped up in that tiny room for eight hours, so get your goons to bring the chair and all the equipment in here."

That last part was pushing it, but he didn't want to risk being locked in the room. At least here there were multiple exits if given the opportunity to escape.

It was clear Ziva didn't like taking orders from Cash. Her

dark eyes bore into him, but she snapped her fingers and Ramón jumped into action. Ziva sat on the couch across from Penny and crossed her long legs.

"Well, Penny, my dear. Looks like you're going to be the little hero who saves your auntie's life."

TWENTY-ONE

Bailey's recon knowledge of the superyacht proved invaluable to Alana as, together, they made their way through the ship. The small gun provided some protection, but Alana would rather have her SIG Sauer P229 when they encountered the guards with assault rifles. Between Bethany and Joan, help should be on the way. But Bailey insisted they couldn't sit around and wait. She didn't need to convince Alana. They had to find Cash and Penny.

"The wheelhouse is the central hub of the vessel. From there, the captain has full control over everything, including communication systems. If we can gain access to the comms inside, we could call for backup, then find Penny and Cash."

They'd made it to the stairs leading up to the top level when Alana heard the distinct *thwop-thwop-thwop* of helicopter rotors. Joan had come through. Backup had finally arrived. She put a hand on Bailey to get her attention. When she turned, Alana cupped her ear with one hand and mouthed, *Listen.*

Bailey paused, then nodded. "There," she whispered.

On the horizon, Alana saw the familiar red-orange of the U.S. Coast Guard helicopter approaching. She shot a look to the roof deck, where an armed guard had a radio to his mouth. Two more gunmen appeared. One with a heavy machine gun, the other with a rocket-propelled grenade launcher resting on his shoulder. "Oh no. Bailey, look!"

Bailey's eyes widened as she saw the weapon, and she took off sprinting up the outside steps to the roof deck. Alana was right behind her. Her heart pounded in her ears as she ran. Machine-gun fire sprayed the side of the helicopter hovering a hundred yards out.

Then Alana heard the piercing whoosh of the rocket's exhaust gasses and the ignition of the rocket motor. A trail of smoke and flame chased the rocket to its target. The grenade blasted through the cockpit glass. A fiery explosion lit up the sky.

Alana's chest tightened as she focused on the helicopter, now billowing smoke from the shattered front window. The chopper whirled in a one-eighty before it nosedived toward the yacht. The helicopter crashed into the water with its rotor still spinning, sending up plumes of spray and foam. Metal screeched against metal as the spinning blades scraped into the hull and ripped it apart.

The force of the impact knocked Alana off her feet. She landed hard on the deck. A sharp pain exploded in her tailbone and stole the scream rising in her throat. Bailey stumbled into the railing and fell overboard.

"BAILEY!" Alana pulled herself to her feet and ran to the guardrail. Where was Bailey? She clutched the rail and searched the churning water for any sign of her. Nothing.

The twisted metal of the helicopter's blade was wedged into the side of the yacht. The hard edge had cut through the hull. The tail of the helicopter jutted out of the water. The yacht creaked and groaned as it began to tilt to one side, the weight of the sinking helicopter dragging it down.

Alana scanned the water, but all she could see was a swirling mass of foam and froth. "No, Bailey, no. Not you too." Her breaths came hard and fast. She slid her hands along the rail and ran past the helicopter, still looking overboard. Then Bailey broke through the surface of the churning waters, coughing and gasping for air.

"Bailey! Hold on, I'll save you!"

"I'm fine," Bailey managed to choke out. "The Coast Guard boat is coming. I can tread, but you need to find Penny and Cash before this boat goes down."

Alana hesitated, torn between staying with Bailey and leaving her to save Cash and Penny. Time was of the essence, and she couldn't risk them going down with the ship. "Hang in there, Bailey! I'm going to save our family!"

Her feet pounded against the floor as she sprinted inside and down the hallway. The floor beneath her feet tilted, making her steps uneven. She held a hand against the wall for balance. The ship was going down fast.

At the end of the hall, a muscled man stepped through a doorway. A gun in his hand.

Alana halted and reached for the pistol in her waistband. Gone.

It must've fallen out when she fell. The man's face was marred with acne scars. He sneered and stepped forward. He raised his weapon.

Alana lunged forward, aiming for his midsection, but he was too quick for her. He sidestepped her attack and swung his gun in a wide arc, catching her across the face.

She stumbled backward, dazed and disoriented. The metallic taste of blood filled her mouth. She pivoted on her heel and landed a roundhouse kick to his gun hand. The weapon clattered to the ground, and Alana planted a second kick in his ribs. He cried out and doubled over, gasping for breath. With a quick and precise strike to the back of his neck, she rendered him unconscious before he had a chance to react.

Heart racing and adrenaline pumping, she pressed on to the main cabin, toward the sounds of muffled shouting. Then Alana smelled it.

Fire.

———

Cash clutched Penny against his chest and gasped for air as the fire from the helicopter spread. The smell of smoke and burning fuel filled his nostrils. The metal blades of a burning helicopter had cut through the hull of the ship, leaving a gaping hole in the living room where they'd been sitting. The flames caught the fluttering drapes on fire and raced across the room. The blaze licked the walls and the ceiling, filling the room with smoke.

Cold water seeped into his shoes. They had precious little time before the yacht sank. That was, if they didn't burn to death first.

Through the smoke, Cash saw a figure running toward them. "Alana!" He dodged debris and flames and pulled her into him with his free arm. He kissed her temple where duct tape covered her eyebrow. "I thought I'd never see you again."

"I knew I'd find you. I had to." She stepped back. "We've gotta move or there won't be any reunions. Help is right outside, but the boat is sinking fast."

"And burning—" Something moved behind Alana in the shadowy smoke. "Alana, watch—"

Alana whirled as Ziva brought a vase down hard on her head. Shards of glass rained down. Alana staggered but put herself between them and Ziva.

"You're not going anywhere, but Penny's coming with me," Ziva said.

Cash turned, shielding Penny from Ziva. She would not lay one hand on his daughter. "If we don't get out of here, we'll all die."

"Fine with me," Ziva sneered. "Without Penny, I'll die anyway."

"Cash, get Penny and get out!" Alana ran at Ziva in a flying tackle and landed on top of her. They grappled in a frenzied struggle on the wet carpet. "Go, Cash!" Alana cried. "Get Penny outside!"

Penny began to cry. He hesitated and shifted Penny in his arms and watched the two women fight even as the burning ship sank deeper into the water. "I...I can't leave you, Alana."

Alana rolled over and pinned Ziva to the ground. She looked up at him. "Bailey fell overboard. She needs you."

He swallowed and nodded. With Penny in his arms, he made his way aft. The ship pitched starboard. Cash struggled to maintain his balance, holding onto Penny as he stumbled across the room.

The boat lurched and a sharp crack echoed through the cabin. It sounded as if the boat had split in half. The floor beneath his feet gave way and he fell. Penny flew from his arms and slid toward the opening in the hull.

"Penny!" Cash lunged forward to grab her. A solid section of the ceiling broke away and came crashing down. He tried to scramble out of the way, but the heavy debris came down hard. Blackness clouded his vision. His head lolled and he watched Penny sinking beneath the water outside the gaping hole in the hull.

"Alana," he rasped over the roaring in his ears. "Save Penny!"

Then everything went black.

TWENTY-TWO

Alana released Ziva and dove for Penny on her stomach, arms outstretched, struggling to grasp her before she sank.

Penny screamed and flailed her hands. "Daaaa!"

"Hang on, Penny, I've got you." Saltwater sprayed Alana's face, stinging her eyes and filling her nostrils with its briny scent.

Penny kicked her feet and arms, but she was treading backward. Away from Alana. If she dove in after her, they could both be trapped under the sinking boat. "Swim toward me, baby. A little farther so I can pull you up."

Alana stretched farther into the water but couldn't...quite... reach. She would just have to go in after her.

The vessel lurched again. Water rushed in, covering half her body. A heavy object fell on the back of her leg. The pain ripped the breath from her lungs—a searing agony that caused her vision to go dark. She twisted to see over her shoulder. A marble-topped end table had fallen on her left leg and pinned her to the ground.

Penny stopped screaming, and her body began to sink. Alana pushed through the pain with gritted teeth and summoned all her strength. With trembling hands, she reached for Penny. Her fingers strained to grasp the girl's limp form.

She couldn't reach. Alana let out a scream that echoed across the sea. "Nooooo!"

She writhed under the crushing weight of the marble table, determined to get it off her leg. Hot tears mingled with sweat and saltwater ran into her eyes. She wriggled and writhed, desperately trying to free her leg, but it was no use. The table had her pinned to the spot.

Her teeth chattered. The water continued to rise around her. Soon she would be underwater too.

Alana heard splashing footsteps and looked over her shoulder to see Ziva emerging from the smoke. Her muscles tensed, and her hands balled into fists, preparing for another fight.

Ziva's eyes bulged. "Where's Penny?"

"She slipped under...under the water. My leg is trapped." Alana began to cry. "I can't...I can't..."

Ziva turned and dove through the hole in the hull, disappearing into the water below.

Alana turned her attention back to the table. She pulled her leg and screamed as pain shot through her hamstring up to her back. Blood bloomed through her pants and clouded the water around her calf. The table had cracked, and a shard pierced her leg. The more she pulled, the more she tore her own flesh.

She brought her left knee up under her stomach. Panting, she paused to bite back the wave of pain. When it passed, she pushed her hips under the lip of the table and pulled her elbows down until she was up out of the water. The table lifted an inch. She pushed harder and gained another inch and pulled her leg free.

She was on all fours, breathing hard, when Ziva broke through the surface of the water with Penny under one arm. Ziva coughed and sputtered water. "Take her. Get her...out..."

Alana felt the weight of Penny's lifeless body as she pulled her out of the water and held her pressed against her torso. "What about you?"

"I can't climb up," Ziva gasped. "Don't worry about me. I'll find a way out." She sucked in a deep breath and disappeared back into the water.

Alana pulled herself to a standing position. With the gash in her leg, every move was excruciating. Time was running out. With shaking hands, she put two fingers on Penny's neck and searched for a pulse. There was nothing.

"Oh God. Oh God, help!" Alana cradled Penny in her arms and swung around, searching for some place flat to lay her. The room was filled up to her knees with water. If she could just get to the back deck, the Coast Guard could see them. Alana sloshed through the water. In a few long strides, she was outside on the deck.

Then Cash was by her side. "Give her to me."

His strong arms encircled the lifeless form of his daughter and laid her on the tilting floor. They dropped to their knees beside Penny and began CPR. Alana tipped Penny's head back and checked that her airway was clear. She sucked in a breath and exhaled into Penny's airway. After five rescue breaths, Cash interlocked his fingers and started chest compressions.

Alana counted. "One...two...three..."

When she reached thirty, Cash paused, and Alana gave two more rescue breaths. They started the cycle again.

Then again.

And again.

"Keep going," he said.

Tears streamed down Alana's face as she watched Cash manually pump blood to Penny's brain. His voice was steady and reassuring. "It's okay. It's going to be okay. Just stay with me."

She wasn't sure if he was speaking to her or to Penny, but

the desperation in his voice was clear. Alana kept counting compressions.

"Spare Penny's life, God. At Your word You can restore life. Do it now."

"Twenty-nine...thirty." Cash paused and Alana breathed air into Penny's lungs.

Penny remained unresponsive. Alana began counting again.

"Come on, Penny," Cash urged, his voice rising in pitch. "You can do this. Breathe for me!"

———

Cash wasn't sure how long they'd been giving Penny CPR, but one thing was certain. He would not quit. There was no giving up on his little girl. But, okay. Time to clear his mind. Focus. No straddling the line of Dad and doctor. He couldn't be her dad right now. Just doctor.

The chaos around him faded into the background.

"Twenty-eight...twenty-nine...thirty." He stopped compressions so Alana could breathe rescue breaths.

"C'mon, God. Do your thing. Bring my baby girl back," he whispered.

Penny's body convulsed as she started to cough and splutter water. He tilted her over on her side. Alana sat beside Penny to keep her from rolling farther.

He waited as Penny cleared her own airway. Finally, she let out a shuddering breath as life came back into her body. Her chest rose and fell on its own. Cash caught himself breathing in and out with Penny and watching the blue drain from her lips.

"Thank you, Lord." Cash lifted Penny into a sitting position and held her against his chest. Emotions he'd been holding back came rushing in, and tears pricked his eyes. "Thank you. Thank you. Thank you." He released a deep breath and let his shoulders sag.

"Daddy?" Penny rasped.

She started to cry. He tried to swallow the cotton in his throat and patted her back. Her crying was the most beautiful sound he'd ever heard. The sound of healthy lungs. The sound of life.

"It's okay, baby. Daddy's here. I'm tryin' to keep you warm."

Penny whimpered. "Where Ah-ah-lana?" Her breath shuttered pushing out Alana's name.

Cash saw the tears on Alana's face. Her red-rimmed eyes were swollen. She leaned in and kissed Penny's forehead and stroked back her wet hair. "Right here, sweetie. I'm right here."

Penny's eyes fluttered and she smiled. "Pretty lights."

Cash glanced over his shoulder to see the Coast Guard rescue boat approaching with flashing lights. A rescue chopper hovered in the distance.

"We're safe. We're going to be okay." With every inch the rescue boat closed, the knot in his chest loosened, allowing him to breathe. He tried to stand with Penny in his arms, but his muscles were slow to respond, and he rocked back on his knees.

"Easy, there." Alana squeezed his shoulder. "You might have a concussion."

"You might be right." His abdominal muscles burned, and his thoughts became fuzzy. There was something he should be doing. Somewhere he should go. He just couldn't remember. His head pounded with the beat of his pulse.

The Coast Guard boat pulled alongside the sinking yacht. "Secure the lines!" The crew leader barked orders. A crew of men dressed in orange and black moved fast and fastened the lines to the yacht's railing. The wind howled around them. "Steady, folks. One at a time. We'll get you out of here."

Two men approached Cash. He was still kneeling with Penny, who had started crying again. One man slipped a life jacket over Cash's head and wrapped a blanket around his shoulders. "It's okay, Dad. We got her."

Cash relinquished Penny to the experienced team. "She needs a hospital, stat. She experienced a near-drowning event but was resuscitated and stabilized. We need to keep her under close observation and monitor her respiratory and neurological functions closely."

"Aye, aye."

He watched as they put her life jacket on and secured it before wrapping her in a blanket. A man shielded her head and carried her to the waiting rescue boat.

Cash looked at Alana, who was lying on the deck shivering. The rescue worker had draped a blanket over her. The man had cut away the fabric of her pant leg and worked to immobilize it. He wanted to go to her, but two men lifted her onto a back board.

The crew leader helped Cash to his feet. "Let's get you off this sinking ship."

Cash's legs turned to jelly. The adrenaline that had kept him going was beginning to fade, and the full impact of their ordeal hit him. The man guided him into the rescue boat. The two men carried Alana onboard behind him.

One officer wrapped another blanket over her, then around Cash, shielding them from the chilly breeze whipping across the water. He leaned over and kissed her on the head. "Are you okay? Your leg—"

"Just a cut. A few stitches and I'll be good as new."

"You're the best CPR partner I could ever ask for, but we're gonna have to talk about your field dressing." He nodded to the duct tape over her eyebrow.

She tried to sit up, but the crew captain touched her shoulder. "Whoa. I think it's best if you stay there until we get clear of the sinking vessel."

"If I lie here on this backboard, I'm going to get seasick." Alana eased into a sitting position. "Now help me."

With the help of Cash and the crew captain, Alana hobbled to the bow of the rescue boat.

A woman with a thick blanket over her shoulders held Penny and planted kisses on her head. "Oh, baby girl, I'm so glad to see you." The woman adjusted Penny's blanket and tucked it under Penny's chattering chin, then turned to Cash.

He saw her scraggly wet hair and mascara streaking her face and gasped. "Bailey!" He rushed to her and crushed her to his chest. This. This was what he'd forgotten. Alana telling him Bailey was on board. "What...are you okay? Why are you here?"

"I'm fine, big brother." Bailey smiled and hugged him again. "It's a long story, but that meeting I had with the leader of the Madrina cartel turned out to be with Ziva."

"Where's Ziva now?"

Bailey and Alana exchanged a look. Alana cut her eyes to Penny. "She saved Penny's life, but..."

Cash wrapped Bailey in another hug. "God, thank you for hearing my prayers and saving us."

When he released her, Bailey looked up, eyes shining with unshed tears. "I'm so sorry, Cash. I didn't mean for—"

Cash's throat tightened as he shook his head. "No, it's not your fault. We're happy you're okay."

Bailey pointed at Alana's leg. "Alana, what happened?"

Alana's teeth chattered, and she pulled the blanket tighter around herself. "Let's save the story for another day. I'm exhausted and freezing."

Cash crouched in front of Penny and checked her vitals. Her pulse was strong and her pupils responded to light. He tickled her side. "Hey, where'd you get that juice box?"

Penny smiled around the straw and pointed to the men untying from the yacht. He kissed her and settled her beside Bailey. Almost right away, Penny's eyes drooped. Cash gave it thirty more seconds before she was asleep in her aunt Bailey's lap.

He sat beside Alana. "Can I take a look at that leg?"

"Maybe later. Right now, I just want you near me."

He held her by her shoulders and looked her in the eyes. "Thank you. Thank you for what you did."

Alana glanced down. "I didn't protect her. She got taken."

He lifted her chin with his finger and looked deep into her eyes. "But you chose her. You almost gave your life for her. That's what I asked you to do, and that's what you did. And I can't thank you enough."

"I did it not because I'm a protector. I did it because I'm a mom."

"And you're a great mom, Alana. The best I've ever known."

Once everyone was secured, the rescue boat headed toward the larger Coast Guard cutter ship waiting to take them back to shore. As they rode the waves, Cash turned to Alana. Her wet hair whipped in the wind and tangled around her shoulders. Water splashed her face and his. Or maybe they were tears. He didn't care. His heart swelled with love for the fierce, brave woman who'd flipped his whole world upside down.

Cash cupped her face in his hands. She looked at him with a sleepy smile. He kissed her eyelids. Her nose. Her curved lips. She wrapped her arms around him. Clung to him and kissed him so long he didn't care if anyone was watching. He just kept kissing her because she had his whole heart. In that moment, he poured it all out to her.

Their kisses slowed with the speed of the boat. When they separated, they looked at each other. Everything had shifted and become permanent. Real. There was no more Elite Guardian and needy father, but two parents. Two people on equal footing.

"Alana, I love you."

She pressed her forehead to his. "I love you too."

He wrapped his arm around her shoulders and gave her a gentle squeeze. "We made it."

Bailey, who had been sitting across from them with a

sleeping Penny in her lap, spoke up. "You know, you guys make a great team."

Cash and Alana exchanged a look, and then he kissed her again, and together, they watched as the yacht and the helicopter sank beneath the waves.

TWENTY-THREE

For the first time in his life, Cash understood why everyone said doctors made the worst patients. Staying overnight in the hospital over a concussion? He thought he'd rather have gone down with the ship last night. Okay, that was a bit dramatic, but still. All he could do was picture Penny's lifeless body and think about how helpless he'd been in that moment.

"Thank you, Lord," he whispered. He didn't think he'd ever stop giving praise and thanksgiving for their survival. It was by the grace of God Himself that Penny hadn't needed to be placed on a ventilator after her close call.

Penny would spend a few days in the pediatric unit receiving oxygen and other medications to support her respiratory and cardiovascular systems and to monitor her for signs of brain damage or other complications. At least he could sleep on the fold-out in Penny's room to be close to her.

A soft knock on his door caught his attention. Bailey peeked her head inside the hospital room. "Hey, can I come in?"

Cash looked up and smiled. "Of course, come on in."

"Where's Penny?"

"Chest X-rays. She'll be right back."

Bailey sat on the rolling stool and scooted herself close to Cash. "How you feelin'?"

"I'm all right. A little sore. Headache from the concussion. Nothing too serious."

Bailey laughed. "Only my doctor brother would say a concussion is nothing too serious. I'm sorry about Ziva. I know she helped save Penny."

"Me too. She was trying to save her life but ended up dying anyway. What will happen with her body?"

"Once the autopsy is performed, they'll release her to the family." Bailey blew out a breath. "Hey, is there anything I can do for you? Bring you or Penny anything?"

"Nah, I'm okay for now. Thanks, though."

Bailey fidgeted with her hands for a moment before speaking up again. "I wanted to apologize for everything that happened. I never meant to hurt anyone, especially not Penny."

"Oh, Bay. There's nothing to apologize for. None of this is your fault. If Ziva slipped past you, it's only because she slipped past the entire FBI taskforce first."

Bailey nodded. "I never realized how deep this whole thing went. The evidence just led me there. Never knew about Sonia and Ziva and the money laundering until a few weeks ago. I didn't want to keep it from you as long as I did."

"Hey, you had a job to do, and you did it. You put your life on the line to stop the guns and drugs pouring into Savannah and killing people." He squeezed her knee. "I'm proud of you."

She gave him a thin smile. "Thanks."

"How did it go over with your bosses?"

Bailey waffled her hand in a so-so gesture. "Everyone we had under surveillance is either dead or missing. The authorities will retrieve the yacht and analyze it for evidence. We'll investigate further and locate the people laundering money for Ziva. But unfortunately, the wheels of the machine will keep turning with or without her. Some other bad guy will take over."

Cash sensed there was something more behind Bailey's words. They were twins, after all. Perhaps a confidential informant. A suspect or a lead they needed to chase down. Her undercover role with the FBI had never allowed her to stay in her hometown for long. Bailey would soon disappear, and they'd be back to the cloak-and-dagger games in order to see each other.

"Well, I'm sure the case will continue. Look how long they've been following the money. Years." Cash hesitated. He needed answers, but he wasn't sure he wanted them. He wanted to put it all behind him, and the only way to do that was to have all the information. "What's the latest on Sonia? Detective Williams said there were no remains in the car."

"Yeah, well. That was before the ERT checked the trunk. They found female remains. Dental records matched Sonia, but a DNA test will confirm it in a few weeks. The medical examiner found a gunshot wound at the back of her head." A tinge of sadness filled her eyes. Bailey and Sonia had been close at one time, and the loss cut them both.

"Ziva was responsible," Cash said. "She all but confessed it to me. Said the FBI was closing in and she had to cut the loose ends."

They were quiet for a moment as he wondered how he'd been so blind to everything in his marriage. So stupid as to let it all crumble around him. Things would be different next time. Things *were* different. He pictured Alana walking through the fire to find him and Penny. Not because it was her job but because that's who she was as a person. A true fighter. Strong and confident, yet soft and kind.

And he knew what he needed to do right this minute. He needed to be there when she came out of surgery. "Hey, can you do me a favor?"

"Yeah, sure." Bailey got to her feet. "What do you need?"

Cash grinned and pointed to the wheelchair in the corner. "I need a ride."

———

Alana lay in her hospital bed, her leg elevated and propped up with pillows. The surgery to repair her torn calf muscle had been successful, but her leg throbbed with pain. She had a stack of magazines by her bed but no interest in reading them. Instead, she was engrossed in a romantic suspense novel by S. M. Warren. Something about the tension and romance in the author's writing sucked Alana in. And it provided a welcome distraction from her pain and discomfort.

Noelle poked her head in Alana's doorway and smiled. "Guess who I brought to see you."

Rocco ran to Alana and threw himself into her embrace. "Mom, I'm so glad you're okay. Your leg...does it hurt? And your face. It's purple. How many stitches do you have?"

"Slow down, bud. I'm just so glad to see you." Alana held him, taking in the scent of his hair and the feel of his arms around her. She could hear his steady heartbeat throbbing. She never wanted to take these moments for granted ever again.

She kissed his head and smoothed his fluffy hair. "You wanna sit up here with me?"

Rocco climbed onto the bed and nestled beside her. "Noelle said the boat you were on sank. Are you sure you're okay?"

Noelle straightened the stack of magazines. "Well, that's my cue to leave. I hope I didn't say anything out of line."

Alana chuckled. "No, Rocco is a smart guy. If we don't tell him, he'll figure it out."

"Yeah, I have Google, Noelle."

She ruffled his hair. "Okay, smarty pants. I'm going to run

grab a cup of coffee from the waiting room. You guys want anything?"

"Oh, bless you, woman. Coffee would be great."

"Can I have a diet soda?" Rocco looked at Alana.

Soda of any kind could be hard on Rocco's kidneys, so they tried to keep it to a special treat. "Yeah, I guess this time would be fine."

Noelle grinned. "I'll be right back."

Alana smiled at Rocco and studied her son's features. "I'm okay, honey. I'm a little banged up, but I'm going to be fine. I'll be on desk duty for a while with my leg like this, but that'll give me plenty of time to tell you everything that happened."

Rocco pulled back and looked at her. "I'm sorry, Mom. I should have been with you."

Alana stroked his cheek. There would be time to explain how wrong he was about that. How being safe with Noelle was exactly where she'd wanted him. It ripped her heart out knowing all Penny had been through, not to mention the trauma she'd have to overcome. "You're here now and that's all that matters."

Alana looked at Rocco's hand and saw the brightly colored pinwheel that he held. "What do you have there?"

Rocco beamed and held out the toy. "It's a pinwheel. I thought Penny might like it."

Could she possibly love this kid any more? "That's so thoughtful of you, Rocco. She's going to love it."

"Can I go see her now?"

"In just a bit. I wanted to talk to you for a second."

"Sure, Mom."

"Rocco, I'm so sorry for being tough on you all the time. I know it's been hard, just the two of us, and I thought I was doing my best. I wanted you to be strong like me. I didn't realize you're already far stronger than I am."

"No way. You're the strongest. You carry a gun and everything."

She smiled a thin smile. "Well, I've learned that strength is more than muscles." She tapped his chest. "You have the heart of a lion combined with the gentleness of a dove. I might've tried to make you tougher, but God showed me that I shouldn't make you more like me. I should be more like you.

"My heart was tough." She tapped her chest. "I'd locked it up tight trying to protect myself, but God showed me I should be a bit softer and let people in more."

"Like Cash and Penny?"

"Yeah. Like them. I thought if I let anyone into our little world, we'd get attached. And then when they saw how complicated our life is, they'd leave."

He scrunched his face. "Why would someone who loved you ever leave? You'd never leave me, would you?"

She hugged him. "No, I'd never ever leave you. But not everyone is like that. But you know what? I think Cash is tough. I think he'd like to stick around even when things are hard."

"I think so too. I mean, Penny can make things tough, and he'd never leave her. I don't think he'd leave us either."

"What I'm saying is, I want to date Cash, but I want to make sure it's okay with you first."

"Are you kidding?" He beamed a smile. "It's what I've been waiting for!"

Alana laughed. "Okay, good. And one more thing. I'm sorry if you ever felt like I was too tough on you. I'm going to work on that."

Rocco leaned closer, pressing himself under her arm. "It's okay. I know you just want me to be the best I can be. I want me to be the best I can be too. And I can't wait to finally have a dad." Rocco nodded to the doorway, where Cash was sitting in a wheelchair.

"Sorry, I didn't mean to interrupt. I can come back." He grabbed the wheels and rolled back an inch.

"No, stay. Please," Alana said. "I was just telling Rocco that we've been through a lot, and I wanted him to know how much I love him." She squeezed her son and whispered in his ear, "I'll always be here for you, Rocco. No matter what."

"I know, Mom. I love you too." He kissed her cheek. "Can I go see Penny now?"

Noelle spoke up from behind Cash. "I'll take him, Alana." She followed Cash into the room and put Alana's coffee on the rolling tray beside her book. "Let's go, bud."

"Cool wheelchair," Rocco said, climbing out of the bed. "My uncle Grey has a better one. He could show you a few tricks."

"You mean like this?" Cash leaned the wheelchair back and turned right, then left before lowering it.

Rocco laughed. "Yeah, stuff like that. How'd you know how to do that?"

"Let's just say there were some long, slow nights at the hospital, and we might have horsed around a bit. Give Penny a hug from me if she's back. I'll go see her next."

"I will," Rocco said. He followed Noelle out of the room, his hand still clutching the pinwheel.

Cash rolled the wheelchair to Alana's bedside and set the brakes. He stood and sat on the edge of her bed. "Alana, I'm sorry for all you've been through. But I know now I wouldn't want to go through life with anyone else."

Alana studied his weary blue eyes. "Honestly, that kind of terrifies me."

His brow furrowed. "It does?"

"Yes, but only because I feel the same way about you. Life with me and Rocco is complicated. I've worked hard to stay in control and keep things manageable. Letting someone in now that I have things stable feels really risky. Especially since trust has never come easy for me." She caressed the back of his hand.

"You know what? Complicated I can handle. I understand complicated."

Electricity burst through her as Cash cupped her face in his strong hands and kissed her. She slipped her arms around his neck and pulled him in for a deeper kiss.

When they parted she whispered, "I love you."

His eyes glistened. "I love you too." He brushed her lips with a kiss and grinned. "Can I let you in on a little secret?"

"What's that?"

"I'm not that smart. I make mistakes and act like a jerk sometimes. So I won't lie to you and say I won't ever hurt you, but I can promise I'll be there so we can work it out together. You make me want to be a better father. A better man. I want to be the man you deserve, and I'll do whatever it takes to protect our family."

Alana smiled, her eyes softening. "I believe you. Neither of us is perfect, which is why we need God as our foundation."

Cash leaned in and kissed her temple. "Wow. You're strong. Beautiful. Kind. Relentless. And smart. How'd I get to be so lucky to find a woman like you?"

Alana smiled. "Well, I don't believe in luck, but I think it had something to do with a little Penny."

EPILOGUE

FIVE MONTHS LATER

Today was a great day, and it was only going to get better. Cash grabbed his gym bag packed with a fresh change of clothes and practically ran from his truck to Alana's front door.

On the porch, a delivery driver had left an oversized cardboard box Alana hadn't brought inside. He slipped the longer strap of his gym bag over his shoulder, squatted, and picked up the box. It was heavier than he expected, and now he couldn't manage the doorknob with his hands full. He reached with his index finger. Couldn't...quite...make it. Now that he had the heavy box in his arms, he didn't want to put it down, so he turned sideways and used his elbow to ring the bell.

Alana opened the door in a white T-shirt, black jeans, and running shoes. His mind flashed to the night he first met her. Her black hair was pulled into the same ponytail with soft tendrils framing her brow. "Hey, I thought we talked about this. You can come in without knocking."

He chuckled and shifted the box. "I couldn't get the door open. My hands are full."

243

"I can see that. What'cha got there?"

Cash paused and planted a quick but firm kiss on her lips on the way inside. "Beats me. It was by the door when I got here. Heavy, though." He carried the box to the kitchen and set it on the counter, then dropped his gym bag on the floor.

Alana dragged her fingers down his chest, then tugged his tie. "You look so very handsome right now." She went up on her toes and kissed him, soft and tender. "Now, are you going to tell me how it went? I'm dyin' over here."

He let his hands fall from her shoulders and looked at the floor. He worked his lower lip.

Alana took his hands. "Oh...Cash..."

"I got it." He looked up and grinned.

"You got it? Really? You're chief of surgery now?"

He couldn't shake the grin and bobbed his head. "I wanted to call, but I thought it would be better in person."

"That was mean." She slapped his chest. "I thought—"

He caught her hands and kissed them. "I'm excited about the promotion but even more excited to spend the day with you. I've missed you." This time he gathered Alana into his arms. Slid one arm around the small of her back, the other arm along her shoulders. He pulled her up to his chest and kissed her. It was a long, lingering kiss that made his heart thud.

"Ooooh...you guys are kissing!" Behind them came the teasing voice of Rocco and muted giggles from Penny. Rocco pooched out his lips and made kissing noises.

Cash grinned and loosed his hold on Alana. She let her hands drag down his chest in a way that made his knees weak. They turned and looked at the mockers.

"Hey, kissing is perfectly normal for two adults who are in love. There's nothing to be embarrassed about." Alana stretched up on her toes and kissed Cash on the chin. Even after five months, his entire body still tingled at her touch.

"I know. I'm just playin' around. Really, I'm glad you guys

met." Rocco wrapped his arms around them both in a quick hug. Before he pulled away, he patted Cash on the back and smiled.

Penny climbed onto a counter stool and pointed to the box. "For me?"

"I don't know. Should we open it and find out?" Alana put her hand on Penny's back and scooted the chair closer to the counter. "Rocco, you want to do the honors?"

"Yeah!" Cash handed Rocco his pocketknife and kept a close watch as he opened the knife and cut the tape.

He'd been nine when his father bought him a Swiss Army knife. It'd made him feel like a real man every time he flicked it open. Alana didn't want Rocco to have a knife of his own yet, but they'd agreed Cash could teach safety and responsibility now, then surprise him on his birthday with the same classic red one his father had given him.

Rocco finished cutting the tape and folded the knife the way Cash had taught him. Cash slipped it back into his pocket. "Good job, bud."

Together, Alana and Penny pulled out thick wrapping to reveal a full-sized white envelope on a stack of books.

Penny peered into the box. "What is it? What is it?"

Cash lifted a book and handed it to Rocco. "Check it out. It's S. M. Warren's latest book. The one where the main character is based on your mom."

"Cool!" Rocco flipped through the pages. "And look! She signed it and everything." He turned the book so they could see Warren's signature scrawled on the title page.

"What's the note say?" Cash nodded to the envelope.

Alana peeled back the flap and pulled out the letter. "Should I read it out loud?"

"Yeah." Cash cut his eyes to the kids, then back to Alana. "If you can."

Alana's eyes scanned the paper. "I think it's good. It says,

'Dear Alana and Elite Guardian family. Thank you for allowing me to author a story based on your harrowing true-life events. I hope I did your characters justice, even if I embellished a bit here and there.

I am thrilled to hear about your plans to create a special place for at-risk youths at the Atlas Gym. The training and instruction they will receive will have a ripple effect throughout the lives of everyone involved in the program. I see the need for such a place and feel very much led by the Lord to support you in this endeavor. Therefore, it is my pleasure to donate all proceeds from the book sales directly to your newly established nonprofit. Enclosed you will find the first check, and I pray there are many more to come. Besides the proceeds from the book sales, I will support the mission with my personal finances on a monthly basis.

Please share copies of this book with the rest of the Elite Guardians and know that I'm thankful to you all.

Warmly, S. M. Warren.'"

Cash smiled. They'd met the author a few times, and her thoughtfulness didn't surprise him. She was charismatic and kind in all the best ways. Alana slid the check out of the envelope and stared at it. Her mouth fell open.

"That much?"

She handed the check to him, and his own mouth fell open a little. "That's...generous..."

"More than," she said. "We should be able to finish the dorms and classrooms."

Rocco held the book against his chest. "You think Penny and I can read this?"

"Let me read it first. As long as it's not too scary, then sure." Alana held her hand out and Rocco handed her the book. "Now, you two run get ready for the game. We don't want to keep Aunt Christina and Uncle Grey waiting."

"C'mon, Penny," Rocco said, helping her down from the stool. "We're going to see Boss too!"

"Boss too!" Penny squealed down the hallway.

Cash tucked the check back into the envelope and handed it to Alana. "I can't wait to read what Warren wrote about that stalker woman. Whatever happened to her anyway?"

"You mean Bethany Gould. Yeah, get this. The whole reason she was stalking Warren in the first place was because they'd met at a writer's conference. Bethany was convinced Warren would get her book published, but then Bethany's husband died unexpectedly. Heart attack, I think. That, coupled with the stress of writing novels and rejection after rejection, caused her to snap."

"And she thought stalking Warren would help how?"

"She thought if Warren would spend a few days going over her manuscript, they could figure out why she was getting rejections."

"And she thought Warren would want to help her after being kidnapped?" Cash shook his head.

"It doesn't make sense to us, but Warren asked the judge for leniency. She said now that she knows why Bethany did what she did, she can sorta relate. Apparently, not just anyone can be a published author."

"I don't know. Sounds to me like this Bethany woman is born to be an author."

Alana scrunched her face. "Why do you say that?"

"You'd have to be a bit crazy to put yourself through all that stress on purpose."

"Hmm, maybe you're right." Alana left two books on the counter and closed the box. "All I know is I'm glad these crazy people keep writing books so I can enjoy a little escape from reality."

Cash tapped the cover. A picture of a woman who resembled Alana had her arms folded. Behind her, a fiery helicopter spiraled toward a sinking yacht. "Yeah...an escape from *reality*."

She smiled and kissed him. "Speaking of reality...go change while I take care of getting the kids ready."

"Yes, ma'am."

Ten minutes later, Cash walked into the living room decked out in team gear. He threw his hands up. "Who's ready for some Banana Ball!"

Rocco and Penny bounced up and down and cheered. Both were decked out in yellow Savannah Bananas team jerseys. Alana had Penny's hair in pigtails tied with big yellow bows. Rocco had a Savannah Bananas team ball cap pulled low over his eyes. Cash was happy to see him wearing it, since he and Alana had scoured every souvenir store in Savannah to find it. The team was so popular that hats were sold out everywhere.

Alana threw her jersey over her T-shirt, and Cash helped her button it. When he finished, she slid her hand around the back of his neck and pulled him in for a lengthy kiss. Cash was breathless when he released her.

"Can I just say again how proud I am of you, Dr. Cash Thomas, Chief of Surgery? It took a bit longer than you expected, but now you finally have everything you wanted."

Cash patted the ring in his pocket. Not everything. Not yet.

————

Alana wasn't a huge baseball fan, but she had to admit, the Savannah Bananas sure made the game fun and interesting. Juliette had scored great seats behind the dugout. Three rows to accommodate the Elite Guardians Savannah branch employees and friends.

The pitcher called a time-out and huddled with the catcher and two fielders on the mound. A popular song Alana sorta recognized blasted over the intercom, and the players began a choreographed dance. Fans exploded into cheers and laughter while the batter struggled to focus on which of the three players would pitch the ball.

Alana leaned to her left to talk to Christina over the music.

"Thanks for coming all the way out here for this silly game. Glad you and Grey could make it. And Boss, of course." The retired military working dog was sprawled out asleep on the concrete in front of Rocco and Penny.

"Are you kidding? I'm having a blast!" Christina nudged her and pointed to the end of the row where Grey's wheelchair was parked beside Cash. Jonah sat beside Noelle in the next row, his body angled to chat with the guys behind him. "Grey said he really likes Cash and Jonah. Between the military and medical stuff, I think they could talk for hours. How do you like Savannah?"

Alana caught Noelle's eye, and her friend smiled and raised her cup of soda in a silent toast. Raven was busy taking photos of the game and the group, laughing at her own jokes and trying to get Juliette to pose for a photo with Rocco and Penny.

"It's only been five months, but you know what? It feels like family."

"Them too?" Christina lifted her chin to indicate Penny and Rocco in the seats in front of them. "Their bond seems tighter than ours at their age."

"Well, you know what I always say. Family is more than blood."

The Savannah Bananas announcer's voice boomed through the stadium. "Ladies and gentlemen, it's time for our Kids Run the Bases event! Bring your little ones down to the field to run the bases with their favorite players! Families are welcome to cheer from behind home plate!"

Penny's and Rocco's eyes lit up. "Can we? Can we?" they chimed together.

"Sure!" Cash waved. "Hurry or they'll start without us."

Rocco and Penny ran ahead, and Cash interlaced his fingers with Alana's. They made their way down to the field where the Savannah Bananas team was lining up on the foul line.

"Look!" Penny pointed.

The team pulled foam banana costumes over their uniforms. They shouted and waved to the children, encouraging them to find a player to run with. Music kicked up, and Alana burst out laughing at the familiar song. The Savannah Bananas formed a conga line with the kids and danced their way to first base.

Cash stood behind Alana and wrapped his arm around her waist. She didn't stop laughing as the line rounded the bases. Rocco held Penny's hand, and she was sure it was their giggles alone that echoed across the stadium.

When the line reached home plate, the team removed their banana costumes and formed a semicircle around her and Cash. Noelle, Juliette, Raven, Jonah, Christina, Grey, and even Boss stood with Rocco, Penny, and the team.

The music stopped.

Everyone in the small crowd, including the entire Savannah Bananas team, got down on one knee and mimed opening a ring box.

Alana gasped.

Was this...was this really happening? Right here on the field?

She whirled around to see Cash kneeling on home plate with a giant smile. Her hands flew to her mouth.

He opened a black velvet ring box to reveal a sparkling diamond. The crowd roared with applause, but she could only focus on Cash.

"Alana, I love you and our perfectly imperfect family." His voice hitched and he swallowed. "Wow, I had a whole thing prepared, but..." He smiled.

She looked at him, eyes filling with tears. "It's okay, just..." She nodded for him to keep going.

"Alana, will you marry me?"

She rushed into his arms. "Yes! A thousand times YES!"

"Yay!" Rocco and Penny ran to them and joined in the hug.

"That was beautiful, you guys." Raven lowered her camera. "I got some great photos of you."

"Did you hear that?" Rocco grinned. "That was our very first family picture!"

"And we'll have many more in the years to come," she said.

Cash put his lips close to her ear. "You've made me the happiest man in the world."

He slipped the ring on her finger, and Alana kissed her future husband.

A NOTE FROM KATE

Dear Reader,

Thank you for joining Alana and Cash on their journey. The idea for this book bloomed from a story seed planted years ago. It started when my sister said she'd caught my nephew sneaking food outside. When she inquired further, he fessed up to feeding a stray cat. That rattled around in my head for a while, and I started to wonder what would happen if Alana had gone outside to see Rocco feeding a child instead.

It's funny how these things said in passing stick with us. I guess what they say is true—be careful what you say around an author, because it might end up in a novel.

One more thing. There's a line in the book where Alana tells Cash recovery teams don't have time to "pore over data". Did you know that it was *pore,* or like me, did you think it was *pour?* I asked fellow authors in our writer community, and they said it was *pour* over data. Well, dear reader, we were wrong, and the editor was right. We all learned something that day, and it reminded me that we're always learning and growing.

If you'd like to keep in touch and hear more about what I'm up to, join my newsletter at www.kateangelo.com.

Blessings,

Kate

Thank you for reading *Vanishing Legacy*! Return to Savannah again with the next Elite Guardians: Savannah romantic suspense, *Hunting Justice*. Read on for a sneak peek!

ELITE GUARDIANS: SAVANNAH

HUNTING JUSTICE

USA TODAY BESTSELLING AUTHOR
LYNETTE EASON
PRESENTS *PUBLISHERS WEEKLY* BESTSELLING AUTHOR
SAMI A. ABRAMS

HUNTING JUSTICE

ELITE GUARDIANS: SAVANNAH - BOOK 2

CHAPTER 1

WEDNESDAY, 5:00 P.M.

The bodies in the Savannah, Georgia county morgue had nothing on medical examiner Dr. Jonah Harris. Tentacles of fatigue wrapped around him and nearly squeezed the life out of him. Finished for the work day, he dragged himself into his private office and collapsed onto the chair, melting into the cushion. He leaned back and ran his hands over his face. Three autopsies in one day had pushed him to his limit, but the young girl who'd died in her sleep had gutted him.

A vacation sounded better by the minute. Maybe he'd take a day to recharge and gain some perspective again. Taking a tour of historic Savannah, simply relaxing at Forsyth Park with a book, or a stroll down the Riverwalk might do the trick. Anything to get away from the stress.

The office phone, somewhere on his desk, rang.

He lifted a handful of documents and peered beneath the

mound of files, searching for the offending noise. A stack of papers slid from the pile and scattered over his desk, knocking his name plaque onto the floor.

Jonah sighed. What a mess. He envied people who had the neat gene. He, on the other hand, struggled with ADD, and one of the side effects was the chaos when it came to his organizational skills. Noelle Burton, a member of the Elite Guardians Agency Savannah office, teased him mercilessly. She'd even gone as far as buying him a framed poster for his office that said *A messy desk is a sign of genius.*

He found the phone and snatched the receiver from the cradle. "Dr. Harris."

"Hi, Jonah, this is Ken."

"Ken, how's it going?" Jonah tilted his head and scratched his five-o'clock shadow. Why hadn't his friend, chief medical examiner Dr. Ken Dodson, called his cell phone?

He smacked his forehead.

Holding the receiver between his ear and shoulder, he stood and retrieved his cell phone from his pants pocket. "Sorry. I turned off my cell phone while in autopsy and forgot to turn it on afterward."

"Appears like you've had a long day."

"You could say that, but let's not go there. How's your day off?" He half listened to his friend and mentor while his phone powered on. Several missed calls and text messages popped up.

"Jonah, I need to talk with you."

Ken's serious tone grabbed Jonah's attention. "Sounds ominous."

"I have something rather important to tell you. Can you come over after you finish at work?" Ken's request sent icy fingers crawling up Jonah's spine and onto his scalp.

He mentally ran through what he had to do before he could leave. "I can be there in about thirty minutes. Can you give me a hint?"

Silence met his ears.

"Ken?"

"I've done things I'm not proud of."

"Haven't we all?"

"No, you don't understand. Once this comes out, my professional reputation will be trashed."

Jonah froze. "Ken, you're worrying me here. Give me something?"

A deep sigh filtered across the line. "I'm ashamed to admit it, but I've falsified autopsy records."

Jonah's mind spun, trying to grasp Ken's admission.

"Jonah, please say something."

"I'm not even sure what to say." He clutched the arm of his chair and lowered himself onto the cushion. "Why?"

"Cecile's treatments were expensive. I made a deal with the devil. Now that my wife is gone, I intend to come clean, but I need your help and for you to stay quiet about it."

Jonah ran his hand through his hair. His friend had dropped a bombshell that would have a rippling effect. "You've put me in a tough position. If I keep your secret, then I'm covering up your crime. But if I tell, you'll lose your license and most likely go to jail."

"I would never ask you to commit a crime on my behalf."

"Then what are you asking?"

"I want you to reopen those cases and set the record straight before you take it public. I have my reasons. That's why I want you to come over. I'll give you the files and tell you what to look for."

Jonah sat in stunned silence. His friend had left him little choice in the matter. He blew out a breath. "All right. I'll be there as soon as I wrap up for the day."

"Thank you."

"And Ken…" Jonah swallowed past the lump invading his throat.

"Yes."

"You could have asked me for the money. I would have given it to you." He would have emptied his brokerage account if that's what it took to help the man who'd become like a father to him.

"I realize that now. I'll see you when you get here." The phone clicked off.

Jonah picked up the metal sign that had fallen and shoved it onto his desk. The notes from his last autopsy required his attention before he left for the day.

The dictation complete, he sent it to the medical transcriptionist to type up and glanced at the wall above the file cabinet. The clock mocked him. Jonah should have left fifteen minutes ago. He had to find out what in the world Ken had gotten himself into.

Falsifying autopsy reports? What had the man been thinking? And now he'd dragged Jonah into his crazy. But there was no need to jump to conclusions until he had proof. Maybe Ken had overreacted. Jonah could only hope.

He powered off his computer and tossed the options to Ken's confession around in his mind. Jonah would listen to Ken's explanation and figure out what he was up against, then he'd call his buddy Detective Matt Williams with the Savannah PD and discuss his legal obligations.

Since Ken held the title of chief medical examiner, that left Jonah in charge once Ken revealed his disreputable actions. Not the way Jonah wanted to earn the position. He shook his head.

After quickly glancing around the room and dismissing the idea of tidying the mess, he grabbed his keys. Ken was waiting, and Jonah wanted to get the distasteful business over with.

He slung his messenger bag over his shoulder and waved at one of the techs as he strolled down the hall. He pushed the emergency release bar on the back door and stepped outside.

The May air warmed his skin. Thank heavens the humidity

hadn't hit swamp levels yet. Give it another month and sweat would be his friend.

With a sigh, he strode to his SUV. He dropped into the driver's seat and stared out the front windshield, wishing he'd never received Ken's phone call.

Might as well get it over with. He cranked the engine and pulled from the parking lot.

Phone connected to his vehicle's Bluetooth, he hit the speed dial for Ken. Six rings and the voicemail picked up. "Hey, Ken. Sorry, I'm running late. I'll be there in about ten minutes." Jonah jabbed the End button, disconnecting the call.

He drummed his fingers on the steering wheel. Why hadn't his friend picked up? He maneuvered through the side streets of town, letting his mind ponder the implications of Ken's admission. But until he knew the facts, he had no way of knowing what to do next.

Ten minutes later, he turned down the tree-lined street that Ken lived on. Spanish moss hung from the limbs, dangling high above the ground. Most days he'd find a soothing calmness about the landscape, but today the greenery reminded him of boney fingers from a horror movie, reaching out to grab him. Ominous?—maybe. A product of his dark mood?—most likely.

Jonah parked across from the pale-yellow two-story Victorian-style house that sat away from the others in the neighborhood. He stared at the home he'd visited multiple times on happier occasions. When Ken's wife Cecile had passed away a couple months ago, Ken had acquired hermit-like tendencies.

But Jonah understood. His wife Cara had died in his arms after a car accident. There he was, an ER doctor at the time—one of the best in the nation—and he couldn't save his own wife. Jonah shook off the memories. He had to deal with Ken's problems and not get sucked into the past.

He stepped from his vehicle and shut the door. Exhaling, he crossed the street.

A boom rocked the neighborhood.

Jonah tumbled backward and slammed onto the ground.

Flames erupted from Ken's house. Remnants of boards and furniture flew in multiple directions. Debris rained down, pelting his arms, legs, and torso.

He sucked in a breath and coughed. Pain shot through his chest, and a high-pitched ringing pierced his ears. His head pounded, but he pried his eyes open. The world whirled around him. Jonah blinked away the daze. Forcing himself to move, he rolled and pushed to a standing position.

Heavy smoke hovered above the back exterior of the house and the few standing walls. Flames leaped in the air, destroying the parts of the once-beautiful home that had survived the blast.

"Ken." His vocal cords refused to function. He groaned. Jonah hoped his friend wasn't inside, but deep down he feared Ken had been home when the house blew.

Dizziness almost took Jonah to his knees as he staggered, but he remained upright. He stumbled over broken glass to his SUV and slumped against the front bumper until his head stopped spinning. Once his vision cleared, he'd call 911, assuming his phone still worked. He just needed a moment to gather himself.

Sirens screamed as the emergency vehicles raced toward him. Someone else must have witnessed the blast and called.

His shoulders slumped, and he released a long breath. Closing his eyes, he dropped his chin to his chest.

"Doc!"

He lifted his head.

Detective Matt Williams strode toward him. "Doc, are you okay?"

"I've been better." Jonah had no idea what injuries he'd

acquired. His brain hadn't gotten that far. But based on his throbbing head, he'd guess a concussion topped the list.

Matt placed a hand on his shoulder. "No kidding. You look awful."

"Thanks a lot." He touched his forehead, then glanced at his hand. Blood dampened his fingers. He'd shake his head at the injustice, but that would only make him dizzier.

"Come on, let's get you to the ambulance and let the paramedics take a look."

"Ambulance?" Jonah glanced to his right. Fire trucks lined the street. Uh, when had the fire department arrived?

"Never mind. I'll have them come to you. Don't move." Matt hurried off before Jonah responded.

Jonah let his gaze wander over the scene. Pieces of Ken's house lay scattered like a child's Lincoln Logs set, covering his friend's property and the neighbors' yards. But why?

The haze inhabiting his brain made reasoning next to impossible. Either the concussion was worse than he thought, or shock had dug in its claws.

A few moments later, Matt returned with paramedic Aaron Quincy in tow. The twenty-three-year-old medic hefted the black medical duffel higher on his shoulder and ran his gaze over Jonah.

"Hey, Doc. How about we get you seated before you fall down." Aaron cupped his elbow and helped him stand. "Let's use the back of your SUV."

"Sounds like a good idea." Jonah extracted the keys from his pocket and handed them to Matt. He hated to admit that the ability to focus and find the right button on the key fob was beyond his capabilities right now.

Matt chuckled. "Doc, I don't think I'll need those. All the windows of your SUV are blown out."

Before Jonah could register his friend's words, Matt and

Aaron assisted him to the back of his SUV and popped the liftgate.

Matt brushed the glass from the interior. "Have a seat."

With his friends' help, he lowered himself onto the hard interior. The weight of what had happened pressed down on him.

"Let's get you checked out." Aaron flashed a penlight into his eyes.

Jonah flinched.

"Sorry about that, Doc." The paramedic continued his exam. "Matt, grab me that blanket."

"What's going on?" Matt asked.

"He's in shock. It's not extreme. At least, not yet."

A blanket was draped over Jonah's shoulders. He listened to the continued exchange going on around him, but the words didn't register in his brain.

The explosion and Ken's confession tumbled in his mind and refused to let go. Were the two linked?

"Doc, look at me. Doc!" Aaron's voice hardened.

Jonah raised his gaze to meet the paramedic's and pulled the blanket tighter. He had to get his act together, or both men would haul him to the hospital without a second thought. "Sorry. What did you say?"

Aaron studied him, then sighed. "I'm sure you've already figured this out, but you have a concussion. I'd advise a trip to the emergency room for a CT scan."

He shook his head and immediately regretted it.

"Doctors make the worst patients," Matt announced like he'd discovered the cure for the plague.

"You don't have to tell me." Aaron slid the blood pressure cuff on Jonah's arm.

"I'm right here, you two." Jonah forced himself to focus. His energy hovered around zero, and the ringing in his ears hadn't stopped. He didn't want to argue with the man, but he had no desire to spend hours at the hospital. "I'll consider it. But for now, the answer is no."

Aaron rolled his eyes and muttered under his breath while continuing to bandage Jonah's scrapes and bruises. "That's not a good idea, Doc."

The antiseptic stung, but Jonah stared at the chunks of wood and parts that used to be a beautiful home. "That may be true, and I'm not stupid. I'll monitor how I feel, but I can't leave—not yet."

Detective Ladecia "Decia" Slaton, mom of the group only because she was a few years older, married, and had three boys, strode toward him. Her somber expression told him all he needed to know.

"Hey, Doc."

"Decia." He swallowed the bile creeping up his throat. "You found Ken?"

She nodded. "The explosion blew his body from the house. He's in the yard. I haven't examined him yet. The firefighters are still working on the blaze."

How had he missed Ken's body? Then again, it didn't take a medical degree to know he was in shock.

"I'm sorry, Doc. He was a great guy." Decia's soft tone squeezed his heart.

Tears burned his eyes. He blinked them away and sucked in a breath. "Thank you."

Decia rested her hand on his arm. "What can we do, Doc?"

He tore his gaze from the devastation. "Catch the person who did this."

Matt placed his boot on the bumper. "Why would you think someone's responsible for the explosion? SFD is speculating a gas leak."

How much should he say? The situation required legal advice, but he had no proof with Ken gone. Jonah glanced at Matt.

His friend raised an eyebrow.

"Let's just say that Ken asked me for help. I left work and headed straight here. Arrived moments before the house blew up. It's a bit of a coincidence, don't you think?"

Decia leaned against the other side of the SUV. "I'd like to hear more about what Ken wanted your help with."

The pounding in Jonah's head chose that moment to increase. He had to figure out the truth before he mentioned specifics to the detectives. He had promised Ken, and he intended to keep that promise. But he had to give them something. "Ken requested that I reevaluate a few autopsies for him."

"Why would he do that?" Matt asked.

"I never got all the details. He died before I found out."

Decia studied him like a bug under a magnifying glass. "Doc, you're a lot of things, but a good liar isn't one of them."

"I'm not lying."

"Maybe so, but you aren't telling us the whole truth." He felt sorry for her three boys when they got in trouble. The woman was tenacious.

The detective reminded Jonah of his grandmother. Not in age or looks, but in how she read people like a human lie detector. "Your boys must not get away with anything."

A cheesy grin graced Decia's face. "Nope. I have a whole police department watching out for them."

Jonah chuckled, then groaned. "Give me time to figure out what's going on. You'll be my first call once I do." But not a minute before. He owed Ken that much. He'd given Decia and Matt the probability the explosion wasn't an accident. He knew the detectives. The information would not go uninvestigated.

"I can live with that...for now." Matt dropped his boot to the ground. Glass crunched under it. "But we still need to take your statement. I'm willing to wait a little while for the shock to wear off and that headache to ease, but it needs to happen sometime tonight."

"I appreciate that." If his head didn't stop pounding, he wasn't sure how much help he'd be.

Aaron packed his medical bag. "I've done all I can do. I hope you change your mind about the hospital."

"If I need it, I'll go." He examined the paramedic's handywork and signed the *refusal to be transported* paperwork. "Thanks, Aaron."

"Sure thing, Doc." Aaron bade Matt and Decia goodbye, then took off to join his partner.

"Would you like a ride since yours is toast?" Matt gestured to the broken windows of the SUV.

"I...uh...I think I'd like to stay for a bit."

"Does your phone work?" Decia asked.

Jonah pulled the device from his pocket and tapped the screen. It lit up. "Thankfully, yes."

"We'll be around until we can get a look at Ken's body. Let us know if you change your mind about the ride."

"Thanks, Ladecia. I appreciate it."

The two detectives strode down the cordoned-off street.

Jonah sat alone in the back of his SUV, staring at the mess that used to be his friend's home. Fire hoses sprayed the remaining flames while the captain yelled instructions to the firefighters. The stench of charred wood and who knew what else burned his nose.

He toyed with his cell phone, pondering what to do next. Ken was gone, along with the explanation behind the falsified autopsy reports.

The urge to call Noelle had his fingers hovering over the speed dial. If he asked, she'd come. That was the kind of friendship they had.

But at the moment, he wasn't ready to face her—or anyone.

We hope you loved the action, adventure, and romance in this riveting story. Discover more exciting romantic suspense from Sunrise Publishing!

GET READY . . . THINGS ARE ABOUT TO GET HOT!

With heart-pounding excitement, gripping suspense, and sizzling (but clean!) romance, the CHASING FIRE: MONTANA series, brought to you by the incredible authors of Sunrise Publishing, including the dynamic duo of bestselling authors Susan May Warren and Lisa Phillips, is your epic summer binge read.

Follow the Montana Hotshots and Smokejumpers as they

chase a wildfire through northwest Montana. The pages ignite with clean romance and high-stakes danger—these heroes (and heroines!) will capture your heart. The biggest question is…who will be your summer book boyfriend?

A BREED APART: LEGACY UNLEASHED!

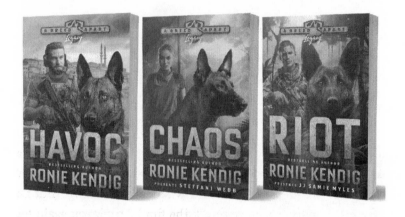

Experience the high-octane thrills, danger, and romance in Ronie Kendig's A Breed Apart: Legacy series.

FIND THEM ALL AT SUNRISE PUBLISHING!

CONNECT WITH SUNRISE

Thank you again for reading *Vanishing Legacy*. We hope you enjoyed the story. If you did, would you be willing to do us a favor and leave a review? It doesn't have to be long—just a few words to help other readers know what they're getting. (But no spoilers! We don't want to wreck the fun!) Thank you again for reading!

We'd love to hear from you—not only about this story, but about any characters or stories you'd like to read in the future. Contact us at www.sunrisepublishing.com/contact.

We also have a monthly update that contains sneak peeks, reviews, upcoming releases, and fun stuff for our reader friends. Sign up at www.sunrisepublishing.com or scan our QR code.

ACKNOWLEDGMENTS

I thank God daily for inspiring me and giving me the gift of words. He is the original author and I'm humbled to be used by Him.

Writing takes a lot out of me, and I'm told this never changes. But I know that having a loving, encouraging, and prayerful husband makes it much easier. Thank you, Jerry, for all your contributions to my stories, and for thinking of me and serving me when I need it most.

Thank you to my five amazing kids and my brilliant little granddaughter. Your support means the world to me. I will always be here for you, even when I'm on deadline. I love you.

I'd like to thank Lynette, Susie, and the Sunrise Publishing team for all their hard work on this book. Lynette helps the story make sense, and she lets me get away with some intense action. I love our friendship, and value her mentorship. Susie May Warren is the inspiration for the author, S. M. Warren, in this book. I think she appreciates how I made her knee injury seem more heroic than simply falling into a hole. But I'm forever grateful for how she pours so much of her wisdom and knowledge into me. Many thanks to the Sunrise team including Lindsay, Rel, Sarah, and more. They do so much behind the scenes to make every book a success.

An incredibly special thanks goes out to my fellow Elite Guardians authors Kelly Underwood and Sami A. Abrams. Thank you so much for your prayers, your encouragement, and your ear when I need to talk through what's not working. I'm so grateful to have landed in Season 3 with you brilliant women! I pray our friendship will last a lifetime.

Thank you to Lily J. Hann and Leona Asper for lending their time, talent, and knowledge to the surgical scene. My research pales in comparison to your real-life experience. I appreciate you both.

It was the sweet disposition and kind smile of a ten-year-old boy named Cash that became the inspiration for the hero of this book. While Cash is still young, I can see he is a strong leader and I know he'll grow up to accomplish amazing things. Cash - Keep your eyes on Jesus. Become a man after God's heart. Let Him guide your steps. Oh, and thanks for taking us up to the top of the Capitol!

I'd also like to thank Representative Mitch and Lynn Boggs for their kindness, love, and support. Thank you for opening your home to us and for the long, spirit-filled talks. We appreciate you more than you know!

And my heartfelt thanks to each reader. I appreciate you, dear one.

ABOUT LYNETTE EASON

 Lynette Eason is the best-selling, award-winning author of over sixty books. Her books have appeared on the USA TODAY, Publisher's Weekly, CBA, ECPA, and Parable bestseller lists. She has won numerous awares including the Carol, the Selah, the Golden Scroll and more. Her novel, *Her Stolen Past* was made into a movie for the Lifetime Movie Network. Lynette can be found online at www.lynetteeason.com

f facebook.com/lynette.eason

⊙ instagram.com/lynetteeason

𝕏 x.com/lynetteeason

BB bookbub.com/authors/lynette-eason

ⓐ amazon.com/stores/Lynette-Eason/author/B001TPZ320

ABOUT KATE ANGELO

Kate Angelo is a Publishers Weekly Bestselling Romantic Suspense author, minister, and public speaker from Southwest Missouri who works alongside her husband championing stronger marriages and families through their nonprofit. As Mom to 5 adult children, she's fluent in both sarcasm and eye rolls. Kate is a coffee addict, tech enthusiast, productivity guru, expert knitter, summer lake fanatic, prayer warrior, dog lover, avid reader, and a known klutz—just ask her doctor. Having aged out of foster care, Kate brings a unique perspective to her writing, breathing life into flawed characters who find hope and healing amidst danger. Subscribe to her newsletter to hear about her pet lion at https://kateangelo.com/

facebook.com/kateangeloauthor

instagram.com/kateangeloauthor

x.com/thekateangelo

bookbub.com/authors/kate-angelo

goodreads.com/kateangeloauthor

amazon.com/stores/Kate-Angelo/author/B09Q6GWHSC

MORE ELITE GUARDIANS

Elite Guardians: Savannah

Vanishing Legacy

Hunting Justice

Guarding Truth

Elite Guardians Collection

Driving Force

Impending Strike

Defending Honor

Christmas in the Crosshairs

Elite Guardians

Always Watching

Without Warning

Moving Target

Chasing Secrets

Made in the USA
Middletown, DE
14 October 2024

62582218R00172